ONLY AFTER DARK

SCARLETT MORO

ONLY AFTER DARK

SCARLETT MORO

DEAR READER

At the back of my print books are several blank lined pages.

I don't know about you, but I'm hard on my books. They're well-loved. They get dog-eared. They get written in. They probably have a coffee stain or two. I highlight words I don't know. I bracket things I love and things I hate. Squiggly underlines draw attention to the incredibly moving bits. If you're a writer, a note-taker, a doodler, a scribbler ... those blank pages are for you.

If you prefer to keep your books in pristine condition, fair enough. Ignore them and enjoy your like-new books. I won't judge you too harshly.

CONTENT WARNINGS

This vampire-esque tale features age-gap love, arranged marriage, forced kissing/proximity, and fighting/violence. As with all my romance, it is *spicy*, meaning there are scenes of a graphic sexual nature.
It's intended for a mature audience.

ONLY AFTER DARK
SCARLETT MORO

Whether dictated or forbidden, love means nothing but pain ... for a monster.

Despite our clan leader announcing my betrothal to Markos, I can't marry him.

I *refuse* to marry him.

And I only have two full moons left until the wedding. That's why I agreed to this mission.

If I can find the hunter who's killing our kind, I can beg to have the marriage called off. Intel says they're at Citrus County University, where I'm now trying to pass as a regular student.

But I have three goals, and they aren't a degree: Find the killer, don't let anyone see me after dark, and keep as far away from my hot professor as possible.

EPILOGUE
PART ONE

The poem's words echo through my mind, sung in my mother's voice.

> *The little bee*
> *Up in the tree*
> *Works happily*
> *For he is free*

Always in her voice.

It's one of the only clear human memories I still have, and I cherish it. Except that the poem, like many children's tales, isn't the happy little story it initially appears to be. I remember my mother explaining the meaning; We should maintain happiness even amongst our darkest struggles because we always have freedom in the recesses of our minds. I didn't see the dreariness of it then.

How awful that the only place we should experience true freedom is in our heads.

I look at the window pane, watching the tiny creature crawling up the glass. It isn't a bee, but a seven-spotted lady beetle. Its red shell shines in the incoming sunlight, and I know it longs for its freedom, to be like the bee in the poem.

Keeping it trapped here means certain death. I chuckle at the absurdity of my having been so often responsible for life. I scoop the critter from the glass and open the window, watching as it grows into a tiny dot against the blue sky. I'm alone again, but at least one of us is truly free.

There's no freedom left in my thoughts.

All they do is circle back to the absence of *him*.

CHAPTER 1

*R*emember *what you're there to do.*

Markos's words reverberate through my mind as I stare at myself in the cheap mirror hanging on the backside of my new room's door. The maroon teddy I'm wearing has long sleeves and a neckline low enough to aid in my quest for information, and paired with a plaid wool skirt it has me looking deliciously ready for my first day of university.

Disgusting.

I hate the look. I miss my leathers. I miss my boots. And I really, really miss my sword.

I slip on the tan knee-high fashion boots Vanthony picked out for me and slide a dagger into the right boot, reveling in the way the cold steel feels against my leg above my short sock. Of course Vanthony was able to pick out clothes to assure a seamless transition into school; Fashion is his mortal calling. It's Markos who I dread seeing me like this. He's always pining after human girls, toying with them the way a cat does a mouse.

Disgusting.

I fight to swallow my disdain and grab my long coat, the one that's just perfect for the early-morning bite the September air now holds.

Not the kind of bite I'm aching to enjoy.

I ponder how long it's been since I felt the warmth of skin on my fangs, fangs I thankfully don't ordain in daylight, as I walk briskly to Citrus County University. Lochfort, the quaint town that houses it, is as beautiful as it is strikingly ordinary. Gold and yellow leaves litter lawns and walkways that lead to cheap, historic houses. Welcoming neighbors live on all corners, the kind of folks who want to do right by God as much as they want to pry and gossip.

The kind of neighbors a creature like me need be wary of.

"Hey Sara!"

I turn my head, my long, dark locks flipping over my shoulder. A slender blonde waves frantically as she runs toward me. I recognize her from the series of profiles Mrs. Gentry, my landlord, showed me of the other women who live in the rooming house I'm staying in for the duration of my assignment. Luckily, in a town this quiet, it was easy to secure housing a short walk from the only university.

The woman gulps in air as she reaches me, fighting to catch her breath. For a human of such small stature, I'd expect her to have better stamina.

"It's Sara, right?" Her face is beaming, the subtle glow of fair skin shining out from behind a barrage of freckles. "You're the new girl that moved into 1042 Marr Street, right? I'm Angel. I was going to ask if you wanted to walk to school together, but you were already gone by the time I came out of my room."

Angel? Could she have a more cliche name? I wonder if she's a stripper in her spare time.

"Sara, yeah," I say, feigning a warm demeanor as I hold out a hand that she shakes far too vigorously. "Sara Summers."

Markos picked out the name; *Sara Summers*. I like the innocent ring to it, but I'm yearning to get back to the real me.

I need to hurry up and get this assignment over with.

"It's so great to meet you!" she gushes, still shaking my hand.

Maybe she's not a stripper, this girl seems starved for attention.

"I wonder if we're going to have any classes together! You think? What are you taking? I'm in the arts wing, myself. Here on a music scholarship. I've been playing flute for as long as I can remember. But I also have a minor in French. My parents are from out east, so we've always spoken French at home. My brother hates it though. He says it's pretentious and the accent sounds stupid. Can you believe that? I think French accents are nice. I don't have one, though."

I take a deep breath as the mousy girl continues yammering as we walk. Despite the half-dozen questions she's asked me, I've not had the chance to answer a single one. Fine by me, I'm not apt to force myself into remembering elaborate details surrounding my false persona.

"Oh gosh, I'm so sorry! I'm talking too much, aren't I?"

Angel cocks her head up at me and I just smile. "It's fine."

"You didn't tell me what you're going to school for."

"Majoring in English, with a minor in Psychology."

"Ah." My answer, it seems, has finally awarded me a little silence. Angel pouts, continuing as our boots touch the edge of the campus greenery. "I doubt we'll have any classes together."

"What a shame," I say, my eyes taking in the scene. The campus is buzzing with the eager energy of a new year. Students hang about in various spots on the grass and at picnic tables, while others pour in and out of the sets of doors in sight. It feels crowded, busy. The kind of place I tend to avoid, even amongst my own kind.

My gaze is drawn to a group of students near the west doors. They're huddled in a circle to the left of a wide walkway, one girl holding a megaphone and shouting as she pumps her fist in the air.

"We need to stand up for what's right! We should have a say in what we're being taught! Our money funds these people's salaries! We have RIGHTS! The RIGHT to an education free from the abomination of the gay agenda!"

The crowd around her cheers as I sigh.

"Terrible, isn't it?"

The voice comes from behind me, bringing with it an unusual warmth for this time of year. I turn as he steps beside me, a tall, well-dressed creature. He stands a good half-foot taller than me, if not more. His hair is mottled with bits of gray that give him a distinguished look, further complimented by his dress shirt and sweater vest. Blue eyes stare down at me from behind dark-framed glasses, and a rolled up sleeve reveals the beginnings of a plethora of tattoos. His other arm is draped by a long coat, and I wonder if it's tattooed as well.

Yum.

My stomach tightens at the thought and I scold myself. I don't have any use for humans, especially good looking ones who look too old to be attending university. I watch as he continues to observe me, a slight smile on his lips.

"I suppose."

"You suppose?" He seems amused by my answer as he smiles wider, adjusting his glasses. "Do you agree with what she's saying then?"

My eyes burn and I realize I've been studying him, unblinking, wondering what's driving him to force this conversation between us. Wishing I hated it more.

"I don't have much interest in ... politics," I reply dryly.

"That's a shame."

He's standing right next to me, a vicinity that would have me on high alert around most humans. But something about him is warm, welcoming. His presence somehow feels safe, and the gentle breeze is carrying with it scents of him and his cologne. I shudder.

"And why is that?" I ask.

And why do you smell so good?

"Just always interesting to see what makes the first year students tick," he replies. "Perhaps I'll see you around the school." He offers a polite nod as he makes his way inside, taking all the air around me with him. The absence of him leaves an uncomfortable gnawing in the pit of my stomach, a sensation I fight to shake off as I hike my bookbag farther onto my shoulder.

"Who was *that*?!" Angel's voice is shrill and unwelcome.

"Beats me," I mutter. "Doesn't matter."

But it feels like it does ... Why?

"Well I hope I get him for at least one of my classes. He was pretty dreamy."

"He's one of the teachers?"

Angel cocks her head and smirks, the look immediately irritating me. "Have you never stepped foot on a school campus before? Older guy, sweater vest, carrying a briefcase? Obvs one of the professors, Sara. So don't go trying anything."

"*Trying* anything? Excuse me?!" My response comes out colder than I intend, and Angel's smile immediately fizzles away as she visibly shrinks.

"Relax, gosh. I'm just kidding."

I won't be able to relax if I have to have any more interactions with that human. Why am I getting so defensive? It's not like I have any intentions of 'trying anything'. I'm here on an assignment, a very specific assignment. One that doesn't involve him.

"Right. Sorry. You said he was carrying a briefcase?"

"Yeah, a leather one. Anyway, I should head inside. If you're not busy after school, we should totally do something! Have you been to Bumpy's? The little cafe a couple blocks that way? They have the best mac and cheese there. They bake cheese and breadcrumbs on top of it and they put diced tomatoes and chives and this proprietary, super secret seasoning blend. It's amazing and—"

"Sure, sounds great," I reply as my phone buzzes in my jacket pocket. I take it out and see a message from Markos.

> Don't forget our meeting later. Can't wait to c
> ur human clothes.

Ugh, what a creep.

I wave a dismissive hand. I need to get away from this girl and find my first class, lest how little I actually fit in here become obvious. "Find me later."

"Okay!" Angel calls as I jog up the walkway leading to the school's main doors.

Thoughts of the professor swirl through my brain as I make my way inside, silently reminding myself that I need to stay focused. Leader Taryn is expecting my expeditious report on this assignment, and I'll be damned if I let some human distract me. He could have picked from at least a dozen others for this, but he chose *me*.

I have to find the human who's been tracking and hunting our kind for the past two decades, and I can't afford any distractions. Which makes it concerning to me that I didn't even notice the professor was holding a briefcase. I need to pay more attention.

And stay the hell away from him.

CHAPTER 2

I've made it through all of my classes but one. The last class is one I'm actually excited for, an introductory creative writing class that intrigued me with its cheeky description, a description I'd easily committed to memory after reading it several times.

The classroom is tucked neatly into the far recesses of the literary wing, nestled into the corner in a way that makes it tricky to find. I sneak into class a few minutes late, praying no one notices as I take a seat in the back.

"Ah, so nice of you to join us!" a familiar voice calls from the front of the room. "You must be Sara. That's the only person on the attendance list who wasn't accounted for."

My stomach lurches as dozens of eyes turn to look at me, and I realize amongst them is a set I recognize. I can't appreciate his scent from this distance, but the glasses and sweater vest are unmistakable, as is his sultry voice.

The professor from the courtyard stares at me, that familiar smile creeping over his features. I can feel the looks of all my classmates, but they feel hazy and distant, a stark contrast to the way the attention from *him* feels.

I swallow hard.

"Sorry I'm late, I—"

He raises a hand to silence me, but there's a sympathetic edge to his features. "It's alright, Sara. There's inevitably a few stragglers in the first couple days who struggle to make their way here. I know this room can be tricky to find."

Straggler?! Struggle?! I've never struggled with anything in my life! If I wasn't on this damn assignment, I'd tie you up and watch you struggle while I sipped your soul from your body!

His words infuriate me, and I doubt how much my face hides it. I can feel the pinching of my brows at his poor choice of words.

"It wasn't a *struggle*," I hiss. "I was merely using the restroom."

"Ah," he gives a knowing nod, his glasses flashing as he adjusts them. "Happy your reason for tardiness isn't because you were lost, then." He's grinning like a fool, and the roaring sea in the pit of my stomach is a mixture of annoyance and intrigue. On one hand, I like the way his attention is fixed solely on me and don't want it to end. On the other, I need this class to get started so it can end and I can get the hell out of here, as far away from him as possible.

I need to talk to someone about dropping this class.

I'm not here for the grades anyway. I'm not actually here trying to get a bachelor's degree like all of the other new students. I don't care about how well I do in any of my classes, though it's not in me to genuinely do poorly. My effort here will be minimal, and no doubt still yield top-of-the-class results. For humans, this is hard work. For a draul, regurgitating information is effortless. Our minds are truly steel traps.

Which is why I've already committed his features to memory.

My hands clench at the thought. I tear into my bag and

pull out a notebook and a pen, desperate to be distracted from the way he keeps looking at me. The way he's *still* looking at me. I feel as though he's waiting for my rebuttal, hoping I have some smart remark so we can keep up this silly banter. Taunting me, baiting me to toy with him in front of the whole class.

He'll be sadly disappointed then. I'm not giving him the satisfaction.

"Sorry," I say again, the word a throatier growl than apology.

"It's all good," he replies, letting his gaze on me linger several seconds longer before finally turning to address the rest of the room. I think I see his eyes drift down my chest ever so slightly, but it's hard to tell from this distance, at least with my day vision.

I guess the top Vanthony picked out is a winner.

"As I was just explaining to the rest of the class, my name is Dr. Ross Haven and I'll be teaching your Introductory to Creative Writing class for the duration of the semester."

Yeah, until I drop this class. You get one day, sir. One.

"I'm excited to have you all here. I hope you're equally excited to be here, and if not," his eyes shift back to me, their intensity pulling my gaze to him and refusing to let go, "then I guess you're always welcome to drop this class and try your luck elsewhere."

What the hell? Is he reading my thoughts?

"Though, you might be hard pressed to find any decent classes with availability. All the good ones fill up early and, not to brag, but you have to be a pretty early bird to get into any of my classes."

He flashes me that cheeky grin yet again and my body fills with a mixture of rage and need. I want to fly to the front of the room and bite that smug look right off his lips. He's irritating and arrogant and looks good enough to eat. The perfect concoction for a soul feast, especially when everything about him makes me so ravenous.

It's been too long since I fed. That's why I'm reacting like this.

I release an audible sigh of relief as he continues on, rambling about expectations, rules, and the structure of the course outline. He takes time to point out the major assignments, indicating which ones hold the greatest weight towards our final grades.

But I'm already here on an assignment, of much greater importance than your silly writing activities.

"And I want you all to know that I do something a little differently in my class than most of the professors here at CCU. I don't dock marks for anything that's handed in late." Half the class erupts in a loud cheer. "But," he continues, ushering everyone back to silence, "I don't give feedback for anything handed in late. And I give *extensive* feedback."

I'd let you give me extensive feedback, Dr. Haven. But not on schoolwork. I bite my bottom lip hard to stifle the intrusive thought. *Jesus, what the hell is wrong with me?*

"So I highly suggest, if you want to get the most out of this class and see some genuine improvement in your writing and critical thinking, you show up, give a shit, and hand your stuff in on time."

"I didn't see 'Giving A Shit' on the grading rubric," I call out. "How many marks are awarded for that?" My outburst generates a few snickers throughout the room. Dr. Haven smiles, and I immediately regret asking. I hate it when he smiles at me, hate how hungry and flustered it makes me. His brows raise well above the tops of his frames as he stares at me, head cocked and looking far too scrumptious for someone in a position of authority and supposed power.

He has no idea how powerless he'd be if he ever saw me after sundown.

That's the thing about humans, their perception of power is so sad and trivial. They think power comes from money, from owning stuff. From being complacent in some little job where they get to boss other humans around for a few hours a day. They have no idea how weak and useless they truly are. And that's why I shouldn't feel bad for soul sucking.

Besides, I only do what I need to do to survive. I do the bare minimum to sustain myself, and beyond that I only do what my clan needs, what Leader Taryn orders me to do.

If I don't, I'll be banished. And if that happens ...

"And how would you suggest I detect and mark whether or not someone gives a shit, Sara?" His voice pulls me back into the room. I'd nearly forgotten about my smart ass comment.

"I think it'll be apparent in each assignment by the quality of the human's work." My answer draws puzzled looks from several of my classmates, the ones who are paying attention at least. I study their faces, watching, waiting. Any one of them could be the hunter, the person I've been sent here to sniff out and report to Leader Taryn.

Rumors circling through the clan indicated the trail led here to CCU, and specifically to the arts department, but there was no intel about how long they'd been involved here. I doubt it's any of the first year students, but many of them have ties to other students here, so it could be that they were hanging around here by association.

I wish Leader Taryn could have given me more to go on, but the intel didn't derive from any of our clan members, not even our kind. Whispers came from the next clan over, a group of hideous cave dwellers hiding up in the mountains. We're hospitable, but I wouldn't exactly describe our clan's relationship with them as wholesome. It's more out of necessity, a symbiotic connection bridging a gap with the Ancestors.

Dr. Haven's brow twitches in amusement, his curiosity seemingly piqued. "You think that 'Giving A Shit' qualifies as merely meeting the requirements, or would you say it's reserved for exemplary work?"

"I'd lean towards exemplary." I pause to admire Dr. Haven's grin. The way he watches me is enthralling, seeming to hang on my every word. "If someone does the bare minimum, they haven't really given much of a shit, have they?"

"I suppose not." He scratches his chin. "Alright, then. From here on out, I'm offering you the chance to be awarded up to five bonus marks on any assignment for exemplary work. Or, as Miss Summers has so eloquently put it, for 'giving a shit'." A few hollers and a bunch of clapping erupt throughout the class. Dr. Haven smiles at me, but it isn't the cheeky grin from before. This smile is different, sultry even, and I feel a rush of heat to my face as he holds my gaze a moment longer.

Fuck.

"I'd like to point out that the assignment need not be perfect to be awarded these marks, as long as an extraordinary amount of effort is recognizable. People willing to go above and beyond in their work deserve to be rewarded. Wouldn't you agree, Miss Summers?"

I shift uncomfortably in my seat. The fact that he's shifted from calling me Sara to Miss Summers hasn't gone unnoticed, and it seems my body hasn't missed it either. I squirm, fighting to find a comfortable position with the unfamiliar sensations that have ensued. The gnawing in my stomach has shifted down into a tingling of my inner thighs, and I need it to stop so I can focus.

And I need it to stop NOW.

"Yes, I'd agree with that," I say coolly, ignoring my body and mind's mixed signals. "Especially if they're choosing to give your assignments that extra attention, as opposed to ones from their other courses."

Dr. Haven smiles again. "I do appreciate extra attention."

So I've noticed.

And it seems the sentiment is mutual.

CHAPTER 3

I try to listen as Dr. Haven continues on, presenting us with a preliminary writing exercise he calls *Paragraph of Truth*. The assignment isn't worth any marks, not even 'Give A Shit' marks, but we are tasked with leaving anonymous feedback on three pieces from unnamed peers. It's meant to help us reflect on how others see our work without the pressure of a grade, as well as give us the chance to be the critical eye.

We can write on any topic we want, but the piece has to be a full paragraph of non-fiction. Works are typed up and photocopied, with no names attached, so we don't have to worry about someone guessing which piece is ours. It can be as mundane as a blurb about a grocery shopping trip, or as dark and personal as we're comfortable making it.

I, of course, opt for the latter.

A SINGLE TEAR rolled down his cheek as they removed the plastic tubing from his mouth. It was as though he was crying, shedding a tear for his final goodbye, though I knew that was impossible. He wasn't feeling anything. No pain, no joy, no sorrow. He didn't have enough brain function left to be lucid, let alone feel anything anymore. It was good too, because it meant he wasn't bothered by how cold his hands were. I remember as I clasped one that they were like ice, as though he was already gone. And after they'd disconnected everything, his heartbeat fading away with the absence of the life support machine, I hoped that, after all his pain and suffering, the only thing left to feel was sweet release.

AFTER GETTING a copy from the classroom printer, Dr. Haven walks around and gives us each a sticky note to write our name on to keep it off the document itself for the sake of anonymity. It angers me, but I'm secretly pining for us to share a cliche moment of our hands brushing.

We don't. He grabs my paper with an expeditious swipe, barely looking at me as he carries it off with all the others and heads out of the room in pursuit of a photocopier. I exhale, realizing I'd had my breath held the several seconds he was near me.

I need to get my shit together. It's my first day on this assignment and I've already let some human—him—completely rattle my nerves. I'm never going to be able to focus and track down the draul hunter at this rate.

Before I've even had time to gather my senses, Dr. Haven is back. Seated closest to the door, I'm the first stop he makes with the photocopied sets of works. As he goes to set the papers down my hand shoots up of its own volition, my knuckles brushing against the underside of his wrist. He freezes and I fight the urge to scream at the intense awkwardness.

"Sorry," he offers quietly, resuming his stroll around the room. I watch him as he walks through the aisles of seats almost dutifully, not glancing in my direction again. He avoids looking at me as he hands out the last set of papers and retreats back to his desk.

Do I make him as flustered as he makes me? Do I want to make him as flustered as he makes me?

"Now then, if everyone could—"

My phone rings and it's loud enough through my coat pocket that Dr. Haven immediately stops talking and eyebrows me. A dozen other people check their pockets and bags since the tone is a generic preset, but somehow the Doctor and I are all too aware that I'm the culprit.

"Apologies," I groan after wrestling the phone out of its silk-lined holster, "I forgot to turn the ringer off." I silence the phone and set it down on the corner of my desk.

"Thank you for bringing up that excellent pointer, Sara."

Sara? What happened to 'Miss Summers'?

"I have one serious ask for all my students, and it's that you refrain from using your phones in class for anything other than research. I know, everyone's phone is a tiny computer these days. If you're using it to look up facts or spellcheck or find the meaning of a word, cool. If you're answering texts or phone calls unrelated to the day's topic, I just ask that you take it out into the hall and rejoin the class once you're finished, so as not to disrupt the lesson."

My phone screen lights up, drawing me in. My eyes pan down just long enough to see that it's Markos texting. Whatever it is he wants, he's blowing up my phone. By the time I look back up Dr. Haven is staring at me, eyes narrowed and brow cocked.

"Do you need to take one of those opportunities now, Miss Summers?"

That's better.

"No, I—" Three more messages pour in. I bite my bottom lip and pout.

Dr. Haven waits. Despite the distance and his glasses, I

can see the way his eyes are smoldering as he watches me. My indecisiveness holds his attention, his bright blue eyes a darker, smokier version of their usual selves. It's as though he's challenging me, daring me to leave his class and address whatever's so important.

Daring me to look away.

"Excuse me," I say as I hastily scoop up the phone and head out into the hall in frustration. I don't even bother reading through Markos's messages before slamming his number into the touch screen and pressing the phone to my ear. I pace up and down a section of the hall as I wait for him to answer, growing more furious and impatient with every ring.

"Hello, beautiful," he coos. I could throttle him through the phone right now. "Have you been getting my messages?"

"What the hell do you want, Markos? I'm in class. You know that, right? Are you trying to fuck this up for me? We both know you were upset when Leader Taryn chose me for this assignment, but that doesn't give you the right to try to fuck me on this."

"Not the way I want to fuck you, Zali," he growls. His voice comes out in a low purr, but I hear the clip of annoyance hanging on every syllable.

He can be annoyed all he wants, two can play at that game.

"If you don't tell me what the fuck it is you want right now, I swear to Lisha I will report you to Leader Taryn, Markos."

"*You* are forgetting your *place*, Zalida!" All hints of seduction vacate his tone. This is the Markos I know, a feral, heartless beast of a draul who is every bit as primal as he is ruthless. A draul who'll kill for sport as easily as he will for survival. A murderous monster, fighting for Leader Taryn's spot alongside the other alphas in the clan.

The draul I am so woefully marked by and set to marry.

I rub the raised skin on the back of my neck. With the announcement of our engagement came Markos branding me with his family rune. Our arranged marriage is one of politics, not love, or even lust. At least, not an ounce of lust on my part. Markos has been trying to cash in on our arrangement ever since Leader Taryn declared it, an offer I have emphatically refused and will continue to refuse until the day we are officially joined and I have no choice but to succumb to his whims.

If I have my way, that day'll never come.

I meant it when I told Dr. Haven I have no interest in politics. Ridiculous, archaic politics are the reason I'm in this mess, and the reason I agreed to this ludicrous assignment in the first place. It's not without obvious danger, a monster seeking out a monster hunter. And all based on the loose threads of a web of gossip and rumors spread by a clan we barely tolerate. In many ways, this is a potential suicide mission.

But if I get into Leader Taryn's good graces, maybe he'll call off this arrangement ... I hope.

There are so many better potential suitors for Markos. Many in our clan are as soul thirsty and animalistic as he, and he has no shortage of females ready to jump at his every beck and call. Why Leader Taryn chose me is still a bit of a mystery. If I had to guess, I'd say it's because a clan is best led by someone level headed, someone sensible. Markos is none of these things, but with a woman by his side strong enough to reign him in and make him see reason, the clan might stand a chance in building our numbers by convincing neighboring clans to join us until we're powerful enough to overthrow the Ancestors.

Until we're powerful enough to *be* the Ancestors.

"I'm *not* Zalida right now, Markos," I hiss. "Not when I'm here. I'm Sara Summers, the bubbly little schoolgirl just here to fit in, lay low, and work on my BA. Now tell me what you want." I grit my teeth. "Please."

I can feel his smile through the phone and it sickens me. "That's my little queen, using her manners," he gushes.

I feel the steel of my dagger, now warm from my skin, and wish Markos was here so I could drive the half-foot blade right into his smug mouth and down his throat. "You'd have to be king for me to be your queen, Markos."

"In due time, my pet." I hear him lick his lips, no doubt aroused by the thought. "I was urgently messaging you to tell you of intel that Leader Taryn asked me to pass on personally."

My ears perk up. "Go on."

"From what we've heard, the hunter is attending CCU and is in the arts wing ..."

"Yes, and? We already knew that, Markos."

"Patience, pet. The bit that we hadn't before heard is that the hunter you're seeking is not one of the university's students. It's someone on the inside, Zali."

My heart freezes in my chest. "What? You're sure?"

"Leader Taryn says the information came from an extremely reliable source. But this is good news. This narrows down your prospects considerably."

Does it ever—This means, rather than literally hundreds of possibilities, it's narrowed down only to the faculty in this specific department, which is around a dozen people at best. I've already met three of them in prior classes today.

And then there's Dr. Haven.

But it can't be him. I know it can't. No one who spends all their free time killing could have as warm and protective of an aura as I experienced in the courtyard this morning. There's no way it could be him. He doesn't strike me as the type, and I pride myself on being an excellent judge of character.

No, it has to be someone else.

"Noted. Thanks for the intel, Markos."

"And Zali?"

I rub the spot between my brows. "Yes?"

"Don't go flirting with any of these humans, or I'll set the entire school on fire and suck the soul from every pathetic creature that flees. You're *mine*."

My hands are cold. Icy. For a moment, I'm transported back to the hospital, back to the room where I held his frozen hand as they took him off life support. I swallow hard.

"Thanks for the reminder, Markos."

CHAPTER 4

I'm relieved when no one notices me reentering the room. My nerves are rattled, my heart racing. My hands still ... *cold*.

I grab my jacket off the back of my chair and throw it over my shoulders, pulling it tightly around me and tying the strap at my waist. The jacket is tailored and well made, an expensive piece that Vanthony picked out because it would "give life to feminine form", or so he said. I might be a bit on the stockier side for a female of our kind, but I have curves. I just train a lot.

Train so that no one fucks with me.

I look down and see the four sheets of paper laying on my desk.

The assignment.

I glance around and realize everyone is quiet at their desks, the room silent. Eyes scan over pages and pens and pencils scratch hand-written sentiments reflecting the reader's thoughts. I nearly forgot we were reviewing each other's work. That phone call with Markos really jarred me. I have to push it from my mind and let myself escape into this mean-ingless task.

The top page is the copy of my work with the sticky note. I assume Dr. Haven gave us back our originals. I look to the front of the room. He's not at his desk, and I feel my heart sink in my chest.

Why should I care whether he's in the room or not? He's nothing but a distraction anyhow.

I move my page to the back of the stack, letting my eyes take in something new. I like this piece. It's simple, but the writing is very clean and the author portrays their feelings well. I would give it near-perfect marks, and much 'Give A Shit' credit. I can tell it was written with care.

The second piece is dissimilar. It reminds me of my own, an intensely personal excerpt from someone's life. Someone who has suffered.

Someone who could still be suffering.

I wonder how long ago what they talk about happened. I wonder if they're still affected by it, or if it's something they've made peace with. Part of me wishes I knew who it was. Maybe we'd have things in common. I'm sure we share a common sense of resilience, if nothing else. On the other hand, I'm glad the project is anonymous. I don't need to be more emotionally mixed up with the humans than I already am.

The professor is making that difficult enough.

Markos is always taunting me for my attachment to "lesser creatures". He thinks it's a sign of weakness, caring for something so naive and fragile. He sees my infatuation with humans as something that holds me back, something that keeps me from the strength required to be a great leader.

And yet Leader Taryn chose *me* for this assignment.

I think the way I can blend in with them without being easily threatened or triggered is a large part of why he chose me. There's no way Markos could spend a day around this many people without sucking the souls from at least a couple. He'd blow his cover well before he collected any valuable information. And we can't afford that, not with the way our numbers are dwindling.

Whomever the hunter is is one of the best we've faced in a long time, and they've only gotten better over the years. They've honed their skills, sharpened their weapons. Ruthlessly took out countless draul and left behind a consuming void in their wake.

Not that we don't do the same.

But it's different for us, I remind myself. We do what we have to to survive. We farm the humans we need to create enough souls for sustenance, maybe a little extra. Sure, there are those of us, like Markos, who kill in excess just because they can. But we're not all like that.

I'm not like that.

I don't remember what it felt like to be human anymore. It's been so long since I was one, all of those memories are faded and dusty, full of holes and worn out by the sands of time. Maybe that's why I insist on these pleasantries with the humans. Maybe there's something, some aspect of myself, that I'm fighting to hold on to. Some soft, fragile bit I'm desperate not to let go.

Or maybe there's memories I don't want to forget.

I flip through the papers on my desk, puzzled. The third and fourth sheets are both copies of my own work. Two copies of my work and no third piece from a fellow peer? Dr. Haven must have made a mistake. I look around, expecting to spot someone looking equally confused, but everyone is peacefully working away with their heads down. Nothing anywhere seems amiss.

The grasp of a hand sets my shoulder on fire. Heat radiates through my jacket and teddy from a strong set of fingers, and I find myself yearning to have those fingers travel over my shoulder and down my chest. I gasp, terrified to turn around and let our eyes meet. I can't mute the way my body is responding, my chest heaving gently with shallow, raspy breaths.

"Can I see you in my office after class?"

It's such a simple sentence, one with no direct implications, and yet somehow it manages to halt my breath and create a subtle dampness between my thighs.

"Am I in trouble?"

What a stupid question! This isn't elementary school. And I'm not even here for school! Who cares if I'm in violation of some idiotic human policy?

"No, not at all. I thought it might be nice to share some verbal insight on your piece, that's all."

"Sure, Dr. Haven."

And if you get too close to me, the piece in my boot will be the last we discuss.

"Great." He unhands my shoulder, the top bit of my collarbone left feeling bare and exposed despite my jacket. Goosebumps travel down my arms, and I beg my body to stop fixating on his touch, to stop craving the pressure of his fingers on my flesh once more. He takes a couple steps before stopping and turning back to me. I can't help but look up and face him. "Just so you're aware, it wasn't a mistake."

"Pardon?"

"Giving you two copies of your own work." His voice is low. No one around is within earshot of us, our hushed conversation not garnering attention. "I want you to reflect on your own work. Tell me what you think about it. Pretend you're reading it for the first time. It's an interesting piece and I'm curious to know your thoughts on it from an outside perspective. If you think you can read it from an outside perspective."

Is this man serious?

"Of course I can read it from an outside perspective, but I thought the whole point was to look at other peoples work, not our own."

"If you think it's outside the scope of your abilities, I can—"

I narrow my eyes. "I never said it was outside my scope, Dr. Haven. I'm merely pointing out that you—"

"Great! Then have at it. And don't forget about meeting in my office after class."

He's smiling again, the smug bastard. Why is he so insistent on getting me in his office? Probably so he can touch my shoulder again in the hopes that I'll ...

I urge the thought away. If I'm so worried about a little shoulder touch, I shouldn't have accepted the request in the first place. But I'm also trying not to make waves here, not until I concretely learn who the hunter is and relay the evidence to Leader Taryn. I don't have to kill them, just find them, report, and let Markos do the rest. Then my work here is done.

We've lost many over the past two decades, but the last three years have been brutal. Not only are the bodies never found, but the draul have been disappearing without a trace, no evidence of their existence left behind. Some go missing while alone, others while in pairs or small groups. The only logical explanation is that the hunter has unlocked some strong banishment magic. We've all heard tales of such magic as children, legends the draul tell their kids to scare them out of venturing into human territory.

But none of us truly believed in it before now.

The hunter has become a sort of bogeyman amongst us. The childish tales have shifted into gruesome warnings. Don't go out at night. Don't go anywhere alone. Don't go anywhere near the humans. And don't go feasting anywhere other than the farm. The rules of survival are simple, and most of us follow them. And yet the disappearances continue.

I wish Markos would disappear. That would solve a lot of my problems.

It would solve all *my problems.*

I bite my thumb as Dr. Haven walks back to the front of the room and sits on the edge of his desk facing the class. He scans the class as one by one the students finish scribbling their feedback on the anonymous work they've each been granted. His eyes stop when they meet mine, the corners of his mouth flicking up ever so slightly.

Damn, he really is handsome.

I remind myself it doesn't matter. That after today I'm dropping this class and won't have to see him again any more than a coincidental passing in the halls. I don't want to, though. I know myself, I know I don't genuinely want to drop this class. For whatever reason, this teacher has gotten under my fucking skin and I don't want to forcefully remove myself from his presence.

But I have to.

I finish jotting feedback onto the last piece, my own, before setting down my pen and exhaling. I don't know what I expected coming to university, but it wasn't this. I wasn't expecting this assignment to feel so heavy right off the bat. I thought it would be easy, a quick in and out that I wouldn't bother investing in. I didn't expect to put any effort into these trivial tasks.

I didn't expect to meet someone like him.

When everyone is finished and all eyes face the front, Dr. Haven gets ready to explain the next bit of his class. "Alright, everyone. How was that? Not so bad, right? As important as it is for us to strive for improvement in our own work, it is equally important to strive for the betterment of our peers. Hopefully the feedback you've all provided has been a mixture of encouragement and constructive criticism. We don't do ourselves or anyone else any favors if we can't keep an open mind and look at things from," he looks at me, "an outside perspective."

My body's tense. The seconds our eyes are locked feels like an eternity, an eternity that I never want to end. I can't make sense of this pull he has on me, this magnetism. It's as though I've stumbled into his presence and landed under some sort of spell, and I can't break free no matter how much I tell myself this path would lead to nothing but misery.

Why does he insist on talking directly to me?

"If you want to leave those sheets on your desks, I'll collect them at the end of class. Don't forget to keep the original copy of your work. Tomorrow I'll give you the copies your peers have read so you can see what they've had to say. I only have one other thing for you today and it's an important one, so listen up."

More important than our meeting in your office later?

"Tomorrow I'm handing out details and rubrics for a project that's going to take place over the course of the entire semester. You'll be working on this amongst our other projects for the next four months. It's a biggie and worth thirty percent of your final grade, so I suggest keeping up on it and not leaving it to the last minute. To help keep you accountable, I'm going to put you all into pairs. We have an even number of students this semester so it'll work out perfectly.

"The project is called *Human Nature*. It's a people-watching assignment. The goal is to get out there and appreciate humans navigating the world. Too often we get caught up in the whirlwind of our day to day lives, especially in uni, so the idea is to carve out a little time to chill and observe. I want you and your partner to plan three meetups and do some people-watching. It can be at a park, in a coffee shop, whatever. Just make sure you note the location.

"The two of you will pick one random person you spot during each meetup and draft what you think their life looks like. Describe their physical attributes, but also note their behavior. Is it common? Unusual? Why did this person specifically pique your interest? After your meetups you'll have three characters you've created, which you'll then put into a short fictional story together. Watch people but don't stare, and for the love of god don't take pictures. Photographing random strangers is creepy. Don't be creepy."

This incites a giggle from most of the class, but I'm not amused. Being paired up with a stranger to go watch other strangers isn't exactly my idea of a good time. Hopefully this assignment, *my* assignment, doesn't take too long and I'm out of here well before having to enact any meeting or human watching.

Wait, aren't I dropping the class?

My chest burns with indecisiveness. Perhaps I'll wait until after this office meeting and then make my decision. Depending how close I can get to the professor, I could use him to garner my intel. Now that we know, or likely know, that the hunter is a faculty member, it'd be useful to have closer relations with someone on the inside.

Or perhaps I'm just seeking an excuse to have closer relations with him.

Either way, this is going to be a long assignment.

CHAPTER 5

The room smells like him and I despise it. It's a noxious mixture of his naturally sweet human scent and the spiciness of his cologne. It smells divine as it surrounds me and leaves every bit of my bare flesh tingling. I hang my jacket over the back of the chair and set my bag on the floor, taking a seat in front of his desk. Dr. Haven shuts the door behind us, his presence brushing past as he circles around to sit across from me.

"So ..." He lets his voice linger, and it hangs in the air alongside his scent. The scent that has me breathing slow, shallow breaths not because I hate it, but because I *don't*.

"So?"

"Your work." He slides a copy of it across the desk to me. "The piece that you wrote today." He eyes me, those blue irises once again beginning to grow smoky as they watch me from behind their lenses.

I glance down at the sheet, faking disinterest. "Is there a question in there somewhere, Dr. Haven?"

He points to the handwritten note.

> *Feels try-hard and potentially insincere. Likely fictitious despite the brief being non-fiction.*

"Do you care to elaborate on the piece, or on your feedback? You'd really assume this paragraph was fictitious if one of your peers wrote it? Seems unlikely to me."

I scoff. "I suppose you were right about me not being able to grade it from an outside perspective, then, Dr. Haven."

It feels as though he can see right through me. Part of me, something deep in my gut, warns me that he already knows too much. That somehow, despite having just met me, he can sense how desperately I want him to ask what it's about. Not to finally get it off my chest. Just to know someone's curious enough to wonder.

Just ask me.

"The assignment was to write a paragraph of non-fiction, Miss Summers."

My body quivers hearing him speak my name as we sit here, alone, his desk a mere slab of wood between us. A slab of wood I could splinter into a million pieces with ease if I wanted to.

And I want to.

"Are you saying you think I made this up?" I ask, eyes squinted.

He cocks his head, the smokiness leaving his eyes. It's replaced with something else, a sadness, I think. As though I've just accused him of something terribly hurtful and offensive.

Maybe I have.

"No, I don't think you made it up."

"Then why are you bringing it up? Why drag me into your office to talk about it?" My tone is frostier than I intend.

Like my damn hands.

As if he can hear my thoughts, Dr. Haven reaches across his desk to where my hands sit clasped together. He places one of his on top of them, the warmth of his skin setting me alight. My breath catches, and I clear my throat to fight the chances of him noticing. His hand sits there, burning, as his gaze softens and he looks deep into my eyes.

"Is there anything you feel you need to talk about, Sara? Any secrets you've been keeping since you arrived here? I just thought perhaps there might be things you'd like to discuss. You know, things to get off your chest."

I swallow hard. "Like what?"

"You tell me."

"There's nothing to tell," I spout, yanking my hands out from beneath his. I regret it immediately. My hands are once again frozen, clammy. I shove them into my lap, pinching them between my thighs. "There's no good reason I wrote what I did. It's not even true. I just wanted to write something that would shock people, make them a little uncomfortable. Isn't that what we're here for? To shake things up and make people question the world?"

His hand is still on the desk where I left it, as if he's patiently waiting for me to replace mine into his grasp. "Is that the reason you're here, Miss Summers? To 'shake things up'?"

I desperately wish his words didn't affect me. My thighs clench, locking my hands between them as hunger travels down from the pit of my stomach to between my legs. He smells so good and it's overwhelming. The cuffs of his shirt are rolled up just past his elbows, and I notice that there aren't tattoos on his other arm. Not that it matters. He's perfect the way he is, and right now I want nothing more than to lunge across this desk and suck the soul from his sweet flesh.

I'm so fucking hungry. He's *making me so hungry.*

A surge of panic courses through me as I feel my self control teetering, fading away bit by bit the longer I sit within this proximity of him. I dart from the chair, tripping over my own feet. I notice his leather briefcase sat on the floor as I catch myself on the corner of his desk, but Dr. Haven snatches it up, shoving it out of sight.

The foreign feeling of embarrassment hits me as my cheeks burn and I return to standing. I lean down to gather my jacket from his chair and my bag from the floor, eager to escape this office, to escape him and his smell and whatever it is he's doing to me. He steps out from behind his desk and I immediately take a large step to put some distance between us. Dr. Haven's eyes follow my movement, grazing over my chest as I bend down to grab my things.

Why did I have to wear such a low cut top?

I throw my bag on my shoulder and my jacket over my arm. "Thank you for inviting me to this completely useless meeting, Dr. Haven, but I really must be going. I've things to do, places to go, people to see."

A brow cocks above his frames. "What sort of people?"

"Marko— ... er, friends. Yes, I have a coffee date with my roommate tonight, and I shouldn't keep her waiting."

"No, I suppose not," he agrees. "Would you like me to walk you out?" He steps forward and I step back, but there's nowhere to go. The door greets my back.

The question catches me off guard. "No!" My voice is high, vehement. I sound shaky and uncertain, but I clear my throat and force my composure. "I mean, no, thank you. I'm sure you're a very busy man. I can make my way out of the school. Thank you."

"Miss Summers?" he calls as I turn and grab the door-knob, the smooth metal bringing with it that familiar iciness. The way he says my name flows through the air until it hits my nostrils and I breathe it in. Warmth sails through me, filling me with lascivious desire. It travels my body and courses through my fingertips. Blood pumps fiercely as my heart rate spikes, and for the first time I can remember since that night in the hospital, my hands actually feel *warm*.

"Yes, Dr. Haven?" I don't turn to look at him. I can't.

"In case there was even a modicum of truth to what you wrote, despite your insistence otherwise, we have great resources here at CCU that you can reach out to. There's an anonymous hotline run entirely by student volunteers for people who just need someone to talk to and—"

My internal warmth is replaced in an instant. A fiery rage takes its place, and I spin on my heels as a hissing noise escapes my lips. "How *dare* you!"

"How dare I?" Dr. Haven looks genuinely shocked. "Sara, I'm only trying to help you. That piece of writing—"

"Was fictitious, Dr. Haven! Made up! Complete nonsense! I only wrote it to get a rise out of you and the rest of the class, and clearly it worked! You've no reason to concern yourself with me or my overactive imagination. Thank you for your concern, Sir, but if you've nothing else to discuss then I really must be going."

He bites his bottom lip, and I wonder what he's preventing himself from saying. "Very well," he says matter-of-factly. "My apologies, Miss Summers. I didn't mean to upset you."

The temperature of my blood drops with his words. A gentle sigh escapes my lips as I stare at him, wishing I could tell him the truth whilst feeling so incredibly foolish.

He didn't invite me to his office because he likes me. He pities me. He pities me and thinks I need some kind of human counseling to deal with unfaced trauma, as if I'm some poor, bruised little lamb in need of rescue. He has no idea that it's he who is the lamb and, to his kind, I'm nothing more than a monstrous wolf.

"Thank you, Dr. Haven."

The words feel so final as he watches me say them, his gaze fixated on my lips. I wait until his eyes once again find mine. He looks so sad, as if he too can sense the finality, but he doesn't say anything. Despite how my eyes must beg him to, he doesn't say anything else or try to convince me not to leave. Instead he lets us stand there, in silence, staring at one another for what feels like too long and not nearly long enough.

"Have a nice coffee date with your friend, Miss Summers."

I need to leave his office, the already-familiar hunger he causes gnawing at my insides. I look into his eyes, mustering up what little conviction I can. "Where'd you go today?"

"Sorry?" His eyes gleam, and there's that smokiness again.

"When I came back into class after my phone call today, you weren't there. I didn't see you leave the room, though."

"Ah, that. Yes, well ... I needed to use the washroom, so I excused myself for a minute. You must have been distracted by the importance of your call." He bridges our gap, stopping dangerously close to me. The way he moves makes the world feel as though it's in slow motion. His smooth steps paired with the way he watches me leaves me breathless and frozen. I stand there, my brain screaming at me to turn and run out the door as my body boldly declines all sense of reason, paralyzed.

The feel of his stature next to me is deliciously over-whelming. Neither of us blinks as we stare at the other's face. I know I shouldn't trust any of the humans so easily, but his features radiate with sincerity as he watches me. His still-smoky eyes pull me in, and the merciless urge for him to kiss me overtakes me as he rests a warm hand on my cheek.

"Are you sure there's nothing you want to talk about, Miss Summers?"

I shake my head gently, ignoring the way the heat from his

hand is filling me. Ignoring the ravenous bits of me begging for his soul. "There's nothing."

His hand pulls my face a little higher. I can almost taste the salt from his skin in the air as I lick my lips. "Please know I'm here if that changes, Miss Summers."

I bite my lip to keep from kissing him. "Thank you. I ... I really must leave, Dr. Haven."

And I can't stand what being this close to you is doing to me.

He releases me and the moment he does I swing the door open and force myself through, out into the hall and away from his office. Away from *him*.

"Goodbye, Miss Summers," he calls as I urge my legs to walk, each step feeling so incredibly heavy. I make my way down the hall, not daring to look back. Not answering.

Goodbye, Dr. Haven.

CHAPTER 6

A cold wind nips at my bare hands, so I shove them into my jacket pockets. It's nearly nightfall. The park's miniature street lamps have all come alight, casting little full moons along the cobblestone path. I wait in the darkness of the trees, their leaves rustling above me. I can't risk any of the humans seeing me now, not on the cusp of nightfall.

The last bit of sunlight creeps down below the horizon, blanketing the world in darkness. My vision improves, everything now crystal clear. I have to be careful. It'll be easy for a human to spot the yellow glow of my eyes against my pitch black surroundings. My fangs protrude down and invade my mouth, the feeling like welcoming an old friend. I slide my tongue over them, marveling at how much I subconsciously miss them during the day.

"Zali ..." I feel his hands grip my waist from behind.

"Hello, Markos."

"Hungry, are you? I can smell it. Should we find a little snack in the park?"

I wiggle free from his grasp and snap around. "Markos,

don't you dare," I growl. "Leader Taryn said we will not hunt here. Not while the hunter is still at large and I'm still trying to fit in at that ridiculous school."

He places an icy hand on the side of my neck, his long, thick fingers pressing against the dull throbbing of my pulse. He eyes me up and down, his face contorting into a scowl. "Where are your human clothes? The ones Vanthony picked out for you?"

I opted to run home to drop off my school bag and change clothes before coming to meet Markos. I didn't need him seeing me in those revealing clothes. He's dicey around me as it is now that we've been declared spouses. He already views me as his property. I don't need him losing control. Not now, not after I've spent so long dodging his advances.

"What's wrong with black jeans and a t-shirt, Markos? These are clothes Vanthony picked out for me. He said these were low-key. Casual clothes, meant for blending in. We're in a public park in a small town where everyone's seen my face, Markos. Are you hoping to get me killed?"

His thumb stretches out across the front of my throat as his grip tightens slightly. "Now why on earth would I want that, my pet? We haven't even gotten to consummate our marriage yet."

"That's because we aren't married yet, Markos," I say, forcing the words out through struggling breaths.

He unhands me and I immediately grab my neck, rubbing away the feel of his skin on mine. "Fine," he snaps. "But you can't deny me forever, Zalida. You have until our wedding night only to decline me. Once you're my wife, I *will* have my way with you ... whether you like it or not."

I feel sick at the thought. Part of me can't understand Markos's obsession with me when there are plenty of drauls in our clan, male and female alike, who'd be more than happy to mate with him. But then, for creatures like Markos, I know the real thrill comes from the chase. Whether it's souls or sex, Markos thrives on taking things by force. It's what he lives for, what makes him a good leader in the sense that our clan will never know scarcity with him at our forefront.

He lives for the hunt.

But while Markos is busy hunting me, someone out there is busy hunting us. Someone I have to locate soon so they can be dealt with swiftly and harshly by Leader Taryn. Someone who has taken out far too many of our kind, and now needs to pay the price for what they've done.

"Don't you have something to tell me?" I ask, fitfully needing to change the subject. "Why did Leader Taryn tell you to come here anyway?"

"He wants me to keep an eye on you," Markos growls. He closes what little distance lies between us. I can feel the heat from his breath on the side of my cheek. "And he wants a report."

"A report?! I've been here one day, Markos. One freaking day! How much of a report is he expecting I'm going to have?"

Markos presses his body up against mine, the weight of him pinning me against a nearby tree. "I would suggest you have something good to tell him after the fuss you made about being assigned this role."

"I didn't make a fuss," I argue, "I merely volunteered and pleaded my case."

"You were hellbent on me not taking this assignment, Zalida!" Markos's voice is raised, and my eyes dart around the park to make sure there's no one within earshot. "You swore to Lisha that if I got this assignment you would take the decision to the Ancestors! *You* questioned Leader Taryn's authority! *You* questioned his ability! He had no choice but to pick you, lest you bring ramifications down on us all!"

"*I* didn't care who Leader Taryn chose as long as it wasn't *you*, Markos!"

His hand is back on my neck so fast it rattles me. I suck in a single gulp of frightened air before I stand there, helplessly pinched between his overwhelming size and the rough bark of the tree. He grips me, his hand clenching shut tighter than before. I wheeze, but I let my eyes show no fear. I keep my brows furrowed and my body stiff with resolve. I can feel Markos's excitement pressing against my stomach as he leans harder against me.

He brings his face to mine, licking from the corner of my chin up the length of my cheek. "You will learn to watch your tongue around me, Zalida," he purrs, his voice husky and raw with feral need, "or I will cut it out of your pretty mouth."

"But then ... how ... how will we have these pleasant talks ... my king?" I cough the words out from under his grip.

Markos smiles. "I like hearing you call me that." His hand finally leaves my throat, snaking around to the back of my neck. He plants a soft kiss on my lips as his fingers trace my branding. "Do not forget who owns you, Zalida. You *will* succumb to me, and you *will* obey me. Won't you, my pet?"

My stomach burns and my neck throbs. I feel queasy, but there's no sense in arguing. Not here, not now. "Yes."

I feel his excitement growing against me as he smiles, his pelvis pressing against me harder. He kisses me again, a gesture I neither fight nor reciprocate. "Good. Now, did you find anything I can bring back to Leader Taryn?"

Telling him anything will be a death sentence for whomever I point to.

"I don't have anything concrete yet," I say, trying to ignore the way Markos keeps his hips pressed firmly against me. "I have some inklings on a couple faculty members, but I need more time to gather proof."

"And what's your plan for that?" he asks, his words a rolling growl in my ear.

"I'm going to take turns following a few humans after school. I'll wait for them to come out and I'll follow them for a night, see where they go and what they do. The hunter will no doubt be up to shifty stuff in weird places. It won't take long to figure it out."

"Good." He presses his groin against me harder. "Are you sure you want to wait until our wedding night, Zalida?" he hisses. "You could help relieve this ache I have for you right now, right up against this tree. You act like you don't want me, but your body will submit. You'll see. You will make a perfect queen, Zali, and those hips will be perfect for bearing my children."

I refrain from throwing up as I strain against him. My arms are free, free enough that as I bring my right leg up a touch, my hand is able to slip into my boot and retrieve my dagger. Markos gasps as I press the tip of it against his side, resting it firmly on the sheer fabric of his cotton shirt. I leave it there as I keep my narrow eyes fixated on his.

"If you so much as reach for your zipper, Markos, I will cut what little appendage you have straight off your body."

"Little?!" He scoffs. "You'll be in for a surprise on our wedding night, my fiery pet."

It's true, I can feel the falseness of my words through his pants, but I can't give him the satisfaction of acknowledgment. "Try me, Markos."

He backs away, hands raised in mock defense as he smirks at me. "As you wish, my queen. I will follow the draul code and wait for our wedding night ... and not a single night more. You've only two full moons to witness before I make you mine, Zali. And while I would prefer you submit willingly, it is fine if you don't. You will be giving me children regardless. And," he licks the corner of his mouth, "we will make many."

He disappears into the trees, leaving nothing but the light of the full moon behind. I sink down to the ground, the coolness of the grass seeping through my jeans as I rest my head back against the tree and close my eyes. My heart is racing, and I feel the sting of tears forming behind my eyelids. I have to find the hunter and report them to Leader Taryn quickly, and then beg Leader Taryn to assign Markos a new wife.

I've only got sixty days until the wedding.

And I'd rather sacrifice my life than be forced to marry that monster.

CHAPTER 7

The banging on my door startles me, and I'm normally not easily startled. I swing it open with such force that Angel jumps back, eyes wide and lashes fluttering. "You're alive!" she cries.

"What? Why wouldn't I be?"

"Last night, silly! What happened to you? We were supposed to go to Bumpy's but you never showed! You weren't there, you weren't in the cafeteria or library at school, you weren't home! What time did you get home? Did you just come home this morning? I got home pretty late and you weren't here. It was after ten. At least I don't think you were here. I didn't see your shoes at the door. Are you okay? Did you get busy with something?"

Angel's verbal assault at this hour of the day is truly unholy, but I can't tell her that, especially after no-showing for our coffee date. She stares at me, her eyes big and puppy-like. Her freckles are muted by the dimly lit hallway, but the look of genuine worry on her face is unmissable. "I'm sorry, something came up." I exit my room and shut the door behind me. "I would have called, but I realized too late that we failed to exchange numbers yesterday."

"Oh my god!" Angel slaps both her cheeks with such force they begin to flush. "I noticed that too! How stupid is that?! We're roommates and we didn't even think to trade numbers! I texted Mrs. Gentry but she didn't get back to me. She was probably already in bed. With the time difference, she's in bed by like five o'clock here."

"Right, I forgot she doesn't live in town. Do you care much for her?"

Angel looks at me, puzzled. "Mrs. Gentry? Yeah! I mean, sure, I guess. Why wouldn't I?"

"No reason," I say. "She mentioned you'd been living here a long time. So I figured you must be fond of her."

Angel blushes, the rouge in her cheeks deepening. "She's my nan."

"Oh. She didn't mention that to me when I rented the room."

"No, I know. I always ask her not to. I don't want anyone living here to think I get special treatment or something. I do pay rent, just for the record. That's why I work at the bookstore in town square. Well, that and I just really like books. What about you, do you like books? I mean, of course you like books, everyone likes books. What kinds of books do you like?"

I glance at my phone. "I'm sorry, Angel, but I really must be going."

"We should walk to school together! Let me just get my—"

"No time, sorry!"

Nor do I want to walk alongside someone who can't keep quiet for two seconds.

"I have to be in class a bit early to discuss a project from yesterday."

"Wow, you already had a project? Whose class was it in?"

"Dr. Haven's."

Angel's eyes light up. "The dreamy professor? No way! And no fair! I'm not in any of his classes. I'm definitely signing up for some next year. I'm so jealous! I totally would have taken one if I'd known what a dreamboat he was. What's he like?"

I scoot past her, jacket flapping and bag bouncing as I fly down the stairs. "So sorry! Chat later!" I call up to her, yanking my shoes on at the door before she has the chance to ask anything else. Dr. Haven is the last person I feel like talking about. He's also the last person I feel like seeing, but I don't think I have a choice. Though it pains me to admit, he could very well be the hunter. He seemed overly protective of his suitcase yesterday in his office, and the fact he managed to slip past me in the hall undetected makes me nervous.

Was I that engrossed with Markos's phone call, or is there something more going on here?

The smell of the school is becoming familiar. It hits me as I enter the doors; Fresh paper, ink, the sickly sweet scents of the many humans. But it isn't until I enter the classroom that I smell *him*. His very distinct sweetness, like a freshly cut pear in summer mixed with the spiciness of cinnamon and the woods in autumn.

Fuck.

I take the same seat as yesterday. Dr. Haven's class was last on yesterday's roster, but today it's first. Good thing, too. It means I can get it over with and then force him from my mind while I navigate the rest of the day.

If I can get him off my mind, that is.

"Good morning, Miss Summers." His voice is smooth and brings with it the subtle scent of a bold roast coffee. "Did you have a good evening?"

"Nothing spectacular," I say as he walks past me and

straight to his desk. I'm relieved he doesn't stop anywhere near me, and even more relieved he didn't touch me. I don't think I could handle that right now. Not after yesterday in his office.

"Coffee with your roommate wasn't spectacular?"

I forgot that's what I told him I'd be up to. Not a complete lie, since Angel and I were supposed to go.

"She had to cancel. Feeling a bit under the weather."

"Sorry to hear that." Dr. Haven sits on the front edge of his desk and stares at me, one hand rhythmically rubbing his chin. I don't know what he's thinking about, but whatever it is it's making me nervous. "I'm afraid I've got another piece of unfortunate news for you this morning."

His words halt my breath. "Oh?" I try to sit still and listen, but my stomach is a storm of butterflies. I wrap my arms around myself and gently squeeze, willing the queasiness to stop.

What if he's somehow figured out what I am and what I've come here to do?

"I'm assigning partners today for the people-watching assignment. We had an even number of students, but Emily has had to drop out. She's from France and apparently has to go back there for a family emergency and won't be returning for the rest of the semester. Which puts us in the predicament of having an odd number of people."

"So you'd like for me to work alone?"

Thank Lisha.

"No. That hardly seems fair."

I unclench my stomach, the butterflies subsiding with my piqued curiosity. "You want me to join a pair and form a group of three then? Because I have to be honest, Dr. Haven, I'm not really one for group work. I'd much rather be alone and—"

"I was thinking I could pair you with me, Miss Summers."

"With ... With you?" I swallow hard. "Does *that* really seem fair? I think one could interpret it as an unfair advantage for a student to be working alongside their professor."

"You'd rather work as a group of three, then?" His blue eyes are cloudy and challenging to read. He waits for my answer so patiently. The room is eerily silent around us, save the distant noises trickling in from the busying hallway.

"I didn't say that," I say softly.

This is my chance to get close to him and find out if he's the hunter! Even though I'm sure it's not him. Still, there's a good chance he knows who it is, or would have an idea, at least.

"I'll do it." The words slip out in a voice other than my own. I hardly recognize the lust-filled tone reverberating from me.

Dr. Haven looks intrigued as he smirks at me. "Oh? Okay. Will I offend you, Miss Summers, if I tell you I thought it would take a lot more convincing on my part for you to assent?"

I can't help but chuckle. "No, Dr. Haven. I'm not offended. I do want to ask though, why a project centered around watching strangers? Wouldn't it be easier to have people do group reports on Shakespeare or something?"

"Everyone does that, all the typical professors. I like doing things differently."

"So I've noticed."

"And the freedoms my job grants are one of the biggest perks. That, and meeting ... *unique* ... characters, such as yourself."

I swallow hard. "You think I'm unique?"

"Very," he says, the gnawing in my stomach returning as he smiles at me. My mind whirls with thoughts of his office, of the way his fingers felt on my chin.

I want that again.

"I assure you, Dr. Haven, I am incredibly boring. And working with me will be boring."

"I highly doubt that," he grins. "Besides, I'm looking forward to seeing how you are watching humans. Who is going to be interesting enough to warrant the attention of a woman so curiously interesting herself?" I feel the heat in my cheeks as he smiles, a boyishly coy glow about his features.

"And just what is it that makes me so interesting, Dr. Haven?"

The room erupts in the white noise of giggles and banter as a trio of peers walks in. They pay no mind to me or Dr. Haven as they take their seats. Class is starting shortly, and the room will soon be full of students. Dr. Haven flashes me one more smile, one I can't help but return as I pull my notebook and pen from my bag and hurry to make myself look busy.

You can't escape my questions forever, Dr. Haven. Not if we're working on this project together. One way or another, you're going to tell me what you know. All I have to do is try not to devour your soul in the meantime.

Dr. Haven walks over to my desk and places a piece of paper face down on it. I hide my hands under my desktop to keep from touching him, from letting my fingertips graze over his warm, soft hands. The urge is overwhelming as he lingers there, pausing a moment too long before making his way back to the front of the room.

I flip the piece of paper over. On it is a single handwritten sentence.

First project meeting tonight, 6pm @ Bumpy's

My heart freezes in my chest. I pull my phone out and check my weather app, which calls for a 7:48 sunset. That doesn't leave a boatload of time for us to work on this and me to get the heck out of sight before anyone sees my true form.

And of all the people to see it, Dr. Haven would be the worst. He could be the hunter. He could report me to the hunter.

He could get scared and want nothing to do with me.

The thought is achingly trivial, yet it poisons my mind and makes it impossible to focus on anything else. Dr. Haven's voice is melodic in the background, but my brain is transfixed on our upcoming meeting. I'll have to think up a decent excuse to keep our meeting brief, but not rush it so much as to cause alarm or make it seem like I'm not taking the project seriously. Though I wish it wasn't, some deep-seated part of me is yearning for his approval on this.

And while I'd be lying to myself if I said I wasn't excited for the time alone together, another part of me, an instinctive part, is hailing a warning:

Something bad is going to come of this.

CHAPTER 8

Of all the human niceties, coffee is my favorite. There's something about it, something about the way the bitter notes coat my palate as I drink. The way I can wrap my cold hands around a hot mug and watch the world go by. The way it sinks down to my stomach and warms my soul.

What little I have left.

The transformation into a draul is a simultaneous gain and loss. You gain a poison as you're bitten, a toxin released from the fangs that aids the soul in slipping off its shell. In the way one shucks an oyster, it doesn't want to leave its encasing, but is left no choice when met with forceful coaxing. Then, it's a loss as the feaster drinks your soul. Too much left, and the soul repairs itself over time and the human condition remains. Drained too much or completely, and death becomes imminent.

But with the right conditions, just the right amount of poison mixed with only a fraction of soul left, you get something in between. Something that's human during the day, or appears to be, but is a different creature entirely after dusk.

Something that has little stomach left for anything other than souls.

A monster, like me.

I sip the coffee, swallowing down the bit of nausea that accompanies it. It's a small price to pay for the pleasantry, a sacrifice I'm more than willing to make.

Especially if I get to make it sitting across from him.

Dr. Haven enters the cafe. I don't need to look up to see that it's him. The bell above the door chimes only a moment sooner than his scent hits me, a scent my body can still make out over the aromas of roasting coffee and cooking food. A scent that brings with it the familiar quivering of my thighs and the storm of butterflies in my stomach. I sigh.

"Miss Summers," he says as he takes the seat across from me in the booth. "I was going to offer to pay, but I see you've already grabbed yourself a beverage."

Pay? Is he under the impression this is some sort of date?

"I was early and figured I'd go ahead and get started. With the coffee, and the people-watching."

He glances around. "Surely a bit harder to do from a booth than a table, though not impossible."

My cheeks begin to tingle. "I merely picked a booth for reasons of comfort. Not privacy."

"Oh, I wasn't insinuating ... I'm going to go get myself a drink, excuse me." He looks flustered as he grabs his briefcase, scoots off the seat and heads to the counter. I watch, thinking perhaps he'll open the case to retrieve his wallet, but see him grab it from his coat pocket instead.

Interesting. He never leaves the briefcase anywhere near me. Why? Is it a small thing I'm making out to be more than it is? Maybe I'm overthinking it. Maybe it's just out of habit.

I take in several quiet, deep breaths while he's away. Though his scent hasn't left me, it's much easier to breathe when he isn't so close. He returns a few minutes later holding a mug filled with something covered in foam and cinnamon. I eye him and the beverage curiously.

"Pumpkin spice latte," he says, clearly sensing my intrigue.

I cock a brow. "You didn't strike me as a latte kind of hu— ... person."

"No?" He sips his drink. "What kind of human did I strike you as?"

His eyes are guarded, his thoughts impossible to read, but there's a slight smile on his lips. I get the feeling he's gauging my reaction. I swirl the coffee around in my half-full mug.

"I assumed a professor would drink something more ... refined."

Dr. Haven feigns dramatic offense as he grasps his chest. "You think pumpkin spice lattes aren't refined? What would you suggest I drink, then?"

I look up from my mug. "Black coffee? That's all I drink."

"Ah, so you think black coffee is refined and my pumpkin spice drink is ... bullshit?"

I stifle a giggle. "Happy you've said it."

There's a moment of silence, and with it a heaviness. His face is etched with little hints of concern, a concern I can't imagine my razzing his drink choice caused. I hate the way he's looking at me, so I look back into my mug. Something in his eyes looks sad, and whatever it is I've the overwhelming ache to make it go away.

I'd suck the soul from anything that dares dampen those blue eyes.

"Sara, I ... If I asked you something, would you be completely honest with me?" The blue of his eyes has gone smoky and gray again. He watches me intently as I sip my coffee, his eyes trailing down to my mouth and back up. His stare is exigent, something unsaid hanging in the air between us and making the room stuffy. I can't deny what sorts of questions my heart longs for, but my mind is screaming, scolding me and warning me, treating me as though I'm a rebellious, love-struck teenager.

But what if I am?

"I suppose that depends on what you intend to ask, Dr. Haven."

No sooner do the words leave my lips than the weight of a bounding presence joins us, casting a shadow across the table. "Sara! Hi! I didn't know you were here? Are you—" Her words cut off as her doe-like eyes pan across the booth to Dr. Haven. Angel gasps. "Dr. Haven! Are you ... Are you guys—"

"NO!" we shout in unison.

Dr. Haven clears his throat. "Miss Summers and I are merely here sharing drinks over a project I'm helping her with. Miss Summers, who is your lovely friend?"

He thinks she's lovely?

I fight the urge to say, *No one.* "Dr. Haven, this is Angel. She's one of the ladies living at the rooming house I've taken up residence in for the semester."

"You're only staying for the semester?!" Angel shrieks as if I've physically assaulted her. "But what about next semester? You are coming back next semester aren't you? You can't look for somewhere else to stay if you're planning to come back next semester! I won't allow it. We've just started getting to know each other!"

"Angel, while I appreciate your need for this sudden interruption, Dr. Haven and I really have a lot of work to do."

"What *are* your plans for next semester, Miss Summers?" Dr. Haven asks, taking another sip of his pumpkin spice bullshit.

Angel stands there, intently waiting for my answer whilst ignoring my statement completely. Her and Dr. Haven stare, my thoughts becoming increasingly scattered and uncomfortable the longer the three of us remain in silence.

"I don't know what my plans are for next semester yet," I

say flatly. "I have ... family ... who need me. I'm not sure I'll be able to get away with abandoning them for such a period of time."

Angel pouts, her right hip jutting out as she shifts weight from one foot to the next. "I guess that's fair," she whines. "If you have family that needs you, that makes sense. Would you take a semester off and come back next year? It's going to take you so long to finish your degree at that pace. Oh, or I guess you could do online classes in between, huh? Hey, if you did that, I bet we could be, like, pen pals or something! We could have virtual homework dates! How fun would that be?"

"Angel, are you here by yourself?" Dr. Haven asks.

She nods as she rolls her eyes. "Yeah, Cassie was supposed to meet me, but she texted me last second and totally bailed because—"

"Why don't you sit down and join us then?" My stomach clenches into a tight knot. "Miss Summers and I were just about to start one of my class projects, a little people-watching exercise. We see if we can find someone of interest, maybe someone a bit peculiar, and we build a character based around them to later incorporate into a story."

Angel's cheeks mirror my temperament as they flush an incandescent rouge. She smiles at Dr. Haven. "Thanks, but I promised one of the girls back at the house I'd bring her a lavender latte. If you're looking for someone weird though, you should consider that guy across the street at the bus stop. I saw two buses go past while I was walking up the block and he didn't get on either of them. That, and he's just been staring into the cafe the whole time. I don't even think he's been blinking. Something about him is giving me, like ... mad serial killer vibes, or something. It's creepy."

My veins throb with an eerier chill as I lean out of the booth. Angel steps back and points, her narrow finger leading my eyes to him.

Markos.

Fuck. What the fuck does he think he's doing here in broad daylight?

He's sitting on the bus bench across the street, just as she said, staring into the cafe. A wicked grin plays on his features, callous and unmoving. My heart stops, my body gripped with fear. If Markos has become emboldened enough to be sitting there, amongst the humans during the day, it is the precursor to nothing but devastation and chaos.

No one is safe.

"Yeah, him. Weird, right? Maybe you wouldn't want to use him as a character though, unless you're writing a story about a psycho or something."

You've no idea how true that statement is, Angel.

"Anyway, I better get going. Have fun with your ... project," she says, shooting me a cheeky grin.

Angel gets her drinks and leaves. My eyes are still fixated on Markos, but the feel of Dr. Haven's stare pulls me back into the booth. I try to read him as he sips his drink, his eyes remaining focused on me over the edge of his mug.

"What do you think, Sara? Should we make that gentleman our focus?"

I lean back out of the booth and see Angel standing outside the cafe doors. She has her two drinks stacked as she fumbles with her phone to text someone before shoving it in her pocket. Drinks in hand, she makes her way toward our place, and the second I lose sight of her is when it happens; the cafe is released from Markos's gaze as his head cocks in her direction and he grins.

He's watching her!

That sly smile, the slow licking of his lips, it's all too recognizable to me now, even from this distance. The moment seems frozen in time. Everything around me has paused. The cafe is silent, nothing to be heard but the gentle drumming of the pulse in my neck as it begins to accelerate. I feel a bit faint, a subtle dizziness that starts low but quickly overwhelms me. My hands and feet are cold and tingling. I close my eyes for a moment to steady myself, but it's a moment too long.

When I open my eyes again, Markos is gone.

CHAPTER 9

The humdrum of the small town is especially loud today. People are out and about in their coats and scarves, soaking in all the beautiful autumn colors without a care. None of them realize the potential danger they're in. None of them know that an alpha draul, the worst of us all, is roaming the streets.

If they did, they wouldn't be out here merrily shopping and eating and living. They'd be in the safety of their homes with all their windows and doors locked. They'd be hiding in closets, whispering to their children to keep quiet. They'd be hiding ... from me too.

I had to make a quick excuse to blow off Dr. Haven. He looked hurt when I said I had to leave, less so when I explained I was coming down with a terrible migraine. I'm not entirely convinced he believed me, but there was nothing better I could think up on the spot. He said he'd check his calendar and let me know tomorrow when we can reschedule.

And I'm far more eager to do so than I should be.

My breath creates little puffs of faint white as I spring to 1042 Marr Street. These human boots aren't made for running, chewing into my achilles and making my feet ache, but the dull pain isn't my focus. I leap over full sections of sidewalk, tiptoeing the line between how fast I can move and how fast would seem abnormal to the surrounding humans.

I get to the house and my breath catches. The front door is open. Not a lot, but enough that it's obvious from the gate. I bolt into the house and an eerie silence greets me. I listen, the sound of blood rushing through my veins filling my ears.

I recall the names and photos of Lily and Meredith from Mrs. Gentry's email, the other two women who reside here. Markos could easily make quick work of three human girls if he wanted. He's fast and strong. He'd have them all taken out before they could so much as dial the police.

"Angel? Anyone? Hello? Anyone home?"

I clear the first floor, checking the sitting room, kitchen, bathroom, and Lily and Meredith's rooms. No one is around, and nothing seems amiss. The old house is quiet, eerily so, with only its usual creaks and moans and the gentle humming of the refrigerator to keep me company.

Fuck, where is she? Where's Angel?

I dash back to the entryway, stopping at the bottom of the steps.

"Hello?"

"Up here!"

Angel's voice gives no signs of distress, but I've no idea how effective she is at masking in dangerous situations. She doesn't strike me as the type, but perhaps she's proficient at remaining calm in times of stress. I fly upstairs, my feet barely touching the steps as I use the railing to heave myself a half-dozen stairs at a time.

Angel's bedroom door is ajar, daylight from her window seeping out onto the weathered carpet of the hallway. I walk slowly, carefully, until my fingers caress the wood and I push the door back far enough to see inside.

"Oh, hey!" Angel beams. She's sitting at her computer desk, alone.

"Where is he?"

The mousiness of her features amplifies as her face contorts. "Who? Wait, you thought I had a guy in my room? Why would I have a guy in my room? I don't have a boyfriend or anything. Maybe you didn't know that. Did you think I had a boyfriend? Why are you home already? Did your *not-*date with the dreamy professor not go well? "

I look around the room. The slight opening of Angel's window gently flutters the curtains. Her closet doors are wide open, no one inside. Nothing but a chaotic mixture of clothes and shoes, some hanging, some piled in corners and over suitcases. Her closet looks as messy and frantic as her personality.

"Nothing," I say, stepping backwards toward the hall. "It's fine."

"Are you alright, Sara? You look kinda pale. Did ... Did something happen with the professor?"

"What?!" I shake my head frantically. "No, no. He was great. I thought ... The weird guy from the bus stop looked like he might have been following you home, that's all. Had me worried."

"The weird guy? Oh. No. No one followed me here. There's no one here but me and Mere."

My stomach twists into a million knots.

"What?"

"Meredith. Oh, have you met her yet? Long, dark hair. Kinda like yours. Last I saw she was in her room. She's the one I was grabbing the latte for at Bumpy's."

My hands tremble. I clamp them together tightly to stop them as low, shallow breaths burn in my lungs as I fight to push gruesome images from my mind.

He's taken her. Markos has fucking taken her, the bastard!

"You're sure she was downstairs?" I keep my voice calm, my words heavy as lead in my chest.

"Yeah, why? Sara, you're scaring me. What's going on? Is someone else here? I don't—"

A loud crash rings out from downstairs, causing us both to jump. I'm at the top of the stairs before Angel can rise from her computer chair, then down them in a single bound. My ears burn as I listen. A stifled cough comes from the kitchen, my feet taking me there before my brain has time to register the potential danger.

Shards of broken porcelain are scattered across the floor. A disposable coffee cup—the latte—lay on its side amongst them, its liquid spreading around them like an ocean surrounding little islands. I gasp as I look up and see her in front of me.

Meredith.

CHAPTER 10

The stout girl with red cheeks and long, dark hair looks at me. The faint smell of cannabis hangs in the air as she fights hard to stifle a giggle. Then she bursts into laughter.

"Fuck, my latte!"

A presence on my back makes me swing around. "Did you seriously just drop the entire latte I bought you?" Angel groans. "And you broke one of my nan's good plates! Whatever, those plates are a thousand years old. I'm just not gonna tell her. But you know those lattes are like eight dollars, right? I'm not walking back to Bumpy's to get you another one."

"What?! Oh, please, Angel? I'm sorry! Lil and I just smoked a j out in the backyard. I was gonna make something to eat but I ... I dunno. I dropped everything somehow." She bursts into another fit of giggles. "Fuck!"

I eye the two girls curiously, my heart still pounding.

Do they think this is funny? Some kind of joke?!

"I'll be in my room," I murmur, not wanting to witness another second of trivial chaos.

"Oh, hey, you're Sara, right? Sorry, I'm Meredith. It's nice to finally meet you. I swear I'm not always stoned." She laughs again. "You can meet Lily later, she's in her room. You're really pretty. Do you smoke?"

"I ... No. I don't smoke." My eyes are burning, my head reeling from all the panic. "I'm sorry, I need to go lie down. I don't feel well."

"Oh no! Are you okay, Sara? Do you need anything? Advil? Water? You're not catching that flu that's going around school, are you?"

"I'm fine, Angel. Just tired."

"Are you sure? Do you—"

"I said I'm fine!" The words are brazen and harsh, pushing past the lump in my throat. My stomach feels queasy, and a familiar fullness begins in my mouth.

Sunset.

My fangs are protruding, my vision growing hazier under the incandescent kitchen lights. "Goodnight," I hiss, not daring to look at either of them. I don't want them to see the yellow glow of my eyes. I don't want them to see my fangs.

I don't want them to know I'm a monster.

I race up the stairs, craving the darkness. The solitude of my room blankets me in safety as I shut the door and let out a breath. I turn the lock on the antique brass knob. I don't need anyone coming in or bothering me. What I need is to rest.

The cool breeze from my open window sends prickles all over my skin. A cold sweat licks my brow, my stomach flopping as I turn and look around.

I don't recall leaving the window open.

I make my way over slowly, taking each step with deliberate care. The room has fallen dark as the remaining dusk greets me through the window. I shut it, locking it tight, but it isn't enough. The feeling growing in the pit of my stomach makes it obvious.

I am not alone.

I turn to face him as he slinks out of my closet, the darkness doing nothing to hide the sheer size of his frame. "Hello, Markos."

He moves like a large cat, stalking me until we're mere inches apart. His hand snakes around my neck, cupping the back of my head and forcing me to look up at him.

"Hello, my pet." His mouth is on mine before I can protest. I keep my lips pressed together tight as his tongue glides across them. I don't kiss him back, and can feel his frustration in the way his grip tightens amongst my hair. "Did you not miss me?"

"Must we play these games, Markos? I grow tired of this cat and mouse chase."

He swings his other arm around me and plants it on my lower back, pressing me against him. "You think what we have is a game, Zalida?" His breath tickles my ear. "I would never play with my queen in such a way."

"You need to talk to Leader Taryn, Markos. Tell him you need a new queen announced. I prefer my role in the field, taking care of assignments. Fighting. You deserve a wife who wants to be your trophy, who wants to bear your children. Who will do well to raise the next generation and build you an empire. There's many women in our clan who would make a better wife than me."

He scoops me up in his arms as though I'm weightless, sidestepping to my bedside and slamming my body down on the mattress. I let out a squeak, but his hand clasps my mouth tight. I cry out against his grip as my arms flail, punching at his back and shoulders to no avail.

"*You* will be my queen, Zalida. Leader Taryn has made it so. We will not go against his word." His weight crushes me as he lays on top of me, his hips digging into mine. His manhood presses into my pelvis as it grows, his hand pushing my head upwards to stretch and expose my neck. His mouth latches to me, sucking so hard it hurts.

He's marking me.

He lets go of me as his mouth releases me. "Besides, I *like* the fact that you will need discipline to become the perfect queen. I could make you bear my children here and now, Zalida," he grins. "You could get it over with, submit to me." He laughs. "You might even enjoy it."

"I doubt that highly, Markos." My voice is a seething whisper. "And if you're not careful, my roommates will hear you."

His grin widens. His bright yellow eyes are streaked with lusty red veins. "I could take care of them right now, if you want, Zali. Then you and I can have this big, empty house to ourselves for the remainder of the assignment."

"You will not touch them, Markos. Not today, not ever. And you are not even supposed to be here. What were you thinking, hanging around in broad daylight like that? My roommate saw you staring into the cafe like a creep! Our clan has relocated too many times for you to pull these stunts! Have you considered this? Stop being so selfish, Markos!"

"Argh!" Markos clamps his hands around my biceps and squeezes tightly, forcing a whimper. "You think just because you're around the humans that you can talk to me like this, Zali? Is that what you think? I will be harsh as a king because it is the only way to ensure obedience. And *you*, like all others, *will* be obedient to me, whether you are my queen or not!"

His head shoots down as his mouth clasps the opposite side of my neck. I feel his fangs, long and hard, penetrate my flesh. He doesn't suck, but merely laps up my blood as it trickles into his mouth. His pelvis grows harder, throbbing through his leather pants. Pain radiates from my neck down into my collar bones, and my hands grow all the icier as his grip on my arms impedes blood flow.

"Markos, stop!" I beg. "Stop! You're making it impossible to blend in here! To ... to ... to finish the assignment. Leader Taryn won't be impressed!"

As if a spell has been broken, he raises his head. His hands release me, and my arms immediately fold across my chest defensively. I see the blood all over his lips and teeth as he grins at me, his eyes having transformed from their usual golden hue to a bloodthirsty red.

I am terrified for our wedding night.

"Leader Taryn's days are numbered," Markos says, his words accompanied by a sinister sneer. "Once you complete this assignment and the hunter is taken care of, I will be orchestrating a meeting with Leader Taryn and the Ancestors. It's time a new leader be chosen, and Leader Taryn be granted a seat with the Ancestors. Our clan has only one Ancestor on the roster. It's pathetic."

"And if he refuses?"

Markos smiles. His eyes are wild. His chest heaves as if he's just run a marathon. His breathing is heavy and ragged, labored by the lust and hunger swelling within him. I wonder how long it's been since he's fed. Lochfort might be in far more trouble than a small town could ever comprehend.

He stares down at me, one hand cupping the side of my face while the other snatches up one of my hands and pins it above my head. His breath is hot on my face as he hovers, then he leans forward enough to plant the softest of kisses on my lips.

"*No one* refuses me, Zali," he whispers.

CHAPTER 11

I keep my place by the tree and watch, tucked safely behind its trunk as he sips his coffee.

Or, more likely, some nonsensical pumpkin spice beverage.

The leaves rustle gently above as the smell of autumn floods my nostrils. Across the street, Bumpy's is well lit as the evening hours kiss the sun farewell. I've already shifted, becoming the monstrous version of myself that I hate so much, which means I have to be careful now not to let any of the humans see me. Thankfully, the park is especially quiet tonight and it's made my task of waiting and watching significantly easier.

I pull my scarf tighter around my neck, wincing at the way I throb. The large purple bruise on one side is balanced by the bruised fang punctures on the other. Markos left me heavily marked yesterday, and it'll be at least a week before these fade. But I can't worry about that now. I can't worry about him, or the impending wedding.

I need to focus on finding the hunter.

Dr. Haven takes another sip of his drink, his hand gripping the top paper of the stack in front of him. Student work, I figure. He looks so peaceful sitting there by himself, and I find the gnawing of a certain hunger growing in the pit of my stomach. He's still wearing his gray overcoat and his briefcase sits on the floor beside him, my heightened night vision drinking in every detail as he works, completely unaware of the fact he's being watched.

Silly human. He could so easily get himself killed being that oblivious.

His hands are perfect, and I watch them as he meticulously sets down his mug and picks up a pen, writing something before shifting the paper to the bottom of the stack. He adjusts his glasses before picking up another paper and his drink and continuing.

I wish I could be what those soft, strong hands are holding.

The thought infuriates me, and I almost don't notice the couple coming down the park's well lit path until their chatter is far too close to me. I crouch down and ready my legs, leaping up into the cover of leaves above me. I keep low on one of the branches, closing my eyes as the couple passes to keep from drawing attention to their glow.

Fuck, that was far too close. I need to get my head on straight. I don't need Dr. Haven and his nice hands blowing this for me.

I try to peer into Bumpy's, but I can't see anything through the leaves. My only option is to wait until I'm sure the couple is far enough away and hop back down. My feet are silent as they hit the ground, my body snaking around the tree just in time to see Dr. Haven exiting the cafe. He clasps his briefcase tight as long strides carry him away from me, my heart pounding in my chest.

I spent all day in class watching Dr. Haven closely, looking for anything suspicious, any sign that he might be the hunter. Nothing stood out to me as unordinary. He, like all my other professors, seems far too normal to be lurking around at night killing drauls. But the intel from the Yedora clan in the mountains led me here, and it can't be mistaken. Can it?

Visions of Professor Gibbons flash through my mind. He's one of my psychology teachers, a tall, slender man with a wide nose and prominent eyebrows. Something about him strikes me as odd, though I haven't quite placed my finger on it. Perhaps it's how indifferent he always seems. Almost as though he has more important things on his mind than whatever is happening in class.

Which would make sense, if he's the hunter.

Just as Dr. Haven is about to turn a corner and disappear from sight, I move. I'm lightning in the darkness, eyes glowing as my feet carry me with a speed impossible to spot with the naked eye. The naked *human* eye, at least. I leave nothing but a subtle breeze behind me as I cross the block in a matter of seconds, stopping at the entrance of a narrow alley situated between an old brick apartment and a convenience store.

The blood rushing through my veins brings a stinging to my neck, my hand snaking up under my scarf. The frozen touch of my fingertips soothes the skin, but it does nothing to slow my pounding heart. Dr. Haven freezes, my pulse mirroring him. I duck behind a dumpster, tucked safely out of sight as I imagine him turning to look around, addressing the eerier sixth sense that someone might be following.

I wait, listening close.

My eyes shut tight as I focus, waiting for the gentle thumping of polished shoes against the alley pavement before I dare peer around the dumpster. Dr. Haven is on the move, his form easy to spot under a street lamp as he exits the alley and makes his way across a field of yellow, overgrown scrubland.

I keep a safe distance as I follow him through the night, stopping and waiting as needed. Hiding. He turns to look around every so often, but I never let him spot me. I'm an excellent predator, as all drauls are. Patient, cunning, silent. We were made to hunt prey, to be killers of the night. We can find food and obtain it with unparalleled stealth, not that we need to now that we have the farms.

Human farms.

I shudder. I don't like what we do to them, but what choice do we have? We need to eat like anything else, to sustain ourselves. Still, I can't blame the hunter for doing what they do. For killing us off. After all, I would likely be doing the same if I was still human.

Or maybe I'd actually be a student, living a normal life and working on a bachelor's degree and falling in love. Having a family.

I scold myself for getting lost in such thoughts. I forfeited all this years ago, these fantasies. Drauls aren't made to procreate. We can, but the offspring are always vicious. With no bit of human soul to speak of, they don't contain any level of humanity. They're hard to bear, and even harder to tame. This is exactly why Markos wants them so badly, and exactly why I don't.

My breath catches as I reground my focus in reality. Dr. Haven has crossed the wide field and led us into some industrial type area with big concrete buildings and scattered street lamps, many of which remain unlit despite the dark hour. My pulse flutters. What would a simple university professor be doing out here at night? What could he possibly be up to?

My brain races for an innocent answer, something mundane and easily explained that would rule him out from being the hunter. But I've got nothing.

I keep watching, keep waiting. I sneak around buildings and posts and always keep a safe distance until I watch from afar as he enters through a big, steel door on the back of a short, weathered building. Some of its windows are boarded up and it looks like it's been forgotten amongst the larger surrounding buildings.

Like someone wants it to be forgotten, to go unnoticed.

My heart slams in my chest alongside the steel door as it swings shut behind him, sealing him from my view.

Whatever he's up to ... please don't let him be the hunter.

CHAPTER 12

I snake along the side of the building, crouched low. The window is near impossible to see through, caked with years of dust and rain spots, but it also serves as good cover while I watch him.

Dr. Ross Haven.

Just thinking his name makes me shudder. There's a familiar pull in the pit of my stomach, an aching that makes its way down my upper thighs as breathing grows slightly more difficult. I wish being in the vicinity of him didn't affect me like this.

But it does.

I creep up to the window and peer inside, squinting my yellow eyes to shield as much of their glow as possible. I can see the backside of Dr. Haven's gray overcoat as he stands over a desk, rifling through papers. There's no way I can make out what any of them say despite my enhanced night vision, but he seems set on finding something specific.

His hands trace up along the little shelf at the back of the desk, his fingertips kissing the spines of the thick books lining it. He pulls one half out and then slips it back, then another, and another. Finally, he lands on a hefty book with an emerald green cover looking well worn from time. He flips it open and hunches over slightly, pushing his glasses farther up his nose as he reads.

I watch in silent curiosity as he flips through the green book, my breath held in my chest. The book he's reading looks extremely old, and while I could surmise that a professor might read a lot of old books, this one looks ... different. Like it's from a different time, a different place.

Maybe a different race.

My skin prickles as I hear the distinct sound of footsteps behind me. They're a ways off in the distance, but I don't dare wait for them to get closer. I shuffle around the side of the building, keeping myself tucked and out of sight as I wait to see who else could possibly be roaming this vacant area at night.

I make out the form of a man before his features become visible under the streetlamp.

Professor Gibbons? What is he doing here?

He walks directly up to the building like an old friend, not once slowing his pace. I wait until I hear the slamming of the steel door before making my way back around, my heart pounding in my chest.

I'm becoming convinced that Professor Gibbons and Dr. Haven either *are* the hunters, or *know* the hunter. But while my brain is screaming at me to text Markos and have him meet me here right now, there's another voice, a deeper one, keeping my ice cold hands from taking out my phone and sending the message.

And in a single moment, it hits me as to how desperately I don't want it to be Dr. Haven.

I don't want him to have anything to do with this, and maybe he doesn't. Maybe he's being coerced by Professor Gibbons. Maybe he owes a favor or a debt and is operating out of duty. Maybe he doesn't know anything about the hunting, and the two of them are just out here researching old texts in an abandoned industrial zone at midnight.

Okay, I can admit that that last one is far-fetched.

I go back to spying, but keep my eyes nearly shut. Dr. Haven is still facing away from me, but Professor Gibbons is facing the window and could easily spot my yellow eyes if I open them fully. I watch as he waves his arms emphatically, pointing at the book and then at Dr. Haven before folding his arms over his chest. Whatever they're talking about, he looks frustrated, exasperated even.

I close my eyes and see if I can't make out some of their conversation. The night air is howling through the overgrown grass of the fields, and the air smells distinctly of oil and metals. Concentrating, I press myself against the building's cool concrete alongside the window, listening keenly as I ensure I remain unknown.

"I'm telling you, I've looked ... no more to be found ... want me to do?"

Dr. Haven's voice pulls me in, soothing my mind while simultaneously igniting my body.

"I don't care! We can't do the enchantment without it! I don't care who you have to rob or kill to get it, *find some*! Otherwise the deal is off! This is your end of the arrangement!"

Professor Gibbons's voice rings clear through the window as he shouts. I can imagine his arms flailing about again, his tall, narrow frame jerking here and there.

The two men seem to be arguing about something, something lost or inaccessible. An enchantment? So, they're trying to do some sort of magic. It must be something important for Professor Gibbons to be this upset about it. What the hell is so important that they're discussing it in private at this hour? And what did he mean by the deal will be off?

"I told you ... growing more ... time to mature."

Dr. Haven's voice is like liquid honey, thick and sweet and smooth as he calmly answers. It amazes me how he so easily keeps his composure while Professor Gibbons is acting so hostile. I don't know what they're referring to, what they're potentially growing, but something tells me I'm not going to like the answer when I find out.

And I have to find out. It's my duty to find out for the sake of our kind.

I close my eyes and lean the side of my face closer to the windowpane, fighting to make out their conversation more clearly. I hear Professor Gibbons mumbling something, his voice now dangerously low. I concentrate harder, hold my breath in my chest. Listen.

"Let me see it, Haven."

"I told you, it isn't ready."

"I've not seen it since you said you had it. Let me see it. Now."

"Fine, fine. Keep your knickers on."

I open my eyes a pinch and see him grab his leather brief-case from the floor. He sets it down on the table beside the green book, his fingers hovering over it. Slowly, he opens it, exhaling deeply as one of his perfect hands reaches inside and withdraws something with a subtle blue glow.

I gasp. "It ... It can't be." My voice is a pained whisper, fear clenching my throat and choking up my words. "How did he find it? The Ancestors had it sealed away."

Dr. Haven's hand wraps tightly around the handle, the dagger's ornate blade humming as a dim cerulean light radiates from it. I've heard of the Drauldin blade before, but last I heard the Yedora clan had it safely in their keeping. Leader Taryn never said anything about it being stolen. Did he not know it'd been stolen? Has he been keeping it a secret on purpose?

Regardless, I have to tell him. That dagger is something bitty draul nightmares are made of. The tales are woven throughout our folklore, stories about how a famous monster hunter named Jalvana enchanted the blade with her blood, killed her own mother for being a draul, then spent years training with it and becoming one of the most adept hunters of all time. Legends say she killed over four thousand draul, traveling continents and mercilessly hunting us and dwindling our numbers despite the fact that she herself was half draul.

She's also the only record of a half-breed ever existing.

But it's more story than historical fact to our kind. There's no concrete proof she ever existed, as she supposedly died over three hundred years ago. The blade itself was known to exist, but various clans have different theories on where it came from and how it came to be enchanted.

One bit is agreed on though: The Drauldin has a magic so powerful woven through it that one kiss from its steel is sure to disintegrate even the most powerful draul. The blade glows bright blue when powered with the right conditions, an incantation and the blood of a half-breed. And pressed to the skin of a creature, it shifts from blue to red as it sets the draul ablaze.

I shudder as I wonder if that's all true.

My heart leaps as Professor Gibbons's head snaps in my direction, his eyes landing directly on the spot I'm occupying. I'm fast, ducking out of sight and crab-crawling alongside the building a few steps until I'm far from the window.

Did he see me? I don't think he saw me. He couldn't have seen me. I'm too quick.

Footsteps and rustling echo from inside the building. My normally near-dead pulse is racing, blood pounding in my ears. I can't let them find me here. If my cover gets blown then the mission is a wash, and there's no chance of escaping Markos.

And I'd rather die than marry that monster.

I'm a blur in the night as I move with a speed no human can replicate. I let my feet carry me twenty, fifty, a hundred feet away from the concrete building. The overgrown grass and shrubbery of the surrounding fields serves as excellent cover as I lay my body on the cool ground. My human clothes do little to keep the cold out, but my blood pumping furiously warms me as I wait. I'm still wary of my eyes, their golden glow too much of a heat score for my liking.

Professor Gibbons stands there, gawking around with narrowed eyes that I only catch glimpses of through the swaying brush. My breathing blends into the whistling night air, but I keep my breaths shallow and slow for good measure. Dr. Haven steps out into the night, the glow of the Drauldin fading away into the security of an inner jacket pocket.

The breeze shifts into a direction that carries his scent. A shiver courses through me, but it isn't from the cold. He smells heavenly, like a subtle soap mixed with a woodsy sweetness, and my thighs involuntarily clench together as I close my eyes and fight to make the feeling go away.

I open them again and watch as he and Gibbons exchange words, the two of them nodding as they continue looking around. Looking for *me*. They seem set to find something, but I'm certain they won't be able to spot me from this distance. Not with the cover of nightfall and the tall grass.

The wind is bittersweet as it stops any possibility of eavesdropping on their conversation while also aiding my cover. I let out a gentle sigh as Dr. Haven retreats back into the building. It's only Professor Gibbons standing there now, his head moving left to right and back again as he scans the horizon.

I watch as he takes one step forward, then pauses. I can reckon he's wondering whether his mind is playing tricks on him, whether he actually saw something move outside the window or not. The Drauldin makes it clear they're the ones who've been hunting us, though I'm still not certain which of them is doing the actual killing. Maybe both.

I really hope it isn't both of them. Dr. Haven is an academic, and an unlikely killer. He's warm, and I can tell how much he cares about his students. Someone like that can't be running around spending their nights murdering innocent creatures.

Are we innocent, though?

My thoughts run back to the farm and my stomach pulls. It's been too long since I've fed and it's clouding my thoughts and judgment. I need to head back to camp and report my findings to Leader Taryn and the clan. But just the thought of this makes my heart ache with a heaviness that shakes me to my very core.

I don't know if I can bring myself to do it.

I don't know if I can bring myself to report Dr. Haven's involvement.

At least now I know why he's always so protective of that damn briefcase. The Drauldin is nothing to toy with, and I can imagine acquiring it was a feat. I wonder where he found it. Something among all those old books must have led him to it, must have helped him in tracking it down. As far as I knew, the Yedora clan had it deep in the earth being guarded by their strongest drauls, and it hadn't been seen in over two centuries.

There's more to Dr. Haven than what sultry bits meet the eye, that's for sure.

Professor Gibbons pulls a pair of leather gloves from his coat pocket and slips them on one by one, taking his time as his eyes continue surveying. I need him to go back inside so I can resume spying on them, but just as the thought occurs Dr. Haven reappears, setting his leather briefcase down as he locks the heavy, steel door.

I need to get the Drauldin, and I need to get into that building and see exactly what's all in those books.

I watch as he crouches down and zips the key safely into one of the front briefcase pockets, picking it up as he stands to face Gibbons. The two stand eerily close together, Gibbons leaning in to talk as if he's worried someone might hear them, out here, in the middle of nowhere in the middle of the night. They shake hands, a stiff gesture mixed with an air of professional tension.

Then I watch as Professor Gibbons takes off into the night with unexpected speed.

An inhuman speed.

A *draul* speed.

CHAPTER 13

The pain in my chest gnaws its way up until it forms a lump in my throat. My room is dark save the light of my laptop screen. I don't want Angel or the others to know I'm awake. I can hear their chit chat from downstairs wafting up in periodic fits of giggles.

And not only do I not want them to see my true form, but I have work to do.

I stare at the screen, reading each line slowly. An article from two years ago based in a town several hours north of here. It's where my clan had been situated before we moved to the outskirts of Citrus County. Before we were raided and forced to move by the hunter. Before we were forced to move by *him*.

No, I can't think that. Just because he's working with Gibbons doesn't mean he's killed any of us. They've made some sort of deal, Gibbons said it himself. Obviously Dr. Haven's been roped into this somehow ... and now it's up to me to get him out.

The thought sinks down to the pit of my stomach and sits there, heavy and nauseating. I can't assume that Dr. Haven wants or needs my help. I can't assume that he wants to be relieved of whatever transaction he and Gibbons have going on, and yet ... I *need* to believe it.

I let my eyes continue down the article, taking in the points about the disappearances. Every time we have to relocate, which has only become more and more frequent over the past decade, we have to set up a new farm. And with no way to stealthily relocate all the humans in our current farm, or with the farm often being raided, it means capturing an entirely new batch of humans.

But we don't take children. We don't destroy families. We've always done this as humanely as possible.

The article talks about a town, Manning, having a series of disappearances. 27 locals vanished over the course of a couple months, mostly couples in their twenties or thirties, and all of whom had been hiking in the nearby forest. And then, as abruptly as they'd started, the disappearances stopped. The local authorities surmised the cause was an animal that then either died or relocated.

But that's because they don't know what's actually out there, lurking in the dark. In the trees. They don't know we exist.

We've kept our existence a secret from the humans for such a long time, but it's getting harder and harder. The hunter keeps tracking us and forcing us to move, and every time we have to catch new humans and disrupt a new area. We try to move far enough away that the connections are never made, but the process is a slippery slope and Leader Taryn is expecting an avalanche if we can't take the hunter out once and for all.

I open another tab on my browser, one I've got set to a separate article. This article is about an oil company granting a sizable donation to Manning College. The article shows a picture of the CEO of the donor company standing next to the dean and there, not far in the background, are Dr. Haven and Professor Gibbons.

Fuck.

This can't be a coincidence. It just can't be. How long have Dr. Haven and Professor Gibbons been working together? How long have they *known* each other? This picture is from three years ago, but this can't be as deep as I can dig. I have to find out more.

I search the name *Bentley Gibbons* and watch as dozens of links pop up. The name doesn't appear overly common as my eyes rifle through various headings. I click on one that talks about a contribution of research in the psychology of people with PTSD. Sure enough, the article is headed by a photo of Gibbons standing in a line of people, clearly celebrating as they all hold glasses of champagne in front of what looks to be a school. He and four others stand there, all with wide smiles, their faces aglow with the light of a streetlamp.

And then it hits me.

It's night time in this picture, just as it was in the industrial yard. And Professor Gibbons is unnaturally fast, but his eyes don't glow. And he didn't sound like he was speaking past fangs. So ... what is he?

There has to be an explanation, but I can't risk getting closer to Gibbons, not while I have no idea what he is or what he's capable of. Which means there's only one logical solution, though it's one I'm convinced is neither easy nor the best idea.

I have to get closer to Dr. Haven.

CHAPTER 14

I try not to fixate on his hands as he tidies the papers on his desk, rearranging them into neat piles. The way he's very particular about it intrigues me, and curiosities of how neat and organized his place must be start to creep into my mind. And the way his hands look so strong and smooth, I can't help imagining what they'd feel like running along my cheeks, down my neck ... then lower.

For fuck sakes.

As if I have time to think of such things. His desk, his house, his hands. None of that matters while he's aiding a hunter who's taken out dozens of our kind. It makes sense that Gibbons is the one killing us with how fast he is. Dr. Haven might not be doing the hunting himself, but he's working alongside Gibbons, and Markos and Leader Taryn aren't going to extend any amount of mercy if they find out.

That's why I have to warn him.

There's that pull in my chest again, the one that seems to be constant any time he's close. As hard as I've tried to fight it, and as hard as I've tried to reason with myself, nothing seems to alleviate it. And nothing makes being in his presence any easier, especially when he always smells so damn good.

"Show me the notes," he says, and I hand them to him.

"I figured it was fine to get a head start on the project since you've not had any time to meet up. You seem to be very ... *occupied* ... as of late, Dr. Haven."

He eyes me up and down, a gesture I wish didn't make my thighs clench together in my seat. His gaze lingers just a moment too long on my chest, and then again on my mouth before his eyes finally climb back up to meet mine. The top I'm wearing, another Vanthony special, is a simple, white button-up blouse. It isn't low cut or revealing, but it seems incredibly distracting all the same.

Dr. Haven clears his throat. "Yes, well, I'm always busy this far into the semester."

"With grading?" I narrow my eyes ever so slightly. I don't expect him to tell me the truth, not yet, but I'm not about to make keeping his secrets easy.

He easily kept his composure as Professor Gibbons yelled at him. Let's see if he can do the same sitting alone with me in his office.

"Largely. But I also have meetings, putting things together for upcoming courses, tweaking current ones, student visits. There's never any shortage of work around here. At least, not until I get time off in the summer."

I won't still be around by then. And if you're not careful, Dr. Haven, you won't be either.

My lips part slightly as I debate asking him what his plans are for the summer. Childish fantasies of us drinking coffee at Bumpy's on a sunny afternoon flood my brain, and I sigh in response.

"I'm sorry if you feel like I've been too busy for you."

His voice is soft, dangerously genuine as his eyes sink into mine. His blue eyes swirl with bits of soft gray as he watches me, focused solely on me as he waits for my response.

"It's okay. I ... I know you're busy, Dr. Haven."

His arms extend out across his desk and I sit there, so desperately wanting to place my hands in his. He seems to be studying every feature of my face, memorizing every detail as we sit there together, the room heavy with things left unsaid.

Fuck it.

I take my hands out of my lap and place them on the desktop, letting them rest inches from his. It's a bold but quiet move, daring him to touch me so I can revel in the way his skin feels against mine. My eyes plead with him to give in to whatever this is, this thing between us that is so frightfully wrong in every sense. Not only is he my teacher ... but he's out to kill me.

And I don't care one bit about either.

My breathing stops as he grants what I was hoping for and scoops my hands into his, his warm skin melting against mine as he squeezes gently. I'm lost in his eyes as he watches me from behind his glasses, glasses I wonder if he'd keep on or take off if he ever made love to me.

"I said I would assist you with the project, Sara, and I meant it. I'm glad you had the chance to get started on it on your own, but I promise to make time to watch the next two people with you. It's just hard for me as I've had ... other things on the go."

Is this his way of pushing me to ask for more? Does he want to confess what he's been up to? To let me in?

"More classwork?" I ask softly, not wanting to push too hard.

His head hangs heavy, like he couldn't bear to hold eye contact with me while lying. "Something like that. More like ... a personal project."

Now's my chance.

"Something I can help with, Dr. Haven?"

His eyes look so sad as he looks at me once more. The

swirling grays have turned to a gloomy storm in his eyes, and he suddenly looks tired, as though keeping all the secrets is starting to take a toll on him.

I know the feeling all too well, Dr. Haven. That's why I need to be rid of this assignment and this school and ... you.

Dr. Haven pulls his hands from mine and my heart stings. He clears his throat and adjusts his glasses, as if realizing who I am and where we are and the absurd inappropriateness of it all. "No, I ... Thank you, Miss Summers. I appreciate the offer, really. I've just got a lot of hobbies that have become a bit time consuming and bogged me down. I'll be fine once this semester is over."

Why, what's happening come the end of the semester? Are you retiring from being Professor Gibbons's aid?

"Of course," I say. I bite back the irritation I feel from him taking his hands off mine and shove them back in my lap as they return to their icy state. "I just thought, you know, if there was anything I could do for you to alleviate some stress ..."

My vocal chords betray me as the words slip out chock full of need. I didn't intend for the insinuation they've mustered. I feel my cheeks burn as his eyes grow dark and hungry. I fight to keep my thoughts from pulling in wild directions, directions where I make quick work of his desk so there's nothing left between us as I get down on my knees in front of him.

"Miss Summers, I don't ... I mean, I don't think there's anything—"

"Good, that's good," I cut him off before he can say anything else. "I just wanted to see if there was anything you might need help with. You know, research or ... whatever."

"Whatever?"

I need to get the conversation back on track. I need information,

Dr. Haven, not to sit here fantasizing about doing unspeakable things to you.

"I imagine you've no shortage of research required for classes or ... personal projects."

Fuck, how am I failing so miserably at making this not sound sexual?

He eyes me up and down again. "Of course there's always research to be done, Miss Summers. But I'm quite adept at handling it myself."

Then what do you need Professor Gibbons for? Just the hunting?

"I see." I tuck my frozen hands between my thighs and squeeze, savoring the heat that radiates from between my legs any time he's near. "Okay."

"However there is something ... No, never mind."

My heart jumps. "What? What is it?"

"Nothing. I shouldn't have said anything. It wouldn't be an appropriate thing to suggest."

Oh, now you HAVE to tell me.

"Please, Dr. Haven. We're both adults." I let my dark eyes challenge his. "Tell me what you were thinking."

"I don't—"

"Please." My voice is a whimper that pushes past pouty lips as I watch him, waiting. Waiting for him to give in. Waiting for him to trust me enough to be honest, to let me in just a little bit.

"I've been thinking about our people-watching exercise."

'Our'? The exercise you so craftily paired us on?

"And?"

He swallows, and the way his throat moves is divine. Hunger ignites within me and radiates through my whole body, the rest of the room melting away as I grab the edge of his desk to keep from lunging across it and tackling him to the ground.

"And there's a woman who lives in the building across

from me who I think would make an excellent character for the project. She's elderly and has a pet parrot. They sit out on her balcony most afternoons and the parrot talks non-stop. She's eccentric enough that I think she'd make a fun addition to our story. What do you think?"

An unfamiliar sense of nervousness creeps over me as I study his eyes, beautiful and still full of raw hunger. "Are you suggesting ... that I come over to your place so we can observe this lady, Dr. Haven?"

He shifts in his seat and clears his throat, his eyes never breaking contact with mine. "Only if you're assuring me that you're comfortable with that, Miss Summers."

Oh, I'm more than comfortable with that, Dr. Haven. It's you who should be uncomfortable.

"Certainly," I say, mustering conviction in my tone, "for the sake of the project."

"Precisely. For the sake of the project," he echoes, his eyes saying something else entirely.

"When did you have in mind?"

His eyes slip down to my hands which still clutch the front edge of his desk. My fingernails have dug in slightly, leaving eight little imprints in the wood. I cough and rip my hands away, tucking them under my legs and wondering if he'll mention it.

But he doesn't.

He just sits there watching me, seemingly amused as his mouth shifts to a smirk while the usual blue tone of his eyes pours back into his irises. "Are you busy on Saturday?"

Saturday, perfect! Sunday I'm supposed to go back to the farm and meet with Leader Taryn and Markos to update them on my findings. If we meet on Saturday, there's a chance I can steal the Drauldin and return it to its rightful place with the Yedora clan. That, plus the confession of Professor Gibbons being both the hunter and a non-

human, should be enough for Leader Taryn to consider the mission complete and award me relief from this betrothal.

Then a sinking feeling hits me.

Once the mission is over, that's it. I go back to the Osjhka clan and go back to helping run the farm. Dr. Haven goes back to teaching and ... what will he do without Professor Gibbons around? Just be a professor? Hopefully he'll be relieved, happy to be rid of whatever duty he feels to the arrangement.

Either way, his life goes back to one without ... *me.*

"Miss Summers?" I relish the way his hands move as he adjusts his glasses, staring at me quizzically. "If Saturdy doesn't work—"

"Saturday is perfect, Dr. Haven. Does two o'clock work?"

He nods and the smile that creeps over his lips is down-right scrumptious. "Two o'clock is perfect."

"Perfect," I repeat, letting the word linger on my lips. Dr. Haven's looking like an afternoon snack sitting across from me, and this room is feeling stuffy as hell. I need to get out of here. In three sleeps I'll be inside his place and will no doubt have ample opportunity to do some proper digging.

The hard part is going to be refraining from digging my fangs into his perfect neck.

CHAPTER 15

"You can't sit there and tell me to be calm, Sara! How can I be calm? How is that possible? It's not! There's no way I can be calm about this! And I can't just sit around here and do nothing while Meredith is out there, probably alone and scared somewhere!"

Consoling humans is not one of my strengths.

I don't know what to say to Angel. I don't have any perfect words to ease her mind or alleviate her stress.

On the contrary, I believe she has every reason to be afraid.

"Try not to freak out, Angel." I keep my voice unnervingly calm despite the situation that's unfolded since the wee hours of the morning. "Let's go over the details again. Where was the last place you saw her?"

"I told you, I saw her at the campfire! She was at the campground hanging out with those ... those guys! I told her not to hang out with those guys! They weren't from Lochofort, Sara! None of them were. I didn't recognize any of them! But they had drinks and a fire going and she said it'd be fine if she stayed and hung out for a couple hours. Who knows what they've done with her! What if they kidnapped her? They're not even there anymore! Mr. Fulton said they checked out this morning! What if they took her with them?"

"Do you think she was passed out in their RV and they just ... left with her? Why would they do that? They'd have to know she'd be upset when she woke up," I say.

"I don't know! I just know that they've done something with her, something terrible! That's the only way she would have stayed out all night like that. And now it's almost one o'clock and there's still no answer on her phone. It's just going straight to voicemail and she isn't answering any of her texts."

"Her phone is likely dead," I think aloud. "Did those guys say where they were headed?"

"Yeah, to the island. Mr. Fulton says they checked out of the campsite an hour ago. They could be anywhere by now!"

"There's only one highway out of here that leads to the island, Angel. If that's where they're headed, then it's unlikely they'd be anywhere but on that road."

"Okay but they have an hour head start! And what if they lied about where they're going? What if they turn off and head somewhere else? You're not thinking of going after them, are you? You don't even have a car. I guess you could rent one. Wait, do you even have your license?"

"You need to go to class, Angel."

"Excuse me? But I—"

"Trust me. You don't want to send the entire school into an uproar, do you? You go to class, and I promise I'll handle this."

She stares at me, her sad eyes bright with curiosity. "What ... What are you going to do?"

My lips curl up in a grin. "What did you say they were driving?"

❦

THE HIGHWAY IS PARTICULARLY dead this morning. There's a bite to the air as it rushes past my face, nipping at my nose and cheeks. I keep my eyes focused as I race through the woods that run parallel to the highway until I see it, the unmistakable RV with various symbols spray painted on the sides. The various colors of neon paint glow against the backdrop of gray road and yellowed autumn grass.

There's no piece of me that believes Meredith is with these guys. Markos hasn't been keeping away from Lochfort as Leader Taryn suggested, and he made it perfectly clear that he would have no problem meddling with the humans I've been growing closer to. No, if I had to guess, I wouldn't think Meredith is with some random hippies who were traveling through town.

I'd guess she's on the farm.

But I don't know where these guys are headed, and on the slim chance that she is with them, I need to check them out before they get too far away. The farm isn't going anywhere, I can check it after if it turns out she's not in the RV. If Markos took her to the farm, then at least she'll be alive.

For now.

I keep myself aligned with the RV as I fly through the woods, moving far too fast for any of these guys to make me out through the trees should they be looking out a window. I have to get the timing just right, a big enough gap in the trees.

I see my opportunity and grab the side of a tree, my nails digging into the bark as I launch myself out and onto the roof of the RV. The whole thing rattles slightly, but I keep myself pressed down until it steadies. I lay there, ear pressed down as I try to make out the voices inside. I pick up four distinct voices, all male, muffled through the layers of metal. No Meredith.

I could rip the RV open like a sardine can if I wanted to,

but there's no reason to alert the humans to my presence. If I start pulling stunts like that, I'll have no choice but to either take them to the farm or kill them right here. It's too big a risk to leave witnesses when our kind is exposed.

I need to wait for a chance to be stealthy.

And I do. It's almost an hour before the guys finally pull off into a rest stop. The four of them exit the camper and head into the little building that houses bathrooms. There's a few stragglers moseying around, and I have to be careful as I roll to the edge of the roof and climb down the side.

Those humans didn't even bother locking the door, I think as I make my way inside. The camper smells of unwashed laundry and processed snacks. It's nauseating, and I hold my breath as I continue to look around. Nothing looks out of the ordinary. The place is messy, with papers scattered about and clothes hanging off every bit of furniture. It looks like the typical space you'd imagine if you thought of a band of young men living on the road. Nothing spectacular, nothing unusual.

I check the room in the back. The bed pulls up to reveal storage underneath, hiding nothing but a guitar and more clothing. The closets are full of band t-shirts and ripped jeans, and the couch is folded out into a bed with the dining table folded up into the wall. It's not a big space, and there's no viable place for a full grown woman to be hiding.

I creep back outside just as the group reemerges from the rest stop hut. They're laughing, completely unaware of my presence. I creep around to the side of the bus and check the outer storage, but all I find are crates of snowboarding gear. There's nothing amiss here. These are just regular guys traveling together who invited a young woman to join them for drinks at their campfire.

"Hey you! What do you think you're doing?"

I slam the storage door shut and turn around. A gruff middle-aged man is heading over to me, his stride filled with determination. He watches me, a fat sausage-like finger waggling at me as he walks. "What you sneaking 'round that RV for? Is that yours?"

Other humans begin to take notice, and before long there's a small group of onlookers hovering around. I glance around. There are no children. Amongst the bodies is an elderly couple, a trio of women who look to be in their early to mid twenties, and a pudgy, wrinkle-faced woman who I assume is the wife of the gentleman yelling at me.

The four men come out of their RV at the sound of the commotion. "What's going on?" the guy with the wiry frame and an afro asks.

"This young lady was snooping through your stuff!" the man barks. "Do you know her?"

"No," another guy answers, this one stockier. Meatier. "Never seen her." His attention turns to me. "Hey, is that true? Were you going through our stuff?"

I sigh. The gruff man doesn't realize the doom he's fated all these people to.

"I'm sorry," I say.

"Sorry?!" the third guy bellows. "'Sorry' doesn't cut it! Why were you going through our shit? What were you looking for? Food?"

"I'm not sorry for that," I whisper. "I'm sorry for what I'm about to do."

CHAPTER 16

It's Friday. There's only one more sleep until I'll find myself inside Dr. Haven's house, alone with him. It's a thought that's both jarring and far too exciting. I should be focused on the mission, on collecting the Drauldin and figuring out exactly what his role is in all of this. But my brain is busy conjuring a plan of its own. A plan for how I can erase any signs of his involvement and consequently spare his life.

And how I'm going to handle being alone in that close of a vicinity to him without letting the feral bits of me take over. His soul would likely be the sweetest I've ever tasted.

My stomach growls. I need to eat.

Sunday, I remind myself. *I'll be back at the farm on Sunday. And then I can look for Meredith.*

I don't even know if she's at the farm. For all I know, Markos could have carried her off deep into the woods somewhere and just had her as a personal snack. I don't know. He's been especially anxious lately, texting me multiple times a day to remind me that I'm his property and that I owe Leader Taryn a name on Sunday or he's going to pull me from the mission.

And a name, singular, is all he's going to get from me ... I hope.

I haven't fully decided one way or the other whether to expose Dr. Haven's involvement. I can't make the choice until I search around his place and see what I find. Part of me wants to be upfront with him and let him know everything. Tell him what I am, tell him what he's gotten himself mixed up in and how close to death he is because of it.

But I can't.

If he finds out I'm a draul, I'll automatically become his next target. Would he tell Professor Gibbons about me? Would the two of them come after me, hunting me down with the enchanted Drauldin and putting a brisk end to my monstrous existence?

Would that be so bad?

That'd be one way to alleviate my betrothal, that's for sure. Not to say that I wish for death, but I certainly have moments where I wonder what it's like. Is it easier than living in hiding? Is it easier than living with the guilt I feel every time I go to the farm?

The farm.

My stomach is simultaneously ravenous and queasy at the thought. It's been so pleasant playing human for a while, having a break from the clan and their feral energy. It's cute sitting in the cafe having coffee, and working mindlessly through my classes, and staying up late chatting with Angel.

Angel ... Poor Angel. She's an absolute mess with Meredith gone.

The whole school is abuzz with nervous energy. Word's gotten around that Meredith is missing, and there's a noticeable fear in the air. I can smell it every time I enter the building. Even back at the house with Angel and Lily. They've put missing posters up all over town. None of the women walk anywhere alone anymore. Everyone stays together. Everyone goes directly home after school. The air is stagnant as all the humans try to go about their lives as though everything is normal.

But I can't let myself become fixated on the situation. There's only two possibilities in my mind. Either Meredith is alive and at the farm, her soul being harvested bit by bit as they keep her a chained up prisoner, or she's already dead and the memory of her will fade over time as she stays in the roster of missing people files at the local police department.

If she is at the farm ... maybe I can help her. Save her. Though, I'd be risking my own life because if I got caught freeing a human—

"Sara!"

The pitchy voice rattles me, a bony hand extending out beside me.

"Professor Gibbons!" I shake his hand and pretend as though I were reading the poster tacked up on the bulletin board in front of me.

"Thinking of joining the drama club?" he asks, and the way he smiles at me makes my skin crawl.

"No, I was just checking the details for a friend. I'm sadly not much of an actress."

"Ah," he says in a tone that tells me he doesn't believe a word I've said. "I see. That's too bad. You're so pretty, I think you'd make a natural choice for any lead role if you had even an inkling of talent. I'm sure you must have ... *talents* ... don't you, Sara?"

Is he coming on to me?

I refrain from cocking a brow as I grit my teeth. "Thank you, Professor Gibbons, but I assure you that isn't the case. Besides, I'm far too busy with my studies for your class to be taking on any extracurriculars."

"Of course," he smiles again. His arm shoots out until he leans against the wall, blocking me in on the side that would be easiest to escape his company through. A sea of students pours past me on the other side, people eagerly making their way to their next class or wherever else. "I'm happy I spotted you here," he continues. "I was wanting to ask you about something. An opportunity."

Color me intrigued, Professor Gibbons. Perhaps this opportunity will allow me to find out exactly who you are ... and what.

"Oh?" I feign lack of interest. "As I stated, Professor Gibbons, I really am quite busy with my classes."

"This wouldn't take up much of your time," he assures me. "As a matter of fact, I'd only need you for an hour or so in the evening."

"The evening?" I shoot back, my composure slightly shaken. "I'm an early riser, and thus very early to bed. If you mean early evening, I can always make early evening work. But you still haven't explained to me what this is all about, Professor."

His smile forms into a sneer, and I swear I see a hint of red glow coming in through his usually hazel eyes. "I was hoping you could help me look through some old books one night this week. For a bit of research, you know. I could use a fresh set of eyes on these materials. I've been over them so many times, it's as though the words simply melt together every time I read them."

"And you don't have anyone else who can help with this research?" I challenge. "No colleague or friend who might be better suited? Not that I have a problem with research, Professor Gibbons, but as a first year student I hardly think I'd be the most qualified candidate for such a task."

"Oh, on the contrary, Sara, I think you'd be the *perfect* candidate."

His words hang with an uncomfortable air of insinuation, a level of pompous expectation that makes me ill and infuriates me. "And where are you thinking this research would take place, Professor? In the uni's library, I assume?"

His grin shifts from devious to downright wicked. "Actually, Sara, I was hoping you could meet me at my office. Not my campus office, I mean my private office. I think you might be familiar with it, actually."

"Professor, I assure you there's no way I'm—"

"It's in the industrial yard on the northeast edge of town. You know the area?"

Fuck, he knows I was there. "No, I don't think—"

"A bit run down, but it makes for an excellent spot to do work. Quiet. Secluded. The sort of spot where, in the later hours of the day, no one would hear you scream for miles. The perfect spot for discussing things in complete and utter privacy. Do you understand what I mean?"

His hazel eyes grow plumes of swirling red as he watches me, waiting to see whether I answer truthfully. He knows I was there, and he wants me to know it. But why? If he wanted to kill me, he could have baited me to a different place and attempted it. Why show me all his cards by confessing his knowledge of my presence that night?

"Now that you mention it, Professor Gibbons," I growl, keeping my voice low amongst the many students still in the halls, "I believe I do know the area you're talking about. I think I've been there before ... *once.*"

"I thought so," he says, smiling wider. His eyes quickly return to normal, the bits of red smoke dissipating at the edges of his irises. "And since you're acquainted with the area, I trust you'll have no problem finding your way to my office. Sunday. Nine o'clock."

I debate whether this move is in my best interest. He wants to meet after dark, which leads me to believe he knows, or at least has an idea, of what I am. But he could also be picking a later time simply because it suits his schedule. If I push for day time, will it only confirm to him that I'm a draul? Is going at night better, because my vision and senses will be heightened and in better condition to fight him off in the event he's seeking confrontation?

Will Dr. Haven be there?

If he is, and Professor Gibbons attacks me, there'll be no way to hide what I am regardless what time of day it is.

"I think I have a previous engagement on Sunday, sadly," I say, keeping my eyes locked on his lest he try anything funny. "I'll have to see if I can rearrange some stuff in my schedule."

"Yes, well you do that. But I should warn you, I think it'd be wise of you to accept my invitation, Sara. I'm not one for waiting, nor for extending multiple invites to those that decline."

"You're the one asking for *my* help, Professor," I remind him, "if what you're saying is true and this is about your research, that is."

He chuffs, his expression growing sour. "Of course. Fair point, Sara. But I really do think it's best if we do it Sunday. It *is* the full moon, after all."

Shit, is it? Already? That means there's only a little over a month until the wedding. I need to make sure I serve Leader Taryn someone's head on a platter before then. Perhaps literally, depending how this meeting goes.

"And what significance is that?" I ask, genuinely curious.

"Some types of research are best conducted when the moon is full, as you know."

Yeah, the types related to performing bits of magic that have long been banned.

"I don't know if you're fully aware of the amount of truth behind that statement, Professor Gibbons. Unless you specialize in a very ... *exclusive* ... form of research."

"You'd be amazed what I get up to when I'm not busy teaching vagrants the uselessness of human psychology, Sara. I'm not one to let all of my talents be wasted in an institution such as this."

"You think the university is useless?" The halls have emptied, with only a few stragglers here and there passing by. No one within earshot.

"I think humans are useless, Sara."

I feel my eternally cold hands grow clammy. I think of his face in the hospital, his human face, and how sad and fragile it looked in his last minutes. But as fragile as he was, I'd never thought of him as useless. After all, I was human once upon a time as well, albeit a time so long ago now that what memories I have left are few and broken and ... fragile.

"I couldn't disagree more," I say, unable to hide the disdain from my voice. "If that's all, Professor Gibbons, I have a class to get to that I'm now late for."

"Of course!" He waves a grandiose arm outwards toward the hall, removing his other hand from the spot that had me feeling trapped. "As you were."

I start walking down the hall, my brisk pace interrupted as he calls out to me before I'm more than ten feet away.

"Oh, and Sara?"

"Yes, Professor Gibbons?" I ask without turning around.

"On Sunday ... Don't bring Markos. It wouldn't be in either of your best interests."

And just like that, my hands shift from clammy to solid ice.

CHAPTER 17

It's Saturday, which can only mean one thing: No more sleeps. It's officially the day that I am to meet Dr. Haven at his house. At least, I presumed it was a house, but as my boots clack against the sidewalk that matches the dreary tone of today's sky, I see that it isn't a house, but a quaint little condominium.

The building only totals four floors, and straight across the road from it is a similar looking building that's a couple floors higher with balconies hanging in front of sets of sliding glass doors. The buildings are all old and tired, but I couldn't have expected much more from a town with barely twenty-thousand people.

Except I did expect more, I expected he'd have a detached property, something more silent and spacious and ... private.

For a man who's likely a monster hunter, or at least working alongside one, it seems an odd choice. But then, maybe it helps him blend in with all the other occupants. Maybe it's better because he doesn't have any nosy neighbors peeking out their windows and watching him come and go all hours of the night. No doubt the apartment has multiple routes to leave by, keeping his whereabouts and activities concealed.

And how long has he been involved with Professor Gibbons and the hunting anyway?

A woman on a balcony smiles at me, giving me a silent nod. I smile and offer a gentle wave, curious as to why she seems to be keeping such a close eye on me. I keep walking to the building Dr. Haven lives in, and every time I look across the street her eyes are still on me, still following me.

Still watching me.

She's an interesting looking woman, with an oversized fur coat and a large purple scarf wrapped messily around her head. When I look again, she's leaning slightly backwards in her chair and motioning back at the opening in her patio door, but her eyes stay glued to me, and the slight smile on her lips never leaves.

She must be motioning to someone inside.

I make my way through a set of glass doors and find myself in a surprisingly large, open front lobby. The wall on the right is a six-foot high set of metal post boxes, and on the left is a buzzer with a list of names and many yellowed plastic buttons. It has that older apartment smell, musty with scents of various foods being cooked. I swallow hard.

I find Dr. Haven's name near the bottom of the list on the right, beside the number 407, his apartment and buzzer numbers matching. I punch it in and wait, listening to the metallic dialing sound the old intercom system makes before hearing the buzz indicating the inner door is now unlocked.

The elevator is already waiting on the main floor, the doors opening immediately after I press the button, but the ride to the fourth floor feels like an eternity. I shove my hands deep into my jacket pockets, frustrated by the clamminess that's ensued from how nervous I feel.

I don't know whether I'm more nervous about seeing his place, being alone with him, or actively snooping through his stuff any moment he's not watching. Will he even leave me alone anywhere long enough to dig around? I wouldn't leave people unattended with anything important if I were a monster hunter. But I'm not a monster hunter, just a monster. I have one secret to keep ... How many does Dr. Haven have?

I step out of the elevator and find his unit at the end of a long hallway covered in cheap paint and dirty carpet that looks as though it hasn't been steam cleaned since the seventies. My hand hovers in front of the door, ready to knock just below the brass *407* numbers, when it swings open to reveal Dr. Haven standing there, smiling widely.

"You made it!" he says in a way that expresses he didn't think I'd actually come.

"Of course. I said I would come over and work on the project." I step inside and take in the minimalistic surroundings. The inside of the condo is surprisingly nice, far nicer than the rest of the building. It's obvious he's done renovations and updated the space in recent years. "Wow, your place is—"

"Much nicer than the rest of this shithole?" He laughs. "The condo board might not want to spend any money improving the place, but I wasn't about to let them stop me from making my unit less of an eyesore. You should have seen it when I first moved in. Three words: Yellow shag carpet."

"Gross," I laugh. I step further past the entryway and let my fingers trace the smooth granite countertops. The kitchen is small but cozy, with barstools lined up against a raised counter and the rest of the space an open living area. A large bookcase packed floor to ceiling with books takes up most of the far wall, and a black velvet couch sits beside a glass-top table with brass legs. In the corner there's a desk littered with books and papers. Everything sits on beautiful hardwood floors, and the walls are painted a toasty gray.

"It's not always this clean, but I figured I should tidy up before you got here."

"It's very lovely." I inhale deeply, savoring the scent of him mixed with the smell of fresh coffee. "And you made—"

"I figured you might appreciate some coffee."

I smile as he saunters into the kitchen. "I'd love some."

He pulls two mugs from the cupboard and fills them before he sets one in front of me. "What do you take in it?" he asks, opening the fridge.

"Nothing!" I clear my throat. "I don't need anything, I'll just take it black. Thank you."

My stomach can barely handle the coffee alone, never mind cream or any other human food.

He eyes me curiously, cocking his head as he grins. "Okay, then. Black it is. Happy I chose a good roast."

I take a sip, swallowing it and the nausea down. "It's good. Really good."

"It's one of my favorites," he says. He adds a splash of almond milk to his before grabbing his cup and walking over to me. I can feel the warmth radiating from his body as he passes me, all of my muscles clenching simultaneously. "Come on, I want to show you something."

I follow him to the living room where he pulls back a thick, dark curtain, revealing a massive window with a view of the street. Across the road is the taller building I saw earlier, and on one of the balconies is the woman who was smiling at me. A bright green parrot sits on her shoulder, bobbing up and down as though it's listening to music.

"The woman you were talking about," I muse. "I saw her earlier. She nodded at me and watched me the whole time I walked down the street until I got into your building. It was a bit weird."

"See why I said she'd make an excellent candidate for the project?" Dr. Haven laughs and shakes his head. "That woman has lived in that apartment for a long time, longer than I've lived in this building."

"And how long have you lived in this building?" I ask.

"Oh, it has to be over a decade by now. Let me think ... Pretty sure it's been eleven years. Twelve as of January. The year I moved in was terrible, too. The winter was especially hard and there was a lot of snow. Moving in the winter is the worst."

"Agreed," I say, thinking about all the times our clan has had to relocate in the winter months. "Yeah, it's definitely not fun."

Dr. Haven moves away from the curtain, letting it fall. His arm brushes against mine as he turns, sending a shiver down my spine. The coffee smells lovely, but he smells better, and far more delicious. Our eyes meet and my hands instinctively clench my mug, snapping the handle off with a loud crack as coffee spills out all over the floor.

"I'm so sorry!" I blurt, holding the cracked mug in one hand and the handle in the other. "I don't ... I didn't mean to—"

"It's okay, Miss Summers," he says, briskly setting his mug down on the coffee table. "I've been meaning to replace these anyway. These mugs are antique."

Embarrassment stings my cheeks as I watch him take my broken mug and pour the coffee left in it in the sink before tossing it in the garbage. He brings a cloth and I snatch it from him, a look of surprise washing over his distinguished features.

"Please, let me get it," I say as I bend down to wipe up the mess.

"I'll get you another coffee." He heads back into the kitchen, retrieving another cup and pouring a fresh coffee as I watch him. He looks even more handsome from where I'm crouched on the floor as he makes his way back to me, setting my new coffee on the table as he holds a hand out. I put my hand in his, the heat from his soft skin sinking into me as he helps me back to standing.

"Thanks," I say softly, the word a breathy whisper.

"Think nothing of it, Miss Summers." The way he stares down at me makes my body vibrate with need. We stand there, silently staring at one another as the thickness of things left unsaid fills the air around us, making it hard to breathe.

Or perhaps it's just him *making it hard to breathe*.

"Dr. Haven, I—"

"We should probably get working on this project, shouldn't we?" he interjects as he clears his throat. "I mean, that is why I asked you over here after all. Besides, daylight is ticking away."

"Daylight?" I ask as he sidesteps the coffee table and takes a seat on the couch.

"I just mean that you don't want to be here all day and night, do you?"

If only you could handle me at night, Dr. Haven, my answer would be an emphatic 'yes'.

"No," I sigh without an ounce of conviction. I loathe how nervous he makes me. I'm a ruthless killing machine, a feral beast that could tear him to shreds if I wanted to, and yet lying about wanting to spend the night with him is nearly insurmountable.

He pats the bit of couch beside him. "Please, have a seat, Miss Summers. I took the liberty of printing off some sheets that can help us list traits and develop Parrot Lady's backstory and personality. It'll make it easier to figure out how we want to weave her into the final project."

I do as he asks and sit beside him, not too close, and scoop up my fresh coffee mug. I let it warm my hands as I listen to him talk while he shows me the papers we'll use, my focus waning in and out as his melodic voice leads me to thoughts of what his bedroom looks like.

I don't know how much time passes as we sit there working together. Periodically, I go look out the window to view the elderly woman and take in more details. Every single time, she's still sitting there, either smiling while her parrot bobs, or waving at her home when the bird's gone.

"What a bizarre old woman," I think aloud, peeking past the curtain with genuine curiosity. "I can see why you picked her for the project. She'll make such a fun character. No one would believe she's real without seeing her in person. I wonder how old her parrot is. They seem to have an incredibly strong bond. It seems she looks for him constantly when he's not on her shoulder."

"And she's out there every single day," Dr. Haven adds from his spot on the couch. "Except when it gets too cold. When that happens, she sets her folding chair up just inside the patio doors and watches the world that way."

"Downright bizarre," I say. "Does she ever say anything to you? Does she say good morning when you walk past or anything?"

"Nope. Just sits there."

"Does she wave at you? Or nod? She nodded and smiled at me when I walked past. I waved, but she didn't wave back."

I look back and Dr. Haven's eyes sparkle with intrigue. "How curious ... No, she's never waved at me. Or nodded. Not in all the years I've lived here. In fact, she hardly ever looks at me when I pass. She usually just stares off down the street, like I imagine she is right now."

I glance outside again. "Yeah. Yeah, you're right. She's staring down the road as if ... as if she's waiting for someone, or something. Maybe she likes to watch for the post?"

Dr. Haven takes his glasses off, buffing them with his sweater vest before adjusting them back on his nose.

"Maybe, but she sits out there well past when the post would arrive."

"Hmm. She could just be senile." I let the curtain fall back into place and make my way to the couch, reoccupying the seat beside him. I watch as Dr. Haven adds the word 'senile' to the list of potential character traits.

"There's definitely a lot of angles we could work with a senile character, depending on the tone of the story. It could be a tactic to garner sympathy from the reader, for example. Or, could be super fun to work into a comedic piece. It just depends on what you want to do, really. Though, from what you chose to write for the *Paragraph of Truth* assignment, I'm assuming heartfelt is more your lane than comedy."

I twitch at the sharp coldness that suddenly plagues my hands, immediately trapping them beneath my legs. I'd happily forgotten about that assignment with everything that's been going on; Markos's threats, Professor Gibbon's involvement and inhuman qualities, Meredith's disappearance. There's been so much going on that I'd been in no place to dwell.

"You wouldn't be wrong in saying I tend to enjoy more somber pieces," I reply, drinking down the rest of my luke-warm coffee. "But that doesn't mean I don't enjoy other things as well."

"Oh, for sure," he says, biting his bottom lip. I set my mug down and let my eyes meet his. There's that swirling gray clouding out the blue again. He's so fucking pretty that I forget to breathe for a moment as he stares at me with a look flooded with expectation.

"What?"

"Are you ever going to tell me the truth about that?" he asks quietly, his eyes pleading, begging me to let him in. "I don't think you would have written it if you didn't want me to ask."

"Dr. Haven, didn't I already explain to you that that story was made up? Nothing more than a wonderful, heart wrenching bit of fiction. That's all."

He sets his open hands out in front of me, and as if by instinct I slip mine out from under my thighs and place them in his. I love the way they feel, the way they engulf mine and immediately begin warming my freezing skin.

"I don't believe you," he whispers. He looks almost afraid to have said it, his gray-blue eyes silently begging me not to be angry.

And I'm not.

I sigh, his eyes rising and falling with my chest. "Why don't you believe me?"

He squeezes my hands tighter, forcing my breath to catch. I can't help but imagine how lovely they'd feel squeezing other bits of me. Every inch of me.

"Because no one writes stuff like that just for the hell of it. No one says that stuff to show off, at least not in any of my classes. And I've taught a lot of classes, Miss Summers."

My mouth hangs open as I fight the urge to correct him, to tell him my name is actually Zalida Wren, to tell him who I truly am.

What I truly am.

"I ... I can't talk about it," I say sadly. I let my eyes get lost in his for a while, silently praying he doesn't push any further. It's been a long time since I saw the inside of a hospital, smelled the weird, sterile environment encased in stark white walls. I don't want to be there, don't want my mind drifting to a place I've tried so hard to forget.

I just want to be here. With *him*.

"It's okay," he says, letting go of one of my hands so he can take a sip of his coffee, "you don't have to tell me. But I hope you know, if you ever *do* want to talk about it ... I'm here for you."

I watch him as he drinks, his gaze drifting away from mine. I hate how much I immediately miss his eyes on me, so I wait until he sets his mug back down and they return, taking me in once more. I see the way his mouth twitches as his eyes drift to mine, and it takes all of my willpower not to lean over and nibble on his lips.

"Sara, I—"

"Miss Summers," I correct him, and his eyes flash with mischievous amusement.

He clears his throat. "Miss Summers," he says, his throat hoarse. I imagine his voice is emulating the neediness I'm plagued with sitting this close to him, on his couch, in his condo, with his hands clasped around mine. "Would you be terribly offended if I kissed you right now?"

My heart drops down into my stomach. My head feels light as I try to process both the question and how I should dare answer. I know how I *want* to answer. God, do I ever. But a part of me, some stupid, calculated part of me, knows that the mission is fucked if I say yes.

But he looks so damn delicious.

"Sir, I don't think—"

He presses his thumb against my bottom lip and I gasp. The warmth of his touch sends a tingling from my mouth to the pit of my stomach, and I feel my lips trembling against him. "Call me 'Sir' again."

It's not a question, but a command. A gentle instruction that causes an aching between my thighs and an irrevocable pull in my chest. "Sir." His hand is on my cheek before I have time to protest. His skin is warm and buttery as it slides down and cups my chin, tilting my head up slightly as he leans in until our mouths collide.

My parted lips, hanging open with shock, quickly close around his, pulling his bottom lip into my mouth as he suckles my top lip gently. I let him explore every angle of my lips until that ceases to be enough, then I wrap my arms around his neck and pull him into the kiss harder.

He feels ravenous as his tongue presses hungrily into my mouth. I savor the taste of coffee between us, moaning softly into the kiss as I feel his other hand rest firmly on my bare thigh. The wool skirt I'm wearing is knee-length, the same one I wore on the first day of school, but being seated has it sitting more mid-thigh. It's a consequence Dr. Haven doesn't seem to mind.

An involuntary whimper escapes me as his thumb traces up and down along my inner thigh, the rest of his fingers staying planted. I so badly want to feel his hand travel up my skirt, for the tips of his fingers to brush the fabric of my panties and send electric shockwaves coursing through me, but I don't dare move it there.

How badly I want him is both delicious and terrifying, and I feel as though I could scream as my brain fights to decline his advances. I want to let this go on forever, but I know I can't. Regardless of how good it feels, how good *he* feels, I need to remain focused on the mission. After all, Dr. Haven's aiding the person who's out to kill me.

And what if coming onto me like this is all a ploy because he knows it?

Professor Gibbons knows what I am. He must, because he knows about Markos. What are the odds he didn't tell Dr. Haven and convince him to set all this up? Is that all this is … a big setup orchestrated by the two of them to distract me and buy my silence by making me feel special?

The thought makes me literally sick to my stomach. I break off the kiss and fly backward, pinning myself to the corner of the couch.

Dr. Haven looks mortified, but I quickly look away. I can't handle seeing him like that. He looks so lost and so hurt and so … broken. "I'm sorry," I blurt out, "it's just that—"

"No, no! Perfectly fine, Miss Summers. And my apologies, seriously. That was wholly inappropriate of me and I apologize. I don't know what came over me. It's just—"

"It's okay, Dr. Haven," I assure him. "I just … It's not that I don't, I just … Please don't be offended if I say I feel as though we need to keep this relationship strictly professional."

"No, yes, of course!" He jumps to his feet with a nod. "Professional relationships are the only appropriate ones between professors and students, after all. I think … Where were we? What were we going to study again?"

"The woman with the parrot."

"Right! The parrot." He looks down at our notes, then at the couch, then lets his eyes bounce between them as if debating whether he should sit back down. I muster up the courage to look up at him, noting the crystal clear blue of his eyes. All of the smokiness has dispersed from his irises, and a hint of flustered embarrassment reaches the corners of his eyes.

"I think we've done a fairly extensive job on the notes, Dr. Haven. And this coupled with the notes I took on the strange gentleman from the bus stop leaves us with only needing to observe one more person. Do you have any suggestions for where we might find them?"

"Hmm," he ponders. I love the way he looks when he's thinking, head slightly cocked. His cheeks still carry the rouge sheen of embarrassment, but it in no way dampens his features or how handsome he is. "Let me think on it a minute. I have to run to the washroom anyhow."

Perfect! This is my opportunity to snoop around and see what I can find.

The thought immediately pangs me with guilt. I curse the way this attachment to him is killing me. There's absolutely no reason for me to feel guilty about this. I need information, immediately if I want there to be any hope of escaping Markos's grasp, and yet my feelings for this human are clouding my vision and making it impossible to focus on the mission without coming unhinged.

"Of course, take your time," I say, Dr. Haven eyeing me curiously.

Fuck. Why did I say that?

"You don't mind if I pour myself another coffee while I wait, do you?"

"Of course not. Make yourself at home." He smiles slightly, his eyes intensely blue as he watches me. He waits a few moments before heading off through a door that had been slightly ajar and revealing a dark glimpse of the bathroom, the click of a lock sealing him inside.

Move.

I grab my cup and take it to the counter, pouring myself more coffee, hoping Dr. Haven can hear me doing it so there's no reason to suspect anything. I set it back down on the coffee table silently and take in the room. It's a small space with few places to put things. A door beside the bathroom door is closed and I assume leads to his bedroom.

My eyes immediately pan over to the desk, and I let my socked feet glide across the hardwood with a whisper. Atop it are stacks of papers, some with notes and grades scrawled across them in red, clearly student work. I look for anything peculiar, anything that might stand out, but there's nothing of interest.

Next, I check the bookcase. I rifle through titles, most of them fantasy or science fiction novels. All recent. Nothing similar to the books I saw him going through at the industrial office. None of them look old or like they'd hold valuable information.

Fucking hell. There's got to be something here that can assist me. Where is that damn leather briefcase he's always carrying around?

I creep to the kitchen and poke around through cupboards and drawers. The modern space makes it easy for my scavenging to go unnoticed, the soft-close doors and drawers all shutting without a peep. But I find nothing out of the ordinary, nothing that isn't cookware or seasonings or small kitchen appliances. Nothing I can take back to Leader Taryn.

Nothing I need to take to hide any level of involvement.

My stomach tangles in a million knots as I turn and look at the door, the one that remains closed, and take a deep breath. There's nowhere else worth checking. I have to bite the bullet and at least take a quick look in his room. I've no idea when, or *if*, I'll ever be back inside his place. This may very well be my only chance at this.

I move like lightning, my draul senses kicking into full gear. I move so fast that my feet hardly touch the floor, my body liquid as I flow around the furniture of his room. A large set of black closet doors looms to my left, matching the pitch black walls. Their matte sheen glows softly with the late afternoon sun that pours in through the window and guides me to the bed.

My eyes absorb every detail of his bedspread, a warm navy set with two pillows that match the duvet and two that are crisp white. A soft throw blanket hangs messily over one side, and I imagine him tossing it off in the morning before making his way to the bathroom for a hot shower.

And tossing off some other things.

A chair in the corner that matches the couch has a black t-shirt and pair of jeans folded on it, and the thought of him wearing such typical clothing creates a gnawing deep in my belly. He's always dressed in careful professional layers at CCU. This outfit looks to be something he's prepared for the weekend, but he's picked a dress shirt and dress pants for my visit today.

The thought of what he's wearing pulls me back to that moment on the couch, the moment his lips pressed against mine. My body immediately reacts, remembering the taste of him and the way his hand felt on my face as he kissed me. The dampness between my thighs makes it impossible to think, pulling me over to where his clothes sit so I can run my fingers over the fabric. I shudder.

The sound of doors swinging open spins me around. Dr. Haven stands there, brow cocked. Slightly narrowed eyes view me from behind their lenses, and my heart freezes as I realize I've been caught without having found anything of value.

But then ... he smiles.

"I was originally going to wear that today, but it seemed a bit too casual to be appropriate for your company," he confesses.

I look down at where my hand still lays on his shirt, flabbergasted. My mouth hangs open as my brain fights to formulate any decent response. "I ... Well, I was just—"

"It's alright, Miss Summers. After all, I did tell you to make yourself at home. Though, if you wanted to see more of my wardrobe, you could have just asked."

My cheeks flush with a level of heat I've not felt in a long time.

He thinks I was in here to creep through his clothes?!

The defensiveness rising in my chest prickles along the back of my neck. "Actually, I wanted to see what brand of cardigans you wear, Doctor. I was thinking of buying one for my boyfriend."

"*Boyfriend?!*" He chokes the word out through a fit of coughs, removing his glasses to buff them on his shirt a bit before replacing them. "I wasn't aware ... You never mentioned that you have a boyfriend."

"You never asked," I state flatly.

"Fair enough." The heavy silence between us is palpable, the air soured with bitter notes mirroring the dark roast on my palate. "I'm sorry."

I'm unsure if the apology is directed at the kiss, or the fact he never bothered to ask if I was in a relationship before doing so, but I haven't got it in me to ask. I hope, more than anything, he doesn't regret it. I certainly don't.

"Well, thank you for your hospitality, Dr. Haven, and for all of the coffee. It was lovely, an excellent roast, but I should really get going. It's getting late and—"

"Have you got somewhere to be this evening, Miss Summers?"

The question feels a bit like a test. It urges me to pick my answer carefully. "Just schoolwork, Sir."

His eyes flare the moment the word leaves my lips. He shifts his weight from one foot to the other, then back again, as though he's suddenly fighting to find a comfortable position. I swear I see a slight twitch in the front of his pants from my peripherals. But I keep my eyes safely locked on his, fighting every bit of me screaming to glance down.

"Nice to know you're so driven even throughout the weekend," he says, clearing his throat and waving his arm towards the open bedroom door. "Come, Miss Summers. I'll walk you out."

I exit his room, leaving the comforts of his clothes and his dangerously inviting bed behind as he follows me to the front door. He gathers up the sheets of notes and brings them to me as I slip on my daggerless boots. Against my best judgment, I left all my weaponry at home. I figured if anything went awry, I'd be weapon enough, even in the daylight.

"Thank you," I say as he hands me the papers.

"Would you like to meet at the cafe sometime next week to scout our last specimen for the assignment?" He's standing so close to me, I could rest my hands on his chest and stare up at him, urge him to wrap his arms around me and pull me in tight.

But I won't.

As badly as I want to, as badly as I want *him*, I have to let my desires remain fantasies, for both our sakes.

"Sure, that'd be great." I muster a sort of jovial tone, but there's a shakiness to it, an uneasiness. "Are you free Monday after school?"

He shakes his head. "Monday is a long teaching day for me. What about Tuesday?"

"Sure, Tuesday works. Have a good night, Dr. Haven."

"Miss Summers?" he asks just as my hand encompasses the doorknob.

I glance over my shoulder. "Yes?"

"I love it when you call me 'Sir'."

"Which apparently I adopted today, for reasons unknown," I say with a soft smile.

"No. The first time was in my office. The first time you were in my office," he corrects, "but I simply didn't know you well enough to point it out then. When I was asking about your *Paragraph of Truth* piece, you said, 'Thank you for your concern, Sir'."

The words jog my brain, transporting me back to his office. The way it smells like him, the way this condo smells like him. The way he makes me so god damn ravenous for something other than souls for the first time in over a half a century.

"So I did," I agree. "Have a good evening, Dr. Haven. *Sir*."

He bites his bottom lip. "You as well, Miss Summers. See you in class on Monday."

Depending how tomorrow goes.

"See you Monday, Sir."

CHAPTER 18

Death, I mean *human* death, has a scent all its own. It permeates everything around it, carrying hints of mildew and sorrow everywhere it seeps. It has an unmistakable way of making skin crawl, of making stomachs turn, and, much like riding a bicycle, never really leaves you once you've experienced it.

The farm *always* smells like this.

Much like a chicken plant, the odor of decay hits you well before you arrive at the actual facility. If a *facility* is what you can call the abandoned farm where we've set up camp this time. The property is guarded by an outline of mountainous everests that keep us sheltered from the rest of the world. A world that doesn't know about us, and wouldn't want us if it did.

A world that doesn't know how lucky it is that we've thus far preferred to keep to ourselves.

But those days are numbered, and will soon be coming to an end if someone like Markos ends up in power. It's only a matter of time before one of us decides that we've been in hiding too long, that it's time for the playing field between our numbers and the humans' numbers to be leveled.

A shiver runs down my spine and my hands grow cold as I enter the weathered barn. The humans are kept here, magically-induced comas keeping them from making a fuss.

Not that anyone could hear them screaming way out here anyhow.

This farm lies on several acres of fenced and treed property, a property that Leader Taryn has talked about developing into a permanent spot for us ... *if* we can kill the hunter. There's no safety in a consistent residence if the hunter, or *hunters*, can keep tracking us and killing us. That's why we've been on the move so much. But rebuilding the farm means sourcing a new location *and* a whole buffet of humans to harvest souls from.

And the slew of disappearances raises red flags and puts us at risk every time.

"Zalida ..."

Leader Taryn's voice is polished stone behind me, a soft booming that reverberates off the old wood walls.

"Leader," I say as I turn to find him standing in the barn doorway. He closes the doors behind him with a flick of his wrist. Magic is generally banned for our kind. Drauls are a force to be reckoned with without needing the assistance of magic, but it is practiced by the Ancestors and the Leaders, as they're responsible for protecting our kind.

"How lovely to see you back here again. You look pale, my child."

"I haven't eaten," I admit.

"Good, good. You're on a mission. One shouldn't eat where they lay."

"Yes, Leader. I agree. You should try passing that knowledge on to Markos."

"Pass what on to me?" Markos comes in, not bothering to

shut the door behind him. "Zali," he growls as he walks up to me and grabs the back of my neck with one of his oversized hands. He squeezes tightly, pulling me against him as he licks up the length of my neck. "Miss me?"

"We've been over this, Markos," I remind him, my gaze locked on Leader Taryn's. "Besides, I don't think now is the time."

"Leave us," Leader Taryn hisses, waving a dismissive hand as though shooing away a small child.

"But Leader—"

"I said to leave us," Leader Taryn echoes, his brows pinching. "Now leave. Do not make me ask again, Markos. You're aware of how fond I am of having to ask twice."

"Yes, Leader. My apologies," Markos grumbles. He walks out of the barn, never turning his back to the Leader, then takes a bow and vanishes into the night.

"Now ... Where were we? Ah, yes. You need to eat, Zali. We should throw a small feast tonight and celebrate your recent contribution to the farm. That group of people you've brought in are lovely, particularly the four young gentlemen."

I had no choice but to bring them in, thanks to that loud-mouth at the rest stop.

"As well, I'll need whatever information you've uncovered during your time away. You have discovered things amongst the humans, surely, but that can wait until after you've had time to feed. And I'm elated to tell you I've a surprise for you."

"Oh?" I say. Leader Taryn waves for me to follow him, leading me through the barn towards the ladder at the back. I climb each rung, the leather soles of my combat boots thumping softly. I don't dare wear my human clothes here.

I get to the top and turn as Leader Taryn casts himself up from the floor, floating with unearthly grace. He lands beside me, his long, black trench coat swaying slightly as he steps closer and wraps an arm around my shoulders. "Markos brought you a little gift. A wedding present you might say."

"Leader, I don't think—"

"Oh, hush, child. Stop being so modest. You volunteering for such an exacting task should be rewarded handsomely. More so once your efforts are fruitful, but even now. You should be rather excited." His walking pulls me with him, past the rows of humans laying in fitful sleep on rows of hay bale beds. The magic keeps them asleep, but they don't look peaceful. They look pained.

Our short jaunt stops at the far corner of the loft, the glow of moonlight pouring in through the adjacent window. Tomorrow the moon will be full, and I'll only have one more cycle until the wedding to settle this. Time is ticking away at a rate I struggle to manage, and yet my worries feel far more flooded by thoughts of how to spare Dr. Haven in all this than how to avoid Markos.

If it really comes to it, I could always end things between Markos and I another way. Perhaps not before he forces me into his bed, but certainly before he forces me to bear any children.

The bales in front of us bear something hidden by a tarp. It twitches and breathes, the mound moving with the life force of whatever lay beneath. The breath held in my chest burns with anticipation, the sense of dread in me growing until it threatens to swallow me whole.

Leader Taryn waves the tarp off with unnecessary flourish, letting it fall to the floor behind us. His smile is sinister and his eyes blaze with hunger as bits of red drip into the yellows of his eyes until only crimson remains.

"Isn't she beautiful?" he coos softly.

The words are muted by the sound of blood rushing in my ears. My usually minimal heartbeat quickens, firing up from a few beats per minute to a few dozen. I am frozen, waiting, hoping Leader Taryn is going to replace the tarp and escort me away from here.

He doesn't.

"What do you think?" He seems uncomfortable with my silence. "She'll make a nice meal, don't you think? You don't even have to save any of her soul for the barn, Zalida. She's just for you."

Indescribable guilt eats at me as my stomach growls with ferocity. My mouth begins to water, saliva coating my fangs as the moonlight coats her trembling body and highlights the soft skin of her exposed neck.

Meredith.

CHAPTER 19

I sit at the far end of the long wooden table. Six chairs line each side, while I occupy the seventh. Directly across from me in the sole armchair is Leader Taryn, his hands clasped together on the table in front of him.

"I hope you understand I meant no disrespect," I say, keeping my head bowed and my gaze on the scratched table-top. The old farm furniture hardly feels appropriate for a meeting of such caliber, but everything on the property is being utilized. Nothing will be replaced unless the time comes that we take up a permanent residence here.

"You are nothing *but* disrespectful, Zali! You'll be in for a rude awakening once you're my wife!" Markos growls from the seat left of our Leader's. "Wifehood will be a miserable existence for you if you don't learn your place and learn it quickly!"

Leader Taryn places an arm on Markos's to keep him from rising out of his seat. Markos's nails protrude like claws, digging into the mature wood. His yellow eyes offer hints of a feral red glow around the edges, fangs bared as he hisses each word in my direction.

"I want to discuss that," I say firmly, raising my head and locking eyes with Leader Taryn. Markos continues to stare at me, a look of pure murder in his eyes flooding my peripherals, but I ignore him. I have little use for him, and even less respect.

"And what about it are you needing to discuss, Zalida?" Leader Taryn asks.

"I … I want the arrangement called off in return for information leading to the hunter."

Vanthony, who sits in the seat right of Leader Taryn, gasps and covers his mouth. The four other drauls seated at the table all avert their eyes, heads bowed as they inhale sharply and keep their disapproving thoughts to themselves.

Weddings never get called off once a Leader has dictated them, but this arrangement is one of political convenience and has never taken my sanity or livelihood into consideration. I'd be doing myself a mountainous dishonor if I didn't speak up and stand my ground.

Markos jumps from his seat, Leader Taryn's grasp doing nothing to stop him. "How fucking *dare* you, Zalida! How dare you disrespect me like this! *You* are *my* property! You have been ever since the betrothal was declared. Any woman in our clan would leap at the opportunity to marry me! To have *me* as their mate! *You* do not even deserve me! You deserve to die a cold and painful death, alone and forgotten until you sink into the earth!"

"MARKOS!" Leader Taryn's voice booms as he uses magic to amplify his voice throughout the room, so loudly that it shakes the rickety walls and causes Vanthony and the others to flinch. "Sit down, NOW."

Markos sits, chest heaving as he breathes. His eyes are locked on me, and I'm sure there's literal steam escaping his nostrils, but I don't give him the satisfaction of looking at him. I keep my eyes focused on Leader Taryn's, as he keeps his on mine.

"It is not meant as disrespect for your decision, Leader. I hope you know I have the utmost respect for you and have always trusted your choices and guidance for myself and the rest of the Osjhka clan."

"If I thought differently, I would never have agreed to sending you to Lochfort, Zalida. So tell me then, if you have so much faith in my decisions, why are you so strongly opposed to this one?"

Markos starts to speak but Leader Taryn waves a hand and all noise from him ceases. Markos looks equal parts furious and terrified at the loss of his voice, his hands rubbing at his throat as if he can somehow will it back. Angry, he stands up so fast that his chair goes flying as he storms out the front door of the farmhouse.

The room hangs with a heavy silence before Leader Taryn speaks again. "This is why I assigned you to Markos, Zali. He's an excellent warrior, a strong leader for our clan, but he is reckless and stupid. Without a partner by his side whispering guidance and providing him with an ... *outlet* ... for all his energy, our clan is fated to a constant state of war. Markos isn't just soul-hungry, he's blood-hungry."

I close my eyes and take a deep breath. "I understand, Leader. Truly, I do. But surely there must be someone else amongst us, or someone from another clan, who can provide Markos with these things. I have no interest in motherhood, nor in him. And I can be useful to you, in ways other than tracking down the hunter. I can continue taking on missions, build alliances with other clans. Anything you need. I just *can't* marry Markos."

Especially because my heart is longing for someone else.

Leader Taryn hums in his throat, hands unclasping and clasping again as he stretches out the long, bony fingers of a creature who knows he's getting too old to fight these battles. "Very well," he says, "but I want more than just the hunter."

My heart does a hopeful jump. "Anything. Name your price, Leader."

"The Drauldin has been stolen from the Yedora clan. Have you heard of it? It's blade—"

"Glows blue," I finish. "I've not only heard of it, dear Leader. I have seen it personally."

Leader Taryn's eyes widen. "Then you know who the hunter is, and you know this is how they've been so effectively killing our kind. The enchantments on that blade, when regularly replenished with incantation and half-breed blood, make it fatally toxic to our kind. One little prick will erase a draul instantly. I assume retrieving it safely will be of grave difficulty."

"I had thought there were no known half-breeds in existence, Leader?"

"The Ancestors are ... *exclusive* ... with their information, Zalida. Even I am not privy to everything they know. And being that they are made up mostly of members from the Yedora clan, I feel we are allowed even less. Between us, I suspect this is why the Drauldin being stolen was kept secret for so long."

"I see. I know who the hunter is, Leader. I saw him in a building in the outskirt industrial yard of Lochfort, but he ... There's a slight problem. He isn't human."

"Isn't human?!" Leader Taryn shrieks in an uncharacteristically high tone. "What do you suggest he is, then? Draul? Or are you suggesting this is some new type of creature we've not seen before?"

"I ... I don't know. He's fast, like us. But there are no yellow eyes nor fangs on him at night. I don't know anything that can move as fast as a draul. No human comes anywhere close. I don't know what he is, but whatever it is will make getting the Drauldin back near impossible. Do you think ... he might be a half-breed?"

"It's possible. If you can't take what you want by force, then you will have to rely on your wit, Zalida. You are one of the smartest members of our kind. And I mean so sincerely. You don't want to be responsible for Markos, fine. Then you must step up in other ways and earn my debt to you. Only then will I call off the wedding. Oh, and Zali?"

"Yes, Leader?"

"You must do it before the next full moon, or the offer shall be revoked. After all, I can't keep Markos hanging in limbo forever if you fail to produce results."

I nod my head. "Yes, Leader." I take a deep breath, aiming to choose my next words carefully. "I'm afraid I have one more favor to ask of you, at the risk of creating further waves and displaying unintended disrespect."

Leader Taryn cocks his head. "Oh? You've piqued my curiosity, Zalida. Do tell."

"The young woman in the barn loft, the one Markos stole from Lochfort. I ... I'd like to return her. Safely, in unharmed condition."

"Zali!" Vanthony gasps, breaking the silence of the group. "You can't be serious? She's seen too much, knows too much. She'd be a huge liability. How could it possibly be worth the risk?"

I glance his way but ignore his question. "Excuse me for asking, Leader Taryn, but you have the power to erase her memories, don't you?" I ask as he watches me curiously.

"Perhaps," he says, "but I do not get off on using these powers just for the sake of it. This is why magic is banned for anyone in the clans who is not a Leader or Ancestor. It is not a source of power that is meant to be abused. These gifts are bestowed upon us by our Goddess, Lisha, and she does not offer these gifts for use without consequence. Do you know why we pray to Lisha, Zali?"

"She was declared a Goddess due to her abilities to conjure and wield magic."

"Yes, but it was more than that," Leader Taryn continues. "She knew how to harness magic that was so powerful, she could do unthinkable things. Stop time. Heal mortal wounds. Even breathe life and soul back into creatures fated for death. It is said that one drop of her blood could grant these abilities to another living creature. She was the most powerful draul ever known. And do you know *why* she was so powerful?"

I shake my head. "No, Leader."

He leans over the table, bridging the gap between us only slightly. His mouth moves, no words coming out. Then, by magic, I hear his voice whisper in my ear.

"Because she was a half-breed."

The words knock me back in my chair, my back straightening as my scalp tingles. "How could that be? How would everyone not know that?"

"Not everything amongst our kind is common knowledge, Zalida." He smiles, offering a thoughtful nod. "You can take the girl back to Lochfort. Markos never should have taken her in the first place. I warned him against stirring up trouble where you're working, but that draul has a mind of his own. If I wasn't mistaken, I'd say he almost wants you to fail for some reason, Zali."

"He is how he is," I mutter through clenched teeth. "He wasn't happy you granted me the assignment, and not him."

"No, of course not. And his outburst tonight was ... Let's just say I will deal with him in my own way and time."

Vanthony and I exchange glances. He smiles softly, no doubt amused by how much joy he knows Leader Taryn's statement brings me. "Thank you, Leader Taryn."

"Return the girl, but do it quietly. Stealthily. I don't want it known that you found or returned her. Keep yourself completely off the radar of any local officials."

"Yes, Leader."

"If that's all, Zali, I'd say the meeting has concluded. You can go."

I feel my face tense, puzzled. "Don't you want to know who the hunter is?"

"No," Leader Taryn shakes his head, "I've decided I'll trust in you to bring them to me before the next full moon. Deliver the hunter, and the Drauldin, and the wedding shall be rescinded."

"Yes, Leader Taryn."

"Oh, and Zali?"

"Yes?"

"You best hurry. Time is slipping away from you rather quickly, I'd say."

"Yes, Leader Taryn."

And how I wish that statement wasn't so fucking true.

CHAPTER 20

Thirty days and twenty-nine nights.

That's all I have left to settle this. That's all I have left to capture Professor Gibbons and present him to Leader Taryn, him and the Drauldin, or else I'm stuck with Markos for the rest of my days.

"Sara? Sara? Hello, Sara! Are you listening?"

I look over to see Angel staring at me expectantly. "Hmm?"

"Oh my gosh, you weren't even listening! Where did you go? How can you be daydreaming at a time like this? Did you hear what I said? I said isn't it crazy how Meredith just wandered out of the woods this morning? I skipped one of my morning classes to go see her, and the hospital wouldn't even let me in! They said she was still having tests and examinations and stuff done. They said I could come by tomorrow. Tomorrow! Can you believe that? She's my best friend and they're making me wait!" Angel's cheeks glow pink. "I mean, she's *also* my best friend."

The fact she thinks I could be offended by this makes me chuckle. "It's fine, Angel. I don't think being your friend for a month or so correlates to 'best friend' status. And I'm okay with that."

She smiles widely. "Okay, as long as you're not offended because I totally didn't mean to offend you, okay? You're not offended, right? That's what you're saying?"

"Not offended," I assure her.

"Phew, okay, good. It's just that Meredith and I have literally gone to school together and been best friends since grade two, so of course she's my best friend, you know? Do you think it's weird that she just stumbled out of the woods? The hospital wouldn't even tell me if she looked okay! They just kept saying 'All her vitals are good'. What does that even mean?!"

"It means her blood pressure, heart rate, temperature, and perspiration rate are all in the normal ranges," I explain. "I'm sure she's fine, Angel. Trust me."

"Oh. Did you go to medical school? Maybe you should have gone to medical school."

My blood runs cold at the thought of being back inside a hospital. I shove my hands in my coat pockets as we move up the line at Bumpy's. "Medicine doesn't interest me."

"Huh. Well who knows what happened to Meredith out there! The farmer who found her apparently said she doesn't remember anything. But she had all her clothes, even her jacket, so at least she wasn't out there freezing, and hopefully nothing ... you know, really *bad* ... happened to her. She shouldn't have been hanging out with those guys! What a bunch of creeps."

"I don't think those guys had anything to do with it," I sigh. "They seemed fine. Harmless. She probably drank too much or smoked too much and wandered off. Maybe she left to go pee and got lost or something. Anyway, she's back now. We should focus on celebrating that."

"Yeah, yeah. Of course, you're totally right. The important thing is that she's back and she's safe and she's going to be okay. Totally. I just wish they'd let me see her, you know? I just want to talk to her and see how she's doing. Like, really doing. Not just 'good vitals' good. I want to make sure she's good, good, you know?"

"I understand, Angel. You're a good friend."

And a bit of a nuisance, but still a really good friend.

"Thanks," she says with a grin. "Hey, how's that project with the hot professor going?"

Heat rushes to my cheeks, but I dodge the question by approaching the counter. The barista smiles at me, a freckly gentleman with a mop of curly hair and striking green eyes. I figure he must be a recent hire, as I've not seen him here before.

"What can I get you?"

"A large black coffee, please. And ..." I look over to Angel.

"Oh! You're going to buy my drink? Sara, you don't have to do that!"

"Please, it's the least I can do. Consider it a pleasant distraction from the drama of the past few days. A celebratory beverage for your friend's safe return."

"Aww, you're so sweet!" she shrieks, throwing her arms around my neck and squeezing. "I'll take a caramel macchiato. Medium, I guess."

"Make it a large," I correct.

"Seriously, Sara? You're so sweet! The sweetest! No wonder you drink black coffee, you're already sweet enough!"

You have no idea how truly wrong you are there, dear Angel.

"Thanks," I murmur.

"Can I get a name for the order?"

"Sara! Her name is Sara," Angel spouts before I have a chance to answer.

The barista blushes as he watches Angel gush about me some more. She hugs me again, her arms growing tangled in my scarf and pulling it off my neck. It drops to the floor and she scoops it up, holding it out as we side step to wait at the pick-up side of the counter.

"I'm so sorry," she says, holding my scarf. She goes to wrap it playfully around my neck, gasping as she does. "Woah! What is that? Is that a tattoo? Oh, it can't be a tattoo, can it? It doesn't look like it has ink. Oh, is it one of those scar tattoo things? I thought only people in weird island tribes did that. Are you from a tribe?"

My heart pumps fiercely in my chest as I realize I'd completely forgotten about Markos's brand. The geometric symbol, consisting of three triangles and twelve dots, represents the dozen generations of his family tree, and the three amongst it appointed as Leaders. Markos will make the fourth Leader in his family history, and the symbol will change to reflect this.

If Leader Taryn and the Osjhka clan ever agree to him being Leader. If he keeps having outbursts and proving to be unstable, he'll be lucky to see that day come. Especially with no level-headed wife by his side to counteract his rashness.

I snatch the scarf from her hands as she fumbles with it and wrap it around my neck defensively. "I ... Yeah. I mean, no, I'm not from a tribe. But it's sort of a family emblem thing. I don't really like to talk about it."

"Oh, okay," she says softly. "Sorry."

"Just don't tell anyone about it, okay?"

"Okay, no worries. Your secret is safe with me. Wait, what if I tell Meredith? I usually tell Meredith everything, and—"

"*No one*, Angel. I mean it. Please."

"Alright, alright. Lips sealed," she moans, running her thumb and forefinger across her lips. "Telling no one."

"Thank you."

"Here are your drinks, Sara," the barista says, handing me

two to-go cups. I can immediately tell which is my coffee by the temperature of them and give a polite nod.

"Thank you," I reply.

"Hey, are you from around here? I'm new here," he adds. "My name is Tobi."

I hand Angel her drink but keep my eyes on Tobi, who hasn't stopped smiling at me since he took our order. "No, Tobi, I'm not from around here. I moved here recently for school."

"Oh, that's cool! I just moved here to help my aunt out with some work around her place." He clears his throat, his face slightly flushed. "Hey, seeing as we're both new here, do you think you'd wanna ... I don't know. Go do something sometime?"

A familiar scent surrounds me, cloaking me in warmth and spiciness as a comfortable presence pops up between Angel and I. I turn to see Dr. Haven, his slightly furrowed brows twitching as he adjusts his glasses.

"I hardly think a student with a double major such as Miss Summers has time for dating," he scoffs, eyeing the young man up and down. "Besides, you don't even know her."

"Yeah, but I could get to know her, if she agrees to go on a date with me. Is this guy your dad or something?"

I nearly drop my coffee as I fight to swallow down the mouthful I just took. I stifle my oncoming laughter with a forced cough. "No, no. Definitely not. He's—"

"Her professor," Dr. Haven interjects. "At least, one of them."

"Dr. Haven teaches English at the university," I explain. "He's an excellent professor."

Tobi scratches his head. "Cool. So ... Did you wanna go out sometime?"

Electricity shoots up my spine as Dr. Haven's hand presses into my lower back. "Did you miss what I said about her being busy?" His voice is seething, but it's obvious he's trying to keep an air of professionalism. "Or is a basic grasp of the English language not a requirement to work here?"

Tobi looks terribly offended as Angel bursts into a fit of giggles. I hand her her drink, then grab Dr. Haven by the hand and practically drag him through the cafe. "Thanks for the coffee, Tobi," I call over my shoulder. "I'll catch you later, Angel!"

"Catch you later," she echoes, not daring to follow us out.

We're halfway down the block and well out of the sight of anyone inside the cafe before I drop Dr. Haven's hand and turn to face him. "What was all *that* about?" I demand.

He looks equal parts perplexed and mortified as he stares down at me, his blue eyes dazzling from behind his lenses. "I ... I'm sorry, I don't know what came over me. But that guy shouldn't be asking you out like that!"

"Oh, no?" My free hand slams onto a jutted hip as I hold my coffee in the other. "And why is that?"

"Because!"

I raise a brow. "Because?"

"Because he doesn't even know you! He doesn't know anything about you. He doesn't know what you like or dislike. He doesn't deserve to take you on a date."

"And you do?" I challenge his gaze with narrowed eyes. "You think you know so much about me, Sir?"

His bottom lip quivers as his mouth hangs open a moment. "I know enough."

"Oh yeah? Like what? Tell me what all you know about me, exactly."

He pauses. His gaze softens, his eyebrows relaxing as he watches me. My hand still hangs defensively on my hip, waiting for his answer.

Whatever it is you think you know ...

"I know you like black coffee."

"Everyone knows that," I murmur. "It's the only thing I order."

"I know you're smart as hell," he continues.

"I'm in university. That's not a wildly uncommon bit of knowledge either."

"Sure, but there's lots of people who go to university that are arguably unintelligent. I know you're not one of them."

I unhand my hip, taking a sip of my coffee. "Still, not a very personal fact, Dr. Haven."

"I know you've been through stuff. Hard stuff. I know you've lost people you love, or at least one person. And I know you hate hospitals because of it."

I suck in a breath as my fingers grow icy around my coffee cup. I grab the cup with my free hand, trying to warm them both up. "So what?"

"So, I know you're resilient. A fighter. And ..." His voice trails off as he stares at me, his eyes begging me for permission to continue.

"And?"

"And ... I know it was you who brought Meredith back."

Panic chokes me as I try to formulate a response. "You ... You don't know that," I whisper. "You *can't* know that."

"I don't know where you brought her back from, but I have an idea."

"Stop," I warn him, "before it's too late for me to protect you."

"I don't think it's me who needs protecting, Miss Summers." He steps closer and I'm lost in him. Heat radiates off him that eases my chill and warms my hands. The spicy, woodsy scent of his cologne flows from his overcoat and fills me, making me want him as it eases the slight nausea I'd been feeling from my coffee.

His eyes swirl with that smoky gray I've come to recognize as lust, and it feels as though I'm being pulled to him. I nearly forget we're still standing in the middle of the street as townspeople go about their business, the rest of the world seeming to melt away more and more the longer we stand here.

He cups my cheek in his hand and I let him, not caring who sees. Everything about him feels magnetic to me, like his very self carries an inexplicable force I can't resist being drawn to. He stares at me with concern in his eyes, my hands still wrapped snugly around my coffee.

All I want at this moment is for him to kiss me, here, in front of all these people.

But he pulls away, as I knew he would, and clears his throat. He glances around a bit nervously, seeming to have come to his senses and remember where we are. "I just think you could do better than Tobi for a date, Miss Summers. That's all I was trying to say."

"I see."

"Plus, I thought you said you already have a boyfriend." I swear there's a saltiness to the statement, but his eyes give nothing away. Their clear, blue tone has returned, but the concern I saw moments ago still lingers.

"That is what I said, yes."

"So, that's true then?"

I shift uncomfortably. "In a sense."

"How do you mean?"

I sigh, sipping more coffee. "It's a ... a *pairing of convenience*, you might say."

"Ah, I see." He considers my words. "Let me help you, then. I can help you."

"Absolutely not!" I swig the last of my coffee and toss the cup in a nearby bin. "It's way too dangerous. You have no idea what you'd be getting yourself into. And Markos—"

"I'm not afraid of Markos, whoever he is."

So Professor Gibbons knows who Markos is ... but Dr. Haven doesn't? Or is he lying about not knowing Markos? Why would he lie about it, though? What could he possibly stand to gain from that after willingly revealing his knowledge of my involvement with Meredith?

"Yeah, well, you should be, Dr. Haven. Trust me, there's a lot of things out there you should be scared of, and of all those, Markos should top the list. He's ruthless."

"I have skills when it comes to such things."

The pain in my jaw gives way to the fact I've been clenching my teeth. I relax it, rubbing my chin. "Can I ask you one question, Dr. Haven?"

"Only if you call me 'Sir'," he says with mischief in his eyes.

"Alright, *Sir* ... Why are you working with Professor Gibbons?"

His composure stiffens. "I don't ... It's a long story."

"I'm free every day this week, and we still have one more person to study for our project. We could get together this afternoon, right after school. That'd give us plenty of time."

"Tonight is no good, I'm ... I'm busy ... with a boatload of grading," he stammers, shifting uncomfortably. "How about tomorrow?"

"Sure. Tomorrow works."

He smiles. "Great. Tomorrow afternoon it is then. See you in class, Miss Summers." I watch as he walks off briskly in the direction of Citrus County University, shoving my hands in my jacket pockets.

I'll see you in class, Sir, and I'll see you tonight as well. You've got me curious what exactly you're up to ... and I don't think it's grading.

CHAPTER 21

Leaves crunch under my boots as I crouch behind the dumpster in the alley beside Dr. Haven's condo building. I stay low, out of sight. Night has fallen. My fangs are out, my glowing, yellow eyes granting me impeccable night vision. I am even faster and stronger than during the day, and there isn't a car on this planet that could outpace me.

I watch as Dr. Haven comes out the front door. He walks into the alley and I vanish, blending into the darkness in the crevice behind the dumpster. I keep my breath held as he walks past and heads to his car, hopping in and taking off into the night.

I keep a safe distance the whole way, never getting too close, never following directly behind him where he might spot me in the rearview. I take alleys and rooftops, climbing here and there and letting him put distance between us before nearly catching up again. I follow him until he reaches the other side of town, stopping in front of a red brick bungalow.

Professor Gibbons comes out, his eyes panning up and

down the street in either direction as though he needs to make sure the coast is clear. Then he flies to the side of Dr. Haven's car, his feet barely touching the ground as he throws open the door and climbs inside.

The car takes off and I follow it, once again keeping a safe distance. They leave town and head into the blackness of the highway. The woods that run parallel provide ample coverage as I stalk them, whizzing through trees just as I had when following that RV.

Everything feels all too familiar as they travel for over an hour, a sick feeling rising up in my stomach the longer I follow them. We're a little over halfway there when I figure it out, my head reeling as the realization settles in harder and faster with every step.

They're headed to the farm.

I don't know what to do. Part of me feels that the right thing to do is to take off ahead of them and warn Leader Taryn and the others. Another piece of me knows that if I do, there is almost no chance that Dr. Haven will make it out of this alive. I don't care what happens to Professor Gibbons, but my entire body aches with panic at the thought of anything happening to *him*.

We get about twenty minutes out from the farm. I'm still struggling to make a decision when I see them: A pair of eyes glowing in the distance.

Not yellow ... but red.

Markos.

I catch a glimpse of them in the trees, but then they're gone. He's lightning fast, even faster than I am, and I don't have time to process what's happening before I hear the tires squealing and see the car veering off onto a gravel path off the side of the road. The back end fishtails, the small compact swerving back and forth as rocks fly out from beneath the tires in every direction.

A loud crashing sound barrels through the night, birds in nearby trees scattering. I stop and wait, my heartbeat slow and steady as I narrow my eyes. I step out from the tree-line, taking in the scene. Dr. Haven's car sits a few dozen feet off the highway on the edge of the gravel road. The front end is completely crumpled and the car isn't running, but the headlights cast glowing beams around what they've hit.

"Markos!"

He stands at the front of the vehicle, the car's nose wrapped around him in a sick, metallic hug. He's grinning ear to ear, his eyes twinkling with pure menace as he stares at the windshield. The car hasn't left a scratch on him, though his shirt is shredded. He rips it off and tosses it aside, revealing a massive, vascular frame bulging with lean muscles.

I'm at him in a heartbeat, but it isn't quick enough. He's already at the driver's side door tearing it from the hinges. He tosses it into some trees with a loud smash. He rips Dr. Haven from his seat and throws him wildly, sending him flying through the air. I move quickly, but Professor Gibbons is quicker. He beats me there, catching Dr. Haven as they skid along the gravel road.

Markos is already on us by the time I turn around. He reaches for Professor Gibbons's neck, but Gibbons's reflexes leave him a blur as he dodges every attempt. The two continue a back and forth scramble, but Markos can't land a blow no matter how hard he tries. Professor Gibbons parries every move, almost seeming to know a moment ahead what Markos plans to do.

A feral roar screams through the night as Markos's bright red eyes begin to turn a deep shade of maroon, a shade I've never witnessed before. He stands still as his chest heaves, Professor Gibbons taking the opportunity to put some distance between them.

I race to Dr. Haven and take his hand. "We need to get you out of here."

"I can't leave Bentley," he replies, and it takes a second in the chaos to realize he means Professor Gibbons. "I can't re-enchant the Drauldin without him."

Markos watches us, breathing deeply, his body seeming to vibrate with energy. He smashes the car's headlights, darkness cloaking the area. My night vision has everything aglow, but I can imagine that Dr. Haven can see nothing but a pair of maroon eyes floating in the darkness. I don't know what Markos is waiting for, but this may be our only opportunity to escape unscathed.

"We need to go *now!*"

"I'm not leaving," Dr. Haven says, his voice far too low and calculated for the intensity of the situation. He pulls a blade out of his overcoat, the metal glowing a dull blue amongst the darkness.

I gasp. "The Drauldin." The emblem of Jalvana is engraved in the blade, but I dare not touch it. The metal seems to sing, a gentle buzz radiating from it as Dr. Haven grasps it in both hands and takes a fighting stance.

"You'll have one shot, monster," Professor Gibbons declares, "so you best make it worth it."

Markos's gaze shifts between the two men, then to me. "Which one will you kill, Zali?" he hisses, fangs bared and gleaming. "You seem to be protecting that one."

"I need them to maintain my cover and finish the assignment, Markos. You can't kill them. At least, not this one. He knows things about our history and our kind. He has ancient texts. I've seen them. We need him alive for now. He could hold valuable information."

"What were they doing heading to the farm, Zalida?! Going to kill more of us, more of our kind! They seek to take us out! You so much as suggesting I spare them is a betrayal!"

He spits the words like venom, a slight slur resulting from his fangs. "You're a traitor!"

"I'm not suggesting you spare them, Markos! I'm suggesting you spare *one* of them, temporarily. Please, for me. Consider it a wedding gift."

The way Markos laughs, a guttural laugh that spews from his throat in violent outbursts, makes my blood run cold. "I brought you a wedding gift, Zalida," he says, his voice a low growl. "And what did you do, my pet? You sent it back. You gave her back to the poor little human town, without even drinking a drop of her soul. I found her earlier, back at that dilapidated old shack you've been calling home, tucked sweetly into her bed. The other girls were there, too. So pretty, all three of them."

I glare at Markos, struggling to keep my breath steady. "What did you do?"

He laughs again. "Nothing, pet. See, thanks to you, Leader Taryn is all over me and everything I do now. I'm to be on my best behavior ... at least, until you deliver the hunter. Which you're going to do, either dead or alive. *Tonight.*"

I flick my chin towards Professor Gibbons. "I'll take him to Leader Taryn right now, Markos. But you let this one go. As I said, I'm not finished with him yet."

Markos grins, an evil, unnerving grin that twists my stomach into knots. My hands tingle with an icy burn, and an eternity seems to pass before he sighs. "When will you learn that you are not the one in charge here, Zalida? You make life so much harder on yourself."

"I—"

But I don't get a second word out before he's there. He flies at Dr. Haven, who still wields the Drauldin in both hands. One lick of that blade will render Markos alight and he will perish, ridding me of everything currently plaguing my life: him, the marriage, the assignment, Lochfort. All of it can be taken care of with one fell swoop, and I pray to Lisha harder than I've ever prayed before.

Dr. Haven swings the sword as Markos confronts him, crying out into the night. I watch the blade, its blue light flickering and fading out just as it slices across Markos's forearm. And then I hear it—The sickening crunch of several dozen bones as Markos wraps his arms around Dr. Haven and squeezes, letting his lifeless body fall to a crumpled heap on the ground.

I stand there quivering in horror, an involuntary scream escaping my lips.

That's all I can do, is scream.

A bloodcurdling, gut-wrenching, heartbroken scream.

CHAPTER 22

It all happened so fast.

It's hard to make out his features through the tears stinging my eyes. I haven't cried in a very, very long time. I haven't cried since that night in the hospital, the one where they took him off life support. And I swore then that I would never cry again, that I'd never care about anyone enough ever again to let myself be led to this level of devastation.

Apparently I lied.

Everything hurts as I kneel down and scoop his torso into my lap. His body is heavy, dead weight, and his frame moves in noodly, inhuman ways with all the bones that have been broken. I feel so lost and defeated and ... *angry*.

I turn and see Markos standing there. His cackles quickly give way to a roar of laughter, and the fury in me grows with every sound he makes, with every slow, hollow beat of his heart. "I guess you'll have to deliver him dead, Zali," he grins.

This ends now.

I lay Dr. Haven's body gently on the ground and stand to face Markos. My eyes scan our surroundings, noting the wreckage and scattered things. Car bits. Glass. Metal. Dr. Haven's glasses in the grass. And the Drauldin, only a few feet from where I stand.

It has no blue glow left to it, its buzzing has dulled to an inaudible level from where it lay. But I don't care. Enchanted or not, I have to try to end this once and for all. The wrath I'll bring on myself for killing my own kind is a distant afterthought compared to the need to eliminate Markos. Leader Taryn's arrangement be damned, I'm not spending one minute saddled up with this *monster*.

I pace slowly over to the blade and pick it up by the handle, careful not to let any bit of the steel touch my skin, lest any enchantment linger and it be as murderous as I've been warned. It feels good in my hand, surprisingly light for the size of it. I point it at Markos, and he finally stops laughing.

"Your human already cut me with that, Zali," he says, showing me the scar on his arm from the wound which has already healed. "What good is that blade going to be to you? Without the enchantment, it is no more useful than any ordinary piece of steel."

"I don't care," I mumble, the air burning my lungs as I fight to speak through the pain of my loss. "One of us is dying tonight, Markos, and at this point I don't care which. So let's do this."

He laughs again, snapping his jaws at me like an animal. "Take care, my pet. We'll meet again soon. On our wedding night, if not sooner."

"What?"

Before I can press him for an explanation, he takes off running, but not in the direction I'd expect. He runs in the opposite direction of the farm, across the highway and clear through the fields of tall grass that lead towards the mountains.

"MARKOS!"

I want to chase after him but my feet feel like lead, pulling me to the earth and keeping me beside Dr. Haven's cold, fragile body. His eyes are closed, the weird positions of his limbs reminding me of a marionette. I can't leave him here, but I can't take him back to Lochfort either.

I'm at a loss.

"We need to get him to the industrial yard," a man's voice says, causing my gaze to snap in his direction.

"Professor Gibbons." I'd somehow blocked out his presence with my heartache. "Professor, I ... You—"

"The industrial yard," he repeats sternly, as though I'm a child being reprimanded for trivial misbehavior. "Now, Sara. Can you get him there? I need to gather my things from the car. Or rather ... what's left of it."

"He ... He's really dead, Professor. How are you—"

"If you want him to live, you'll save your questions for later, Miss Summers. His body is broken and his heart may not be beating, but his soul is intact, for now. Now, do you want him to survive or not?"

"Yes! Yes! More than anything!"

"As do I. So do as I asked and get him to the industrial yard."

CHAPTER 23

It stinks in here, like musty air and old copper pipes and
stale motor oil. The only saving grace in it is *him*,
though his sweet scent is slowly beginning to fade and
be replaced by the sour notes of death.

I can't stand it.

I can't stand him not smelling like himself. I can't stand
watching the color drain from his face and his perfect hands.
I'm happy his eyes are closed and I can't see the glassiness
that is no doubt quickly replacing the lively twinkle I've come
to expect when those blue eyes look at me.

This better fucking work.

It has to. I'm not accepting any other possibility. The pull
to him that I feel has been there since the first time he spoke
to me, that moment he approached me as I watched the
protestors outside CCU, but I didn't grasp how strong it was
until now. There's an emptiness inside me from having almost
no soul that I've grown used to.

But the emptiness from not having *him* is terrifying.

It's cliche to say that the world is duller without someone,
that colors aren't as bright and smells aren't as rich and music

isn't as grand ... but now I fear it's true. How could anything possibly feel the same? How could anything be as good, look as good, *taste* as good?

Good Lisha, how will I enjoy a cup of coffee sitting in a world without him in it?

The very thought shatters me. I would swear off coffee for good if it meant something, or *someone*, bringing him back to me. And now I have to place my faith in that someone being Professor Gibbons, the very person who's probably been killing off everyone I know for the past couple decades.

Fuck.

"What are you doing? Whatever you're going to do, Professor, I suggest you hurry up and do it. The smell of death is growing stronger on him by the minute."

Professor Gibbons raises a brow at me from across the steel table. In front of him lay various herbs and liquids in jars and vials. His hands work fiercely with a large mortar and pestle. "I can smell the death on him just as well as you can, Sara. If not *better* than you can."

I glare at him. "Just what are you, anyway, Professor Gibbons? I know you aren't human."

My eyes grow wide as he goes into a cabinet behind him and retrieves a small blade, the rough size and shape of a letter opener. He holds his hand above the mortar and slices, letting the blood trail down his fingertips and mix with the concoction inside.

"Not *fully* human, you mean."

A puff of smoke and a bright flash jump from the mortar, quickly fizzling out as he continues to mix for a few more seconds. Then he puts the mixture in a small, mesh ball, which he places in an onyx mug. An electric kettle in the corner flicks off with uncanny timing, and he pours hot water into the mug to brew a sort of tea.

"Is this going to fix him?" I ask softly.

"We hope," he says with a shrug so nonchalant it infuriates me. "I need him alive."

"*You* need him alive?! You're the one who got him into this mess!" I cry, waggling an accusatory finger. "If you hadn't been hunting us, none of this would have happened!"

Professor Gibbons cocks his head, a slight smirk on his lips. "Oh? Is that what you think? That I'm the one who's been hunting you?"

"Yes! Why else would you two be meeting out here? Why else were you headed to the farm tonight? Why else would you have stolen the Drauldin from the Yedora clan?"

"You have so many questions, and so few answers," Professor Gibbons shakes his head, tsking. "And yet, you're so convinced that *I'm* the one who's the hunter."

"It makes the most sense! You're fast, far too fast to be human. And Dr. Haven is——"

"Not as fast?"

"Yes, exactly."

Professor Gibbons's eyes narrow. "And you know this ... simply because you've never seen him move that fast? Is that it?"

My reasoning sounds completely idiotic posed in such a simple question. I fold my arms tightly over my chest. "Dr. Haven is far too sweet of a human to be a hunter," I say firmly. "He doesn't strike me as the type. *You*, however, have always given me the creeps."

Professor Gibbons bursts out laughing. "Oh, well! Excuse me. I didn't realize *giving you the creeps* translated into me being a murderous hunter. My apologies."

I run my teeth over my fangs, annoyed at how little he seems to be taking this seriously. "Just save Dr. Haven. I'll figure out what to do about you later."

He eyes me curiously, picking up the onyx mug and bouncing the tea strainer up and down a few times. "Okay, but before I resurrect him you should know ... it's *he* who is the hunter. My job is purely to deal in magic. Enchantments, curses, healing things. I don't do *elimination*. That is your beloved Professor Haven's job."

"*Doctor* Haven," I correct him.

"Sure, Doctor. Calling him what you want doesn't change what he is. Just like me calling you 'Sara Summers' doesn't really stop you from being 'Zalida Wren', does it?"

I freeze, the tips of my ears prickling at the sound of my last name. They're so uncommonly used amongst our kind, it's weird to even hear it spoken out loud. "How do you know my name?"

"I know a lot about you, Zalida. It's interesting how easily bought information is when it comes to our kind. There's always a power struggle, amongst the Leaders, amongst the clans. Every clan wanting to make up the majority of the Ancestors and be in charge of some imaginary politics. Makes you sad, doesn't it? That every detail about you has such a low price?"

"I don't ... I don't understand."

"Don't you think it's weird that Markos took off and left me completely unharmed?"

The point is a punch to my stomach, a literal blow that knocks the air from my lungs and causes me to stagger back a step. "You ... You've been working together."

"You catch on quick, Summers. You don't mind if I keep calling you that, do you? It'll keep me in good habits. Wouldn't want to slip up around anyone from school."

"Whatever, *Bentley*."

He cringes. "You really are every bit as clever as you are beautiful, Sara. Not the smartest, though. If you were smart, you'd have gone through with marrying Markos. That one is a hunter and a prime mate. Together you could have bred and raised a great army of drauls."

I shake my head, trying to forcefully remove the stomach-turning thought. "I hate Markos. I would never marry him willingly. But why, Professor? Why work with him? What was there for you to gain?"

"The same thing he had to gain from me. Protection. Immunity. He doesn't kill me, I don't kill him. Information about your kind helps lead us to the farms and eliminate you in droves."

"But why would Markos want to help you kill off other drauls? Our numbers are dwindling as it is. We're being pushed to the brink of extinction in some parts. And why did he show up tonight and attack us if you're partners?"

"You're the inferior race," Professor Gibbons shrugs. "You can't hide your identity, not at night. Plus, the more pure the draul bloodline runs through the generations, the more feral the offspring become. Half-breeds are the ones who are really powerful. We're smarter, faster, stronger. We see better at night, even without glowing eyes. We don't need souls to survive, we eat regular food. Plus, our blood conjures up a level of magic no pure blood could ever come close to.

As for the attack tonight ... I have a feeling he's been watching you and is in tune with your affections toward Ross. Clearly, I've not made it obvious enough to him how integral your doctor is to our operations."

Fuck. If Markos didn't know how I felt about Dr. Haven before, he certainly does now. Which means he'll stop at nothing to make me pay.

"So you had no idea he was going to attack? You didn't encourage him to kill Dr. Haven?"

"If I had, would I be saving him now?" he scoffs, rolling his eyes.

"That's yet to be seen," I snap. "And that's what you are? A half-breed? I thought there'd been no half-breeds recorded since the tale of Jalvana."

"Exactly," he agrees. "None *recorded*. That doesn't mean none are in existence."

I gasp. "That's how you have the power to save Dr. Haven. Your blood is the key to harnessing enough power to bring someone back from the dead."

"Precisely. As long as they're not *too* dead. Speaking of which, we should get moving. But as I said before, you should know that Ross is indeed the person who's been killing off the clans, largely your Osjhka clan. Are you still sure you want me to save him?"

I take a deep breath. "I'm sure."

CHAPTER 24

His face is warm as I press my fingertips to his cheek, stroking lightly. There's stubble that's grown in the couple days he's been asleep. I watch him as he lays there, eyelids fluttering, bits of streetlight floating in through his bedroom window.

I haven't left his condo since I brought him home.

Professor Gibbons warned me that the brew would need time to work. Bringing someone back from the dead is no easy task, it would seem. But I vowed I would stay with him and see to it that he remained safe until he woke up, and after sixty hours that time is finally here.

His eyes open fully as he yawns and stretches, letting all four limbs starfish out across his bed. I rise from the edge where I'd been sitting, tucking myself into the darkest corner of the room. His bedside lamp casts cloaking shadows, and I clear my throat as he turns to smile at me.

"Oh ... Hello, Miss Summers," he moans, looking a bit delirious. "How long was I out this time?"

"Two full days and a bit. Wait, *this time*? This has happened before?"

"Once," he says, holding up his index finger on a shaky hand. "I've died once before."

"How did you ... You know what, never mind. I don't want to know. How are you feeling? Are you feeling okay? I don't know what being brought back from the dead feels like, but I would imagine it isn't great."

He laughs, his whole face lighting up. It's good to see him looking like this, with color to his flesh and that familiar twinkle to his eyes. His bright blue irises are radiant, crystal clear and once again full of life. He seems himself, and just being in his presence puts me incredibly at ease.

"I'd compare it to a pretty intense hangover," he says, clutching his forehead. "Speaking of which, there isn't coffee made, is there?"

"There isn't but I can go make you some."

"I can—"

"Please, Dr. Haven," I cut him off, "let me do it. You need to rest."

He looks like he wants to argue, but to my surprise he doesn't push it. "Alright, fair enough. Mugs are in the cupboard above the sink. Coffee and filters are in the one to the left of that."

"I know," I reply, leaving out the part about me having spent the past two days memorizing the layout of the place and everything in it.

"And can you grab me some painkillers from the—"

"Cupboard above the stove. Sure."

His features exude curiosity but all he does is smile. "Thanks."

I go to the kitchen and gather the things to make coffee, a subtle sadness clutching at my chest as I do. My mind can't help but wander to thoughts of what it would be like to have this arrangement all the time, to live in his house and make him his coffee and be there when he wakes up. It's a silly fantasy, but images of the possibilities flash through my head all the same.

I can't torture myself with such nonsense. It's never going to happen, and this doesn't change anything. Dr. Haven being alive doesn't change things between us, doesn't change the fact that he's a man and I'm a monster. If anything, what I know now puts us in a more difficult position.

He's the hunter.

At least, that's what Professor Gibbons claimed. If it's true, I need to hear it from Dr. Haven's mouth directly. And if it *is* true, and he does verify that he is indeed the hunter, then that puts me in an unthinkable predicament.

But it isn't him. It can't *be him.*

The smell of coffee floods my nostrils as bits begin to drip down into the carafe. I try to shift my focus solely onto it, rather than the gibberish in my brain.

Drip. Drip. Drip.

"It doesn't brew faster if you watch it."

His voice is warm and welcome behind me, but it stirs up a whirlwind of insecurity. I run to the wall and flick the kitchen light off, blanketing us in a comfortable darkness.

"There's no need to do that," he says.

"I don't ... You've never seen me after dark, Dr. Haven. I'm ... *different.*"

He chuckles. "You say that like I've never seen a draul before. I've seen hundreds."

"You've *seen* hundreds, but you've never seen *me*. Besides," I turn to face him so he can see the yellow hue of my eyes, "how many have you *killed?*"

The question seems to take him off guard, a pained look overtaking his handsome face. "About the same."

The words are a knife to my heart. I clutch the counter behind me in both hands for support, leaning my weight backwards as I choke down the tears trying to form in the corners of my eyes. "So Professor Gibbons was telling the truth, then. You are the hunter. *You*. Not him."

"He might not do the actual killing, but without his alliance with—Markos, was it?—none of what I do would be possible. None of the drauls would have partnered up with me, none of them would have trusted me. And I couldn't have freed so many without his intel into the camp locations and populations and such."

"*Freed?!* Is that what you think you're doing? Freeing us?"

"A life without a soul is one of pain and torture. You're damned to live out centuries without the capacity to properly enjoy anything. Sex, music. You can't even enjoy food. From what I've heard, none of them are overly pleasurable. How is that a life worth living?"

"I have a soul!"

"So does an earthworm. It doesn't mean it enjoys its existence," he says quietly.

"You think we can't enjoy stuff? That's what this is about?" My heartbeat has quickened, but it's still dreadfully slow compared to his, which I can hear from across the open room.

"When's the last time you listened to music?"

His question challenges my memory, but as I go to answer my mind sits empty and my mouth hangs open. "I don't know. I don't remember the last time. I hear it sometimes, at school or at the cafe, but ... I don't specifically put it on to listen to."

"And why is that, Miss Summers?"

I can't stop the tears from welling in my eyes any longer. "I guess because I don't crave it. It doesn't bring me any real joy."

"Exactly."

"But that doesn't mean I can't enjoy things!" I argue. "I've kept coffee in my life, and I'm sure you know most drauls don't do that. I truly do enjoy coffee. It's why I still drink it even though it tends to make me a bit sick."

Dr. Haven smiles, that wide, genuine smile that still has me fooled into feeling there's no way he could be a killer. "You know, out of all the drauls I've ever encountered, you're the only one who's held onto anything human."

I laugh as I swipe away the tears that have rolled down either cheek. I'm happy that it's dark and he can't see me. "There are certain things I refuse to let go, coffee being one."

"Oh yeah?" He takes a few steps toward me, sidestepping the edge of the kitchen counter despite the darkness. He has the layout of the space committed to memory, the way I have all of his features committed to mine. "What else have you held on to?"

"Memories," I offer gently. "My mother's voice. Little poems and songs she'd sing to me. And ... What life was like. Before. Though, I don't have much of that left."

Dr. Haven stares into my eyes, taking another stride until he's only a couple feet from me. "What about ... the hospital?"

I let go of the counter and straighten my composure. "That memory is one I *can't* forget. And not for a lack of trying."

I wonder if he's going to press me for more information, but he doesn't. "The brain holds onto memories that are correlated to the strongest emotions," he says. "Happy memories, traumatic events. Good things, bad things. It doesn't differentiate. It just ingrains stuff in us that had the most impact."

"What about you? Do you have memories you can't let go of?"

"Sure," he says, taking another step. The smell of death lingers on him very slightly, but most of his scent has returned to the sweet spiciness I've grown so fond of. "My graduation was a big one, though that one's good. The death of my parents was another. That happened when I was very young, and it still haunts me. I dream about it sometimes."

My chest is heavy. I want to tell him things, to be completely open and honest with him, but it's hard now that I know what he is. My head and heart feel so conflicted, and yet ...

Fuck it.

"It was my fiancé."

His eyes grow soft. "In the hospital?"

"Yes."

"What ... You don't have to tell me what happened."

I bite my bottom lip, tucking my icy hands up into my underarms. "I want to. If you want to know."

"I've wanted to know ever since you wrote about it in my class, Miss Summers." His eyes are so big and sincere, his irises overtaken by dark pupils as they seek to let any little bit of light in that might be hiding amongst the blackness.

"I had already been a draul for a while, maybe fifty years or so. And I had never been partnered. No one had ever piqued my interest, and I mostly avoided the clans. I was a bit of a free spirit and didn't want to be involved in the politics. I didn't want someone placing rules and expectations on me."

"How did you survive without the farms?"

"I still had to eat, but I never killed anyone. Similar to the farms, I would take just enough soul to satiate myself and leave the rest to repair. My usual targets were hitchhikers. Wanderers. Solo campers. Nothing that would cause alarm. And I never killed them."

"So you said," Dr. Haven notes.

"Right. But then I found one, a guy camping by himself in the woods ... and I couldn't bring myself to do it. Something about him made me curious. I wanted to get to know him.

So, I did. He traveled a lot and I followed him around the country. I didn't show up every place he was in, I made it seem like a coincidence that I'd be here or there. Eventually, we got to know one another."

"And then fell in love."

I swallow hard. "Yes. It took a long time before I showed him what I was, but I couldn't hide it forever. He was freaked out at first, but he got over it quicker than I expected. He didn't care. He just loved me for me."

Dr. Haven smiles. "I can't say I blame him."

The words force a grin from me despite the sadness I feel as I relive my past. I take a deep breath. "But then ... I couldn't keep him safe forever. Word spread to the clans that a draul and a human were together. We were camping and one of the Yedora clan saw us. Saw me, like this. They told my clan, the Osjhka, and ... and then—"

"You don't have to talk about it," Dr. Haven says, hearing me get choked up. He closes the last bit of distance between us and wraps his arms around me tightly. His body is ridiculously warm, and I love the way his towering stature lets him rest his chin atop my head with ease. He kisses my hair. "Seriously, you don't have to tell me any more."

"I need to," I whisper, letting tears roll down my cheeks as I untuck my arms and wrap them around his waist and squeeze. Something about him makes me want to open up, makes it easier to cry, makes it easier to finally let someone in.

Something about him makes me more ... *human*.

"Okay," he says, snaking one arm up behind my back so he can stroke my hair.

I go on to tell him the rest. I explain how Markos's uncle was the Leader at the time, and how furious he was when he found out a clanless draul was frolicking with a human. How this anger passed on to Markos, who made it his personal duty to hunt us down. How he could have easily killed my fiancé, but instead left him in a magic-induced coma with no way for me to undo it.

"He wanted me to suffer. He felt as though I somehow deserved to for falling in love with a human. When the hospital couldn't figure out what was wrong with my fiancé, and noticed how little brain activity he had, they said the life support was no longer viable. So ... I let him go."

"It was for the best," Dr. Haven says, a response I feel would be the natural reaction of anyone in his shoes. "There was nothing more you could do for him."

"Except turn him into one of *us*. A creature. But I'd have never wished that on him."

"And yet you think it so cruel for me to do what I do," he says.

"There are drauls who don't hate what they are," I reply flatly.

"Sure. But I've yet to meet one who doesn't miss what they *were*." He scratches his chin. "I'm sorry about your fiancé, Miss Summers. Truly."

"And I'm sorry about your parents."

"It was a long time ago. I was very little, and remember only bits about it, and about them. Water long under the bridge, save for the occasional nightmare." He takes a sharp breath. "Miss Summers, can I turn on the light? Please. I'd really like to make a coffee. It sounds like it's done brewing, and my head is still throbbing."

"Are you okay if I go to your room before you do that?"

"You really don't want me to see you that badly?"

"I ... What if you hate how I look like this? I don't look like myself."

"And what if I love it?" he counters.

Part of me wants to dash to his room and hide, genuinely scared of his reaction. But another part of me feels the inevitability of this confrontation sinking in, and something about him and the way his fingers trace through the back of my hair and along my neck is dampening my fear.

"Alright," I agree. "But if you look the least bit uncomfortable or stare awkwardly at my fangs, I'm out of here."

"Fair points, Miss Summers."

His arms leave me as he moves to the wall with the lightswitch, my breath held in my chest as he flicks it. The kitchen light beams down on us, the bright glow creating a glare off the glossy countertops. His eyes take me in from where he stands as bits of gray begin to cloud his irises.

"You ... are ... ravishing," he says, taking a stride with each word until he's back in front of me.

"I'm a monster," I say quietly. I try to avert my gaze, but his hand is on my chin before I have the chance to look away. He pulls my face up toward his, his soft lips landing on mine as he claims my mouth in a gentle but passionate kiss.

"I see a lot of things, Miss Summers, but I do *not* see a monster. And I've seen a lot of monsters."

"You've *killed* a lot of monsters," I correct him. "If Professor Gibbons had his way, I'm sure you'd be out to kill me too."

"That is *never* going to happen," he says sternly. "Besides, you're not like the others. And not just because you still enjoy coffee." He lets me go after pecking my forehead. "Speaking of which, would you like some?"

⚜

WE CURL up on his couch and talk and sip coffee into the wee hours of the morning. As the sun peeks over the horizon, the whites of my eyes lose their yellow glow, and my fangs retreat back into ordinary looking teeth. I am human again, at least in appearance.

"Miss Summers, as much as I'm thoroughly enjoying your company, I think I really, really need a hot shower. If that's alright with you."

It's funny to me that he would even bother to ask my opinion in his own home, but I can't help but smile at the thoughtfulness. "Of course, Sir. After all, it's your house. I can handle sitting in my own company for a bit while you get cleaned up."

He kisses my temple and leaves from where we're snuggled up together and heads to the bathroom. I hear the shower start moments later, the sound of the running water a tease as I think about how long it's been since I've done the same. The door sits slightly ajar, and I wait for him to close it. But he doesn't, and it's not long before steam seeps out of the bathroom and I realize he's already gotten in the shower.

I set my coffee down and lean forward, my bum barely hanging onto the edge of the couch. A big part of me wants to get up and join him, another part of me thinks this entire situation is pure insanity. Dr. Ross Haven has admitted to me that he's the one who's been killing my kind, and all I can think about is how badly I want to go fuck him in the shower.

And he thinks because I don't listen to music that I don't enjoy stuff. I enjoy plenty! And there's quite a few things I enjoy even more than coffee.

I head for the bathroom door, pressing it open a little farther and letting the steam lick at my face. I can make out Dr. Haven's form behind the plastic shower curtain. He's facing away from me, letting the water pour over him as he rinses his face.

I unzip my leather pants and slide them off silently, my matching top quickly following. Then my undershirt and bra go, then my socks go one at a time until I am standing there in nothing but my panties. Their sheer fabric sits atop my hip bones and hugs the natural curves of my body, and I love the way they feel so close to wearing nothing at all.

I want to be as naked as him ... with him.

I slide the shower curtain back slowly, waiting for Dr. Haven to turn around. When he does, a look of surprise washes over his features as his cock twitches and begins to rise. "Miss Summers, I ... Well, I—"

I take my panties off without saying a word, letting my eyes burn into his as he steps closer to the edge of the tub to watch me. He doesn't have his glasses on, and I realize I've no idea how much of me he can really see. I turn and find them on the counter near the sink and hand them to him.

"Thank you, that's ... Oh, wow," he mumbles as his eyes are finally able to properly take me in. He looks me up and down, basking in me a moment as every drop of blue in his irises is replaced by that sultry, smoky gray I've come to crave. "You're—"

"Can I come in?"

It's a simple question he doesn't immediately answer. He stands there a moment, mouth agape, as if trying to process whether I'm serious and this is all really happening. Then he doesn't answer with words. He simply holds a hand out for me to take and helps me step over the edge of the tub.

He moves out of the way so I can step into the water. Its heat soothes me, and I feel no pressure or sense of urgency as Dr. Haven steps up behind me and begins squeezing my neck and shoulders. An involuntary moan escapes my lips as his strong hands massage my skin, easing away the tension I've held there since the encounter with Markos, all of that falling away bit by bit as I let the pain and tightness subside.

His hands leave for a few seconds but quickly return, the smell of lightly scented soap hitting me as he begins at my neck and rubs over my shoulders and then down my back.

He's slow and attentive, washing me carefully as he lathers my arms one at a time.

I shudder when I feel his hands hit the small of my back, then glide slowly over my cheeks as he crouches down behind me. He lets all his fingertips trail down one leg at a time, then moves his hands back up as he caresses my calves, behind my knees, then up between my thighs.

I put my hands on the wall in front of me, hinging forward so the water can cascade down my back as he tenderly washes me. The water rinses me as his hands continue to rub, and it takes everything in me not to turn around and face him. I gasp as I feel his fingertips move back up my inner thighs and onto my lady bits, tracing the curves of my outer lips with painfully light pressure.

My hips instinctively move backward, forcing his hand against me harder. He grasps the outside of my left hip as his other hand explores me, moving past my thighs until he can reach far enough around to begin stroking my clit. A moan escapes my lips, breathy and full of need as I ache to feel his fingers inside me.

I need *him* inside me.

The way he teases me is sweet torture. His fingers rub up and down my button as he presses his thumb inside me, causing me to cry out. My breathing grows ragged as he slides his thumb in and out ever so slowly, his fingers gliding over my clit in sync and causing little shockwaves to run up into the pit of my stomach.

I need him NOW.

I can't take it anymore. I turn to face him, helping him stand up so I can press my bare chest against his. His hard cock presses against my stomach as I stretch up on my toes to kiss him, our mouths colliding in furious, needy pecks as his kisses trail from my lips to the corner of my mouth and then down my jawline.

His hand finds its way back between my legs as he kisses my neck, and I wrap my arms around his neck for support as he slides two fingers inside me. I'm wetter in ways than what the shower has granted, and his fingers move in and out of me easily as his thumb lands on my sweet spot and causes my legs to tremble.

"Is that okay?" he whispers in my ear, but all I can do is nod and press my face into his shoulder. He continues kissing my neck as his fingers glide in and out of me. I feel the orgasm in me building slowly, a sensation no one's brought me in a very, very long time. I love the way his fingers feel, guiding every bit of me to the slow burn of release.

"Please don't stop," I beg him, and he's happy to oblige. I feel myself growing closer and closer, my hips jutting forward to coax his fingers in just a little deeper and his thumb against me a little harder. "Don't ... stop ..."

My nails dig into his shoulders as I climax. He holds me close as my body shakes, my thighs clenching around his hand as heady shockwaves overtake me one after another. I breathe heavily as I stand there with him, crying out as he slides his fingers out of my sensitive, tingling hole.

I look up at him with half-closed eyes, my eyelids heavy with satisfaction. The grays in his eyes have grown dark and urgent, like an oncoming storm you see on the horizon long before it rolls in. He's full of need as he looks deep into my eyes, and all I want right now is to bring him to the state of bliss my head is swimming in.

"Come to bed with me," he says.

The command is stern but gentle, pulling me out of the tub alongside him with an invisible force of intoxication. Human or not, whatever it is he does to me is profound. The effect he has is one I was so hellbent on fighting, but now, having succumbed to it, I'm not sure I'll ever be able to let it go. Nor that I want to.

I go and lay in his bed, my body still damp from the shower. I'm surprised when he stops at the edge of the bed, rather than climbing in with me. He stands there and stares at me, drinking in every detail as though I'm a fine wine he'd cherish on his palate a long while before swallowing.

At this point, I'd let him swallow any and every bit of me he wants to.

He adjusts his glasses and smiles. "You're beautiful."

"So are you," I tell him. And he is. His strong arms look just as perfect for holding me as for pinning me to his bed, and the outlines of tattoos yet to be finished only serve to make him all the more delicious. The perfect angles of his hips lead down to muscular legs, but my eyes can't help but wander between them to the raging cock in front of me.

He's very well endowed, and I already feel the sweet tingle of need returning between my thighs. I want him to take me right here and now, but he stands there and continues watching me as he strokes himself, moaning softly as his fingers become coated in precome. I want to spring off the bed and lick them and him clean, but instead I wait patiently and enjoy the view.

"Play with yourself," he says, and I listen. I let a hand slide down my inner thigh slowly, reveling in how soft my skin is. My fingers find my clit and I gasp, still swollen and sensitive from my recent orgasm. I slide my middle finger along my lips, parting them and slipping it in easily with my wetness. I whimper and his eyes widen.

I need him, need to know how he tastes and how he feels and how different the world would look while he's buried inside me. Everything in me, everything feral, and everything soft, and everything sweetly bruised and wounded and broken, needs to know if it would change anything if we finally give in to this.

He steps over to the side of the bed and I slide over to the edge, hand still pressed between my legs. He holds his thick manhood out in front of me and I wrap my lips around him. He shudders and moans loudly. I let my mouth and throat relax, adjusting to the ample thickness of him as I lick and suck the tip. The sweet and salty taste of his precome has me growing wetter, and I moan down onto his shaft as I take him deeper and slip another finger into myself simultaneously.

I ease my throat down on his length over and over, smiling every time he gasps or moans or presses his hips against me harder. I love the sounds he makes, how audibly he expresses what a good job I'm doing. His hands grow tangled in my hair, coaxing me just a little bit further as his fingers press into my scalp.

"Stop, stop, stop," he whispers, and I do, releasing him from my mouth. He doesn't want to come like this, and I'm elated. I don't want him to either. My body is screaming to have him in me, and I want to know what it feels like to have every drop of his release deep inside me.

He seems happy to grant my wish as he leans his face down to mine. He cups my cheek and plants his mouth on mine, and I don't recall ever tasting more need in a single kiss. His tongue invades my mouth with urgency, but he breaks off the kiss as quickly as it started and climbs onto the bed with me.

He lies down beside me, his hand stroking along my neck and collarbone before once again getting lost in my hair. "How do you want me?" he asks.

I lay back, letting my head fall on the pillows as I let my knees fall apart. "Just like this." The truth, which I don't dare say out loud, is that I don't want anything crazy or wild.

I want *him* to make love to me.

He hears me, scooting down to the end of the bed and sitting himself between my feet. He tenderly grabs my ankles, his strong hands sliding up my calves, then along the back of my legs, until finally his hands come around to grip my hips and pull me ever so slightly toward him.

I'm lost in the way he stares down at me as he positions himself above me. His sultry, gray eyes bore down into mine as he watches me, our gazes locked as he lowers his hips slowly until I feel his head pressing against my wet opening.

His neck canes down as he kisses along my throat and jaw, and I can't help but lift my hips slightly, desperately urging him to press inside. He inhales sharply as just the head of his cock pushes past my lips, tormenting us both with the need for more. The sensation is already so intense, my nerve endings still heightened from my previous climax.

I need him inside so fucking badly.

"Are you sure you want to do this?" he whispers in my ear.

"Yes." The word escapes full of lust, but there's more than that. There's a desperation to it that I don't bother trying to hide. That, at this moment, I'm not afraid to show him.

"I mean ... Are you sure you want to do this *with me*, knowing what you know?"

I don't have it in me to speak. Instead, I answer his question by wrapping my legs around his waist and squeezing tightly, forcing his hips down and causing us both to cry out as I drive him inside me. Both his girth and length are exquisite, stretching and filling me in a way no one has before. He stays still, buried inside me, and kisses me hard.

The way he kisses me tells me he's wanted this as long as I have, since our first encounter outside the school. I let him explore every corner of my mouth as his hips begin to slowly move back and forth, in and out, my body caressing every inch of his shaft as he takes his time with me. He's meticulous in the way he moves, and I fear I already feel myself slipping into the sweet clutches of addiction.

He pulls out slowly, then pushes back in in a way that ensures I savor every single inch of him. It isn't quick or animalistic, the way I assume Markos would take me if he had the chance. It's hypnotizingly erotic, pulling me more and more under his spell as he refuses to break eye contact as he makes love to me.

He kisses me briefly. "Do you want to switch?" he moans into my mouth.

"Switch ... how?" I manage between thrusts.

"You could be on top."

The offer is sweet and, though I'm enjoying the rhythm he's set, too tempting to pass up. The thought of getting on top of him is divine. "Okay," I nod.

We scoot around one another as he replaces me on the bed. I swing a leg over his hips and let my pussy lips straddle him, sliding them up and down his tool as his hands grip my hips. He grasps me tight, coaxing my hips back and forth a little faster, teasing us both as I further coat him in my slippery wetness.

I let my pussy slide along him until not having him inside me becomes pure agony, then I move my hips up and lower myself onto the tip of him. "Oh, fuck," I moan as I slide down onto his length and feel him reach new depths inside me. "Ohhh."

Dr. Haven grabs my face and pulls me down gently, kissing me as I rock my hips back and forth. I feel my clit rubbing against his pelvis as I grind, the mixture of that and the way he fills me driving my mind blank as I process nothing beyond the scent of him and the intense pleasure.

"I ... I'm going to come," he groans, and without a moment of hesitation I begin thrusting myself against him harder and faster.

"Come for me," I beg him. "I want you to fill me ... please, please ..."

His climax is electric as I feel spurt after spurt inside me. It drives me over the edge, my muscles convulsing as another orgasm quakes over me and pulls him just a little deeper inside. I cry out into the quiet of his room, breaking the silence as we lay there blanketed in a sheen of sweat that shimmers in the rays of sunlight coming through the window.

"That ... was—"

"Amazing," I say, finishing his sentence as we both struggle to catch our breath and let our heart rates return to normal. Mine is a bit faster than usual, but his sounds like it might beat right out of his chest. I lay forward and rest my face in the crook of his neck, the gentle thump of his pulse against my lips making me hungry for something else.

I need to go back to the farm and eat.

We lay there together in perfect silence. Tiny birds chirp somewhere outside, and I let his sweet, woodsy scent fill me as I take deep, deliberate breaths. My heart rate descends back down to its usual state, barely there, and I sigh as his arms wrap around me and pin me against him tighter.

This is bliss.

"Hey ..." he says, his voice trailing off with what sounds like the oncoming of sleep.

"Yes, Sir?"

"I ... love you."

Fuck.

I sit up, the move jarring him fully awake. His eyes open, crystal blue and chock full of concern. I let him slip out of me, a dreary sigh escaping me at how much I hate the sudden emptiness, how much I hate not having him there.

"I should get cleaned up," I say, trying to muster a chipper tone to relax some of the anxiety riddling his features. I clamber off the bed and rush to the bathroom through the walk-in closet, closing the closet doors behind me with a loud exhale. I shut the outer door, the one that leads to the main area of his place, then go to the sink and splash some cool water on my face.

Fuck.

Falling in love was not part of the plan. Not him falling in love with me, not me falling in love with him. None of this is okay. And now I'm in a situation where Professor Gibbons knows too much to keep alive, Markos is a traitor, and I'm still under Leader Taryn's orders to marry that psycho unless I deliver Dr. Haven to him in the next few weeks.

And to boot, now he's gone and fallen in love with me.

FUCK.

I need to get out of here. I need to eat. I need to think. I need time to think and process and come up with a plan and—

A knock at the outer door is accompanied by his voice. "Everything okay in there?"

"Yes, fine, thank you. Just ... getting cleaned up."

I use a towel to clean myself up as best as possible, tossing it in the tub before yanking on all my clothes. When I come out, Dr. Haven is standing there in a plush, navy blue housecoat fixing himself another coffee. "Hey," he says quietly, the word ringing with hopeful inflection.

"Hey." I force a smile, trying to act normal. But I've already blown it. There's no way he's going to believe everything's good between us now. He said he loved me, and I didn't say it back. You could cut the tension with a spoon as he heads to the fridge and grabs a carton of oat milk, adding some to his mug.

"Are we ... Is everything good?" he asks, stealing glances of me as he fixes his coffee.

"Yes, for sure. Everything is good. I just realized I really need to get back to the farm. Leader Taryn was ... I mean ... I just have some stuff to do, that's all."

"Fair enough." He leaves his mug on the counter and wanders over to me, a certain sadness clouding his eyes. "Do you ... I could drive you home, if you like."

The thought of spending an awkwardly silent car ride together is less than appealing. As much as I love his company, and as much as a big portion of me wants to say yes, I know it's not for the best.

"You're still recovering. You should rest."

"Really, I'm fine," he insists. "Like I said, this isn't my first rodeo."

"Well, I can't say I've ever met anyone else who makes dying a habit," I say, happy to see that this garners a slight smile from him. "I'll be fine, Dr. Haven. But thank you." I turn and pull my boots on, nearly at the door when I feel the warmth of his hand pressing into my shoulder.

"Miss Summers?"

I swallow hard, turning to face him. The pain in his eyes claws at me. My chest burns and my hands are icy and the thought of stepping through this doorway without him feels like a special kind of hell. But I need to go. Now. Before I can't.

"Yes, Dr. Haven?"

"I ... See you at school."

"See you at school, Sir."

And then I leave, unable to handle another second of the sorrow in his gaze.

CHAPTER 25

My stomach twists in sickening knots as I pace through the barn.

Gone. Everything and everyone is gone.

The knots turn to low growls, my stomach issuing a warning. I need to eat, and badly. But there isn't a soul in sight. The entire farmhouse is empty, nothing but the furniture we found it with. There's hardly three weeks until the full moon now. I'm running out of time, I'm running out of ideas, and apparently I've run completely out of food.

Where the hell did they go, and why didn't Leader Taryn tell me?!

My leather boots thud against the wood laden with bits of hay. The musty smell of old wood permeates everything around me, but the sweetness of freshly drunk souls still lingers, fueling my hunger further and causing me to let out an animalistic cry.

I need to eat.

My stagnant pulse quickens as my head begins spinning. I feel ravenous, hungry …

Feral.

The image of Professor Gibbons pops into my head. It's a crazy thought, I can admit, but maybe there's some way he can help me. Maybe there's a potion or a spell or something he can do to stave off hunger without having to hunt down anyone in the area.

Or maybe I should just travel a few miles out and find a camper or straggler somewhere.

Fuck, this hunger is getting to my head. I swore when I took this assignment that I wouldn't be eating anywhere but the farm. I don't want to attack a random person, and a hunger this strong can cause an appetite that's insatiable. Regularly fed, and my self control is excellent. But with how I'm feeling now, I'm not even sure I could feast and stop in time to not kill someone.

And I don't want to kill anyone. I may be a monster, but I'm not a killer.

I don't know whether or not I can really trust Gibbons. He's been working alongside Markos, the traitor, and he's been using information about our camps to aid Dr. Haven in killing us.

Us.

The word brings a tartness to my mouth. As much as I'm a draul, like all the others, I've never felt a particular closeness to any of them. Vanthony is the only one I even care to make friendly banter with. I preferred it when I was free, clanless, doing my own thing in my own time. But the protection the clan offers can't be disregarded, and being in the favor of Leader Taryn and the Ancestors is something that could later be met with great reward.

But I've always preferred to stay among the humans, that much has never changed.

On top of that, Professor Gibbons took the Drauldin with him when we disbanded after Markos fled. I guess I was so busy worrying about Dr. Haven that I didn't notice. I need to know where Gibbons stands when it comes to Markos. Does his loyalty lie more with him, or with Dr. Haven?

I have so many questions and so few answers.

I leave the empty barn, moonlight dousing me as I step out into the crisp night air. Winter is around the corner, you can feel it, and my arranged marriage isn't far behind. It pains me to admit, but I need Professor Gibbons. I need him to expose Markos to Leader Taryn. That, without a doubt, will be the end of Markos forever.

My frozen hands feel little of the cold as I race through the night. I could head directly to Professor Gibbons's house and confront him there, he's likely to be home at this hour. But there's somewhere I want to stop first, somewhere that might be more useful in my quest for information and proof of Markos's betrayal.

The industrial yard.

It's quiet when I get there. The familiar weathered buildings and dim streetlamps stand in their designated spots, the wind seeming to greet me with an exasperated sigh. I crouch low in the grass, dressed in my all-black leathers, trying to blend as best into the darkness as I can lest anyone be around to spot me.

I'm silent, my movements smooth. No light comes from the office window, and I don't hear anything that has me convinced I'm not alone. The world is quiet, and it's all too apparent why they call it *the dead of night*. And, being not that far from dead myself, I'm comfortable here.

I sneak up to the building and peek in the office window, my yellow eyes staring back at me in the dirty glass. A sliver of moonlight grants an inkling of the interior, my heart clenching when I see it. The bookshelf with all the old texts, the one where Dr. Haven pulled the emerald book from, is empty. Completely barren.

What the hell?

I press on the old window and am shocked when I find it slides open easily. I go inside, greeted by the must and metallic scents I'd encountered when I brought Dr. Haven's lifeless body here. Despite my night vision, I'd rather investigate with the familiar ease of the light. My hands trace the walls until I find a lightswitch, the old incandescent bulb coming alive with a buzzing hum.

Everything is gone. The steel table with all of Professor Gibbons's equipment and supplies, all the things spread about for use in potions and concoctions, has been cleared away. The table is spotless, an unusually clean bit of furniture in an otherwise dusty room, and the shelves have been stripped of all books. Cupboard doors hang messily open, revealing they too are bare.

I take a deep, steadying breath. It seems this assignment is barreling sideways, leaving me confused and angry. Is Leader Taryn also in on the arrangement between Gibbons and Markos? Clearly there's a reason why he suddenly relocated the farm and didn't bother to tell me. I feel like I'm on the outside of some catastrophic joke.

But there has to be an explanation ... right?

Time for Plan C.

I STARE at the brick bungalow, watching, waiting. There's light coming from the room on the front right side of the house, and the curtains are a few inches open. But as I approach the house, my senses become all too aware of it. Multiple shadows. Multiple voices.

Professor Gibbons is in there, but he isn't alone.

I creep up to the outer wall and press myself against it, the cool bricks kissing the side of my cheek as I listen. I hold my breath and concentrate, focusing on the bits of dialogue until I can hear everything clearly through the windowpane.

"You aren't listening. I *need* him. I can't afford to be the face of this operation. If you truly want what you say, to raise an army of half-breeds, overthrow the Ancestors and gain control over all the clans, you need me. I'm one of the only half-breeds in existence, you know that."

"*That* is the only reason you are still standing," the voice growls.

Fucking Markos!

"I've told you, we needed Haven for a time, but that time has come to an end. We don't need him to enchant the Drauldin, only the blood of a half-breed can do that. He's an excellent hunter, I'll give him that, but he is no longer necessary. I can take over the killing from here on out."

"You wielding the Drauldin while enchanted is too dangerous! One touch of the blade and you'll be dead within minutes, minutes that will feel like the slowest torture you've ever endured. It's too risky. And we need Haven to kill off more of your clan before it'll be weak enough for you to overthrow, Taryn included. And potentially, that fiancé of yours. A bit of a loose cannon, that one."

"You will not touch Zalida!" Markos hisses, and I clearly picture the way he forces the words through clenched teeth. "She is *my* bride, *my* wife, *my* property. She isn't like the other draul women. She's strong, she's capable. That is why she must be the one to bear my children."

In a grotesque sense, what he's saying almost sounds a bit sweet.

"And if I have to chain her to a bed to make her succumb to me, so be it."

Ah, there he is. There's the disgusting monster I know.

"I've known she was special ever since I first laid eyes on her. That's why I killed the first human she was in love with.

Besides, a draul with a human? The thought alone is revolting. Not to mention, it's strictly forbidden."

My hands grow icy at the mention of my deceased fiancé. Markos has never mentioned him before, not that I know of. It's an unspoken misery of mine, one I think he knows better than to bring up in my presence.

"How do you expect to raise an army of half-breeds without human and draul relationships?" Professor Gibbons scoffs. "You disrespect my very parents with that statement, you know."

"Humans are weak. Disgusting. *Food*." I hear the way his tongue laps across his fangs as the last word seeps from his mouth. "But the half-breeds are, generally, superior. Stronger. Faster. Able to blend with the humans when needed. I'll breed some human women to build my army, but they'll be disposed of as soon as they're no longer needed."

God, what a fucking creep. So this has been his plan all along. To overthrow Leader Taryn and the Ancestors and build himself an army. Well, he's got another thing coming. He's never going to get away with it once I report this to Leader Taryn. Him and Gibbons are both done for.

"You make it sound like it's going to be so easy," Professor Gibbons snaps. "You should know that half-breed children are extremely rare, even in human-draul relationships. There haven't been any new half-breed births reported in almost a century."

"None reported," Markos echoes, "but that doesn't mean there haven't been any. Who's to say? Any mixed couple would likely be in hiding."

"Drauls aren't able to hide their identities forever. Eventually, someone finds out."

"Whatever," Markos roars. "I grow tired of this conversation. The issue now is what to do with Haven. I killed him, and you went and brought him back from the dead. And worse still, Zalida seems to have grown some sort of affection toward him. It's *sickening*."

What's sickening is YOU, Markos!

"I would prefer to keep Haven around until he finishes killing Taryn and puts you in a better position for the overthrow." Professor Gibbons's voice is smooth and steady, each word audibly curated with the utmost thought and intention. " But the Drauldin is in my care. We can do it your way, if you wish."

"And then? Haven can not be allowed to live. He's a loose end, he knows far too much. I'm not leaving Lochfort while there is still air in his lungs and soul in his body."

There's a silence that seems to linger on forever before Gibbons speaks again.

"Then dispose of him. For good this time."

CHAPTER 26

Looking in the full-length mirror pulls an unexpected sadness from within me. It seems like forever has passed since I was standing here, dressed for my first day at Citrus County University, and yet it's been less than two months. There are no cute human clothes on me today. I'm head to toe in leathers. Both of my combat boots hide blades, and a long blade sits across my back under my jacket.

I am ready.

I slip out of 1042 Marr Street, careful not to wake any of the other girls. It's funny how such an ordinary dwelling and the residents within have become so sacred to me in such a short time. Markos may have made life more difficult here when he took Meredith, but I was relieved when Leader Taryn let me return her unharmed. She's back where she belongs, and none of these girls deserve to be swept up in the war Markos has brewing between the clans.

My mind races with a million thoughts and possibilities, but I needn't focus for my feet to instinctually lead me to his condo. I know going through the park is a bit riskier as far as anyone seeing me, but it's also the fastest way, and it's late enough at night that the risk is minimal.

Even if it wasn't, it wouldn't matter. I have to warn Dr. Haven before Markos gets to him that his life is at stake if he doesn't get out of Lochfort tonight. I need to tell him he can't trust Professor Gibbons, then get him somewhere safe.

I let out a heavy sigh as I enter the park, stopping alongside the cover of a thick tree trunk to catch my breath. I haven't traveled all that far, but I'm winded. It's been too long since I've fed and I've consequently little energy to spare. Asking Professor Gibbons for an alternate solution didn't go as planned, seeing as he and Markos were busy planning Dr. Haven's demise.

What a couple of scumbags, and some friend Professor Gibbons is. I wonder if this has been his plan all along, just using Dr. Haven until he no longer needs him, then sacrificing him to the cause. And to Markos, of all drauls.

I'm about to muster the strength to head the rest of the way when I hear the snap of a twig behind me. I immediately spin around, fangs bared, my lambent gaze landing on that familiar sneer.

Markos.

"Za-li-da," he sighs, enunciating every syllable. His body slinks to me like a cougar stalking its prey. He takes his time, his golden eyes focused on me as they skim up and down the length of my body. "I like you better in your human clothes," he pouts, "but you look like you're dressed for war, my queen. Where on earth might you be running dressed like that?"

"I ... was about to go on a little journey," I tell him. "An adventure, you might say."

"Oh?" I can tell I've piqued his curiosity. "Not running back to your newfound human, are you?"

I cock my head. "I no longer need the humans, Markos. My mission has been accomplished. I know the two humans involved in the executions of our clan members now. All I have to do is go report the names and all I know to Leader Taryn, and my presence in Lochfort is finished."

He saunters over to me, grabbing my chin with an uncharacteristic tenderness. He lifts my face, tsking as he examines me. "You're dark around the eyes, my queen. You look tired."

"I went back to the farm to feed," I tell him, a tone of pleading in my voice, "but Leader Taryn and the others were gone. Everything was gone."

"Why not feast on one of the lowly peasants around here, Zali? You said it yourself, your duty here is done. This place no longer need be forbidden."

I shake my head. "I'd rather get Leader Taryn's confirmation that the assignment is complete before I go making a mess here, Markos. After all, unlike you, I've never been a fan of shitting where I eat."

His grip slides from my chin to my throat and squeezes firmly. "*I* do what needs to be done wherever I go, Zalida."

"Of course," I gasp, and he releases me. I rub my neck, pressing my other hand against the tree beside me for support. "I'm just not as bold as you when it comes to the humans. I prefer avoiding heat scores. Keeping things on the down low. That's all."

I'm in no state to fight him off right now, and he knows it. The sick grin on his features tells me he has me exactly where he wants me.

Even so, I won't make it easy for him if he decides to try anything.

He grabs my chin again, harder this time, and kisses me roughly. His mouth latches to mine and I do nothing to resist, nothing to fight him off. As much as I want to bite his tongue off as it rolls around in my mouth, I can't. I need him to take me to wherever the farm now sits.

I *need* to eat.

"Let me carry you," he whispers in my ear. It's a command. Not a sweet offering, not a selfless act of love or adoration. It's an opportunity for him to keep me with him, to keep me under his watchful eye and ensure I'm not going anywhere near Dr. Haven.

And as much as I want to see Dr. Haven to warn him about the conversation between Markos and Gibbons, there's a pull inside me that's even stronger.

The intense desire to just *be* wherever *he* is.

I just want to exist in the same space, to know he's in bed or in the next room or taking a shower, and that I'm close enough to be beside him in a second. I long to be in his general vicinity and enjoy the comfort I've somehow found in knowing he's close. The comfort I was feeling while at his condo, before I panicked and rushed out of there.

But I'm hungry and weak, and Markos isn't going anywhere without me.

Assuming I'm not too late and he hasn't already killed Dr. Haven, Markos taking me to the new farm might be the best possible solution right now. Not only can I eat and regain my strength, but keeping Markos with me means keeping him away from Dr. Haven.

I'll have to make my way to the condo later. Hopefully nothing happens to him in the meantime. Professor Gibbons didn't seem to want him dead, I don't think he'll go there by himself to do anything.

"Okay, Markos," I sigh. "Take me, then."

He snarls along the side of my neck, his fangs scraping along my flesh ever so slightly. "You should be careful what you ask for, Zali. I could take you right here, right now ... if I wanted."

"It'd be a pathetic encounter with me being this weak, Markos," I shoot back dryly. "You'd be better off taking a human woman, if you wanted something with so little fight and tenacity in it."

He growls loudly against my skin. "You're right, Zali. Now would be a waste of a time to claim you. But time is ticking, my pet. Our wedding is only a couple short weeks away. My wait is almost over."

"As if I need reminding."

And we'll see whether or not you even live that long, traitor.

"Please, Markos," I coo, "enough games. Take me to the farm. I need to speak with Leader Taryn, and I desperately, desperately need to eat. Please."

"I love it when you beg," he replies, turning so his back is facing me. I jump up and wrap my arms around his neck as I steady my legs on his hips. I can feel the muscles of his back flex as he reaches back and grabs me, squeezing my buttocks and pinning me against him hard. I lay the side of my face between his shoulder blades, determined to rest as he races to the new farm location.

The distance is farther than I'd anticipated, and a sense of relief washes over me when we finally arrive. The new spot is an abandoned hotel located on the outskirts of a ghost town. The few dozen humans we feast on have all been neatly laid out on rickety beds in the hotel's many rooms. Somehow, it feels an even creepier setting than the barn, and I shudder as I walk down a long hall, passing open doors and seeing all of the humans in their fitful, magic-induced sleeps.

I find a young woman to feast on, taking just enough of her soul to satiate my hunger before I feel a hand on my shoulder that pulls me from her neck.

"Zali," Leader Taryn's voice is hypnotic to my newly-fed senses, "we need to speak."

CHAPTER 27

"I'd really prefer to talk to you alone."

Vanthony's eyebrows raise as he and the other council members watch me. Markos shoots me a vicious glare through narrow eyes. I'm unsure whether he has any inkling I know about his alliance with Gibbons, but the look in his eyes tells me he knows I know *something*.

"Whatever you wish to say to our Leader, surely you can say in front of all of us, Zalida. After all, Leader Taryn takes the weight of our collective opinions into account to make the decisions that will best benefit the Osjhka. So tell us, what is so top secret that you feel it requires absolute privacy?" Markos's voice is calm, but his eyes gleam with rage.

Death floods my eyes, and I know Markos sees it by the way he flinches ever so slightly when my eyes meet his. There's a burning to my eyes, the stinging pain of a feral instinct ready to tear from the inside out and manifest in a blood bath as I end Markos's treason once and for all.

"Is there anything *you* would like to tell Leader Taryn, Markos?"

Leader Taryn's brows perk up slightly, everyone's attention shifting to Markos as he fights to come up with a response. "I don't know, Zalida. Are you insinuating there should be something to tell? After all, wasn't it you who was trying to protect the very human you're supposed to be delivering here?"

A chorus of muffled gasps rings out, followed by anxious whispers and sidelong glances. "I wanted information from a human," I state firmly, "but it seems you were already fraternizing with him. I assume you're already aware of any valuable knowledge he might contain."

Markos chuckles. "It's true I took on a bit of investigation work myself, Zalida. You've yet to produce any results, despite having spent so much time around the humans. Forgive me if I admit that my faith in you was beginning to waver."

Leader Taryn's expression is solemn, his hands folded together in front of him. Most of the group sits around a round table in the hotel dining room. Markos stands beside our Leader while I stand on the opposite side of the large table. Leader Taryn sighs, placing his hands flat on the table.

"A name, Zalida."

"Excuse me, Leader?"

"Markos has produced a fair point. You've yet to deliver the hunter, and your allotted time is quickly coming to a close. Do you have a name you can present us with tonight, or not? Unlike Markos, my faith in you has never wavered. But ... I'm not keen on disappointment, either."

"Gibbons," I say firmly. "Professor Bentley Gibbons. He's one of the psych professors at CCU. He's the hunter, and the one who stole the Drauldin. He's the creature I mentioned before. It turns out he is indeed a half-breed."

"And why hasn't he been presented to me, Zalida? Did you share this information with Markos so he could bring him to me?"

Markos and I exchange glances, a battle of wills commencing. I can tell everyone right here and now that he's a traitor, but I don't have any proof and he knows it. He's been Leader Taryn's right-hand draul for a long time, he has a level of respect and rapport I've yet to earn. Showing all my cards now, with no concrete evidence, risks no one believing me.

Besides, I can't chance Markos getting away with this.

"There's been an unexpected hitch in the situation, Leader."

Markos's eyes burn into mine, warning me against any idea I have of being bold enough to call him out.

"He's incredibly fast, Leader, and strong. I confronted him, but bringing him will be no easy feat. He managed to escape my surprise attack unscathed."

"Half-breeds," Leader Taryn finishes, a soft smile playing on his thin lips. "Fascinating. Are you sure that's what he is, Zalida? Half-breeds are so incredibly rare."

"I'm aware, Leader Taryn, but I can assure you he is. Professor Gibbons confirmed it himself when I asked. This is why he stole the Drauldin, he knew he could enchant it and use it to kill pure-breeds. I would have tried again to bring him in regardless, but the assignment has left me weak and undernourished most days. My apologies."

"Hmmm," Leader Taryn hums, his bony fingers strumming together as he thinks. "You're all dismissed. Zali, you'll return to Lochfort now that you've fed and bait this Professor Gibbons. I want him here, however you can manage to bring him. Coercion, blackmail, force. Have Markos help you if you need. But I want him *alive*," he shoots Markos a serious glance, "both of you."

Markos nods. "Understood, Leader Taryn."

Leader Taryn waves a hand and everyone begins to scatter from the room, disappearing to whatever recesses of this ghost town they've decided to claim for their own. Markos wears a sickening smile as he leans down and whispers something in our Leader's ear. I know that look and know he's up to no good, but I can't concern myself with that right now.

I have a plan. All I need is a little time and to know someone here is on my side.

"Vanthony, wait up!" I call out as I follow him out of the hotel and into the frozen stillness of the night. He walks fast, not bothering to so much as glance back at me. "Vanthony!"

He covers ground quickly through the ghost town and darts into a small shack. I follow him into the pitch blackness, my eyes cutting through the dark interior and illuminating the tired furniture inside. He flops down into an armchair covered in thin fabric, his hands immediately shooting into his hair and ruffling it.

"What's with you, Vanthony? You hardly looked at me during that meeting, I could barely catch up to you just now. Are you going to let me in on what the fuck is going on around here? Why was the farm suddenly relocated? I didn't want Leader Taryn to think I was questioning him. He must have had good reason for moving us yet again. We were supposed to outfit the farm."

He looks at me. The mixture of despair and concern in his eyes rattles me. "Is it true that you've been sleeping with one of the humans, Zali?"

"What?!" I wish I could mask the guilt that rings so clearly through the word. "No. Why? Who told you this? It was Markos, wasn't it?"

Vanthony sighs, shaking his fingers through his hair some more. It's as though he's trying to shake away a swarm of unpleasant thoughts. "Yeah. He claims he got into an altercation with the hunter and you were there, but you were protecting him. And after this, you disappeared for a few days. He suspects you were healing him. Among ... other things. You slept with this Professor Gibbons fellow?"

My stomach somersaults with intense nausea at the thought. "No! And what do you mean *healing him*? I don't have that kind of power. I don't even think Leader Taryn has that kind of power."

"You know as well as I do, Zali, there are enchantments and elixirs that can be done, especially in the full moon. Tell me all of this is untrue. Please. Tell me you haven't been secretly working alongside the very human who's been needlessly murdering us."

"No! I ... Look, it's complicated," I sigh. "But I want you to know the truth. I need someone to know it."

He stares at me with heavy eyes, their yellow hue seeming dull and tired. "Okay."

"It's Markos, Vanthony. He's a traitor. He's been working with Professor Gibbons, feeding him information about the farm locations and our weapons and setups so that he can take us out. Don't you think it's weird that the hunter has been right on our tails all these years, no matter how far or often we relocate? How could any human track us that well?"

"Except you're claiming he's not human. You're claiming he's a half-breed, which is even more ludicrous."

"I know it sounds crazy," I admit, "but you have to believe me. Markos has been selling us out in exchange for the promise of Gibbons helping him raise an army of half-breeds. He wants to overthrow Leader Taryn and rule our clan before overthrowing the Ancestors and reigning over all the other clans in existence. It's all an elaborate scheme he's been brewing right under our noses."

I wish Vanthony's face would give me some clue as to whether he believes me. After a long bit of quiet, he stands from the chair and walks over to me. He places his hands on my shoulders and squeezes, exhaling sharply.

"I get it, Zali."

"You do?"

"Yeah. I mean, I'd be pretty desperate too if I was in your situation."

His words startle me and I tear away from his grip. "What? What are you—"

"Everyone knows you don't want to marry Markos, Zali. And honestly, between you and me, I don't blame you. Truth be told, he's a bit of a dick and definitely not your type. But to fabricate this whole thing to get out of marrying him, I mean ..."

"WHAT?! Are you fucking kidding me? Vanthony, please. You think I've made all this up just to get out of marrying him? If I wanted to get out of it that bad, I'd just kill him."

"If you could," he sighs. "Markos is strong and he gets pretty ... feral ... at times. Plus, Leader Taryn would likely kill you for eliminating one of the council and disrespecting his order for you to marry."

"Whatever, it doesn't matter. The point is, I'm not lying about this."

"It's just funny, because of all that is almost *verbatim* what Markos said you would say, Zali. He said the last time the two of you had a confrontation regarding the wedding, you threatened to tell everyone he was a traitor to try to have him executed before the wedding took place. The full moon is nearly here, and seeing as you haven't eliminated the hunter and finished the assignment, it only makes sense that you're desperate."

I blink furiously to try to rid my eyes of the hazy burn that's overtaking them. My ice cold hands are balled into tight fists and I can feel my vision beginning to grow red with fury. "I ... am not ... lying." I'm terrified there may be irrevocable consequences if Vanthony and I continue to occupy the same room. "I have to go."

"Zali," Vanthony calls after me as I go to leave, "I'll keep this between us, but you should refrain from spreading this lie any farther and just marry Markos. You could do much worse, really. Besides, you have to admit he's pretty good looking. The two of you will make an unstoppable pair."

I leave and slam the door behind me, unable to listen to another word.

Good thing I have a plan.

CHAPTER 28

His bedroom light is on and I can't help but smile. I scale the side of the condo easily, using balconies and window ledges to launch me up to his floor until I'm outside his bedroom window. I slide it open and the smell of him hits me, woodsy and spicy and sweet and everything I've fallen so hopelessly in love with.

Even if I don't want to admit it.

He's lying in bed reading, his bedside lamp creating a subtle glow that only emphasizes how handsome he is. His eyes widen in surprise only briefly when he sees me, curiously watching as I jump in the open window with graceful ease and shut it behind me.

"I could have let you in, you know."

"And risk someone seeing me like this?" I ask, gesturing broadly at my face. "The last thing I need right now is to send the town of Lochfort into a panic because a fanged, yellow-eyed monster was spotted hanging around your building."

Dr. Haven laughs. He sits himself more upright as I pull off my boots and weapons, piling stuff on his chair before I climb into bed beside him and lay my head back on the head-board with a deep sigh.

"Everything alright, Miss Summers?"

"You can call me Zali, if you like," I say without looking over. "I know you know 'Sara Summers' isn't my real name."

"What do you prefer to be called?" he asks.

I turn my head, instantly mesmerized by the sincerity in his blue eyes. He presses his glasses further up his nose and I smile. "I have to admit, I've grown quite fond of *Miss Summers*."

"So it shall stay then," he replies, dog-earing the open page of his book. I notice red pen marks, underlines of words and sections, and little notes scribbled in the margins.

I feel my nose wrinkle. "Do you always do that to your books?" I ask, pointing.

He looks a tad defensive. "Why? Does it bother you that I fold pages and write in my books?"

"No," I say softly. "It bothers *most people*. I do the same things to mine. I've just never met anyone who mutilates their books as much as I do."

He places the book on the nightstand and lets out a gentle sigh. "Books, like people, are meant to be well loved ... even if that love is unfairly torturous."

I let my head fall back on the headboard again. "Not every aspect of love is meant to be pleasurable, Dr. Haven. Without pain, pleasure would be lifeless."

His hand cups my cheek, but he needs no effort to pull my face toward his. That pull was already there. It's been there since that first time he approached me in the courtyard. It's been there every time I'm watching him teach, and every time we're alone in his office. Every time we've sat across from one another at Bumpy's. Every time we're near each other ... and even when we're not.

I wish his mouth didn't taste so good as he kisses me, but

every ounce of him feels as necessary as air. Every touch of his skin is electric, but I don't want it to be. Someone like him loving someone like me is a death sentence, tenfold if what Vanthony said is true and Markos knows about it. As far as Markos is concerned, I'm his property, and he'll stop at nothing to eliminate anyone who interferes with that.

Just like he did with my fiancé.

My hands grow cold at the thought, but Dr. Haven takes them in his and squeezes as we kiss. It's as though he can read my mind, knowing what I need without me ever having to speak it. He holds my hands tight as he breaks the kiss and stares deep into my eyes.

"I'm sorry, my hands are always so cold."

"I don't mind," he assures me. "Here." He takes them and sticks them in his cardigan pulling me closer as he presses his arms to his sides to hug them to his body. I love how attentive he is, and how giving. Maybe this is what I miss about being human, the genuine affection. The tenderness. The bits that seem to fall away once you become a monster, at least for most of us.

"I meant what I said, you know. Before." I see the worry in his eyes, which only seems to be magnified by his dark frames. "And it's fine if you don't feel the same. But I wanted you to know how I feel, even if it's not reciprocated."

"Is that what you think, Sir? That I didn't say it because I don't share your feelings?"

"No."

I cock my head. "What do you think, then?"

"I think you're scared."

I bite my lip and frown. "You don't know what you're getting yourself into. I don't want to be the one to get you killed. I don't want you getting killed at all, and Markos—"

He presses his lips to mine and, though I'm certain it's just to shut me up, I'm not the least bit upset about it. My hands move to the buttons of the dress shirt he wears underneath his cardigan, fumbling with them one by one until my cool palms press against his chest. My fingertips brush his nipples and he moans into the kiss, letting his hands tangle in my hair.

I want him again so very badly.

But I *need* him again even more.

It's a fight to get all my tight leathers off, but piece by piece he wrestles me out of them until I'm left in nothing but a pair of black lace panties. His cardigan and dress shirt are sent sprawling to the floor, a stark contrast to the way his clothes normally hang neatly on his chair. He doesn't seem fussed about it as his pants suffer the same fate, a sense of urgency overtaking him.

His socks and underwear go last as I lay there in my panties, watching as he stands to take them off and reveal his full nakedness. He's already rock hard as he climbs back on the bed. He pulls the covers back and we slip underneath, his tall frame curling up beside me.

"Roll onto your stomach," he says. "I want to do something for you."

I don't question it or protest. I roll over and let my bare midriff sink into the plush mattress as I grab a pillow, resting my head down as I wrap my arms around it. His hands start at my feet, massaging the soles and arches with a firmness that makes me moan softly into the pillow.

I love how strong his fingers are as he squeezes me. His hands slide up from my feet to my ankles, then to my calves. He rubs the backs of my knees before moving upward with slow, teasing motions. His thumbs knead the backs of my legs, and then all his fingers wrap around until they're gently stroking along my inner thighs. I moan again.

I wonder which of us can keep this up longer, him with the teasing or me enduring it. Part of me never wants this to end, and yet another part of me, a ravenous part, wants him to tear these panties off me and pin me to the bed with his hips and his thick rod. Both sound absolutely delightful, and I silently hope I won't have to settle for only one or the other by night's end.

His hands grip the sides of my booty firmly and I groan. The way he massages me not only feels amazing but also sends shivers of need shooting up my thighs. I wiggle under his expert hands, my booty lifting slightly off the bed as my body begs for more.

His touch trails along my lower back and up either side of my spine as he climbs on top of me. My chin rests on the pillow, but I turn my face to him after he kisses my temple. His lips find mine, planting atop them with tender desire. There's no rush or urgency to his movements. He takes his time with everything he does, letting me savor every small movement before pressing against me.

His fingertips brush against the brand on the back of my neck and I wince, my stomach clenching at the sensation. I always forget the mark is there, unable to see it or feel it in any sense, but it's always a gruesome reminder of things to come when pointed out.

"I'm sorry," he whispers.

I shake my head. "It's alright, Sir. It's—"

"I know what it is," he says. "I know the tradition. I think it's barbaric."

"Mmm, yeah. I'd have to agree. It's ... If I have any say, what it symbolizes will never transpire."

He kisses the mark and my stomach miraculously eases. "I'd do anything I can, anything you need, to help make that come true," he says.

"I know," I mutter softly. I turn my head enough to study his features, features I've committed to memory and yet still never tire of seeing. "Make love to me."

His knees come between mine and open my legs slightly, positioning me in a way that invites him inside. We kiss, and then he keeps kissing me as I feel him at my opening. The way he enters me is perfect. His hips move torturously slow, both of us reveling in the long, deliberate amount of time he takes to slide all the way in and then back out again.

"God," I moan as he fills me and then pushes his hips down to get just a little deeper. I can feel every bit of me squeezing and caressing him, eager to stroke every drop of satisfaction from him once he's ready to give it to me.

"You ... feel ... incredible," he sighs between simultaneous thrusts and kisses.

"So ... Uhhn ... So do you, Sir," I manage between the delicious movement of him going in and out of me. The way his cock fits inside me is delectable, stretching and filling me just the right amount. I wish we could live in this moment together forever and not worry about the danger our worlds are on the brink of.

I squeeze a hand past the front of my thigh and begin playing with myself, rubbing my fingers over my clit in a circular motion as he continues thrusting into me from behind. His arms on either side of me somehow make me feel safe and guarded, a heightened version of the comfort I've come to feel whenever in his presence.

My fingers move faster and faster, and he seems to want to keep pace. He switches from long, slow strokes to hard and fast thrusts as the impending sense of ecstacy begins to build within me. I scream into the pillow as I climax, my hips jumping backward and slamming him deep inside me with delicious force.

He moans loudly as the movement buries his length, my sweet cavern clenching around him and trapping him fully inside. His orgasm seems to pick up precisely where mine leaves off, bits of pleasure fizzling out inside me as he begins to sizzle with his own euphoric release. I lay there underneath him, lost and elated with the feeling of all his come inside me.

He brushes damp hair from my face, kissing my sweaty temple. "I ... That was nice," he says, and I'm sure I hear a certain sadness in his voice.

"It was," I agree.

He wraps his arms around me as he rolls us both over, keeping himself tucked inside me as we switch to laying on our sides. His fingers trace bits of my skin, caressing up and down along my arm, smoothing back rogue strands of my hair. Lulling me gently to a sleepier state as we bask in the afterglow of our tryst.

He pets my hair as we lay there in silence a long while, my eyelids growing more and more heavy. My tongue runs over my fangs, the feel of them smooth and slick in my mouth. It's funny to me now to think I was so worried about him seeing me like this. It clearly doesn't do anything to diminish his attraction to me.

Or to diminish the way he *feels* about me.

"Sir?" I say quietly as he continues stroking my hair.

"Hmm?"

I roll over and face him. His head is on the pillow, his eyelids looking just as heavy as mine. I kiss his nose and he smiles. Then I kiss his lips and he kisses me back.

"I'm sorry ... about before. I'm sorry I didn't say it back to you. It's just that—"

"Please, Miss Summers, you don't have to explain yourself to me. I should have never said it in the first place. It was foolish, reckless, and—"

"It was real," I blurt, not letting him finish. "It's good to be honest about your feelings."

"Yes, well, I'm not convinced that's always the case. Some

things are just better left unsaid, especially when they're not reciprocated. It just leads to regret."

I scramble to prop myself up, my heart thumping with frustration. "Is that how you feel?" I fold my arms across my chest. "You regret loving me?"

Dr. Haven sits up, a serious look on his face. "How can you even suggest that, Miss Summers? I could never regret loving you, I'm just saying I regret *saying* that I love you."

I hop off the bed in search of my scattered clothes. "I don't know why I even brought it up," I snap coldly. "We have way bigger things we need to be worrying about. Professor Gibbons has the Drauldin, and Markos has made it his personal mission to end you. Again."

"Well, none of that is exactly news," he says, pulling the blanket further into his lap as he leans back against the headboard. "Please, I didn't mean to upset you. Just stay with me a while. You can spend the night, if you want. Please." His eyes are pleading, begging me to stay.

But I can't. This was a mistake.

"I actually came here to warn you, Dr. Haven," I say, fighting to get into my leather pants. "Gibbons and Markos aren't just working together. I went to the farm to eat and it'd been moved, so I went to the industrial yard in search of Gibbons. Your entire office there has been cleared out. Books, potions, equipment. All gone."

Dr. Haven looks confused. "So Bentley cleared everything out? Well, he must have had a good reason."

I scoff and shake my head. "I needed to eat, badly, so I went to Gibbons's house. I thought maybe there was an elixir or something he could give me in place of soul. But when I got there, someone was inside with him. Turns out it was Markos, who's pissed that Gibbons resurrected you. Gibbons gave him full-on permission to kill you again. Markos says you're a loose end."

Dr. Haven tuts loudly. "Bentley and I have been doing this for a long while, as I'm sure you're aware. I can assure you his loyalty is to me, regardless of what he's told your friend."

"Markos is *not* my friend," I hiss through gritted teeth. "He's my fiancé, and his days as such are numbered. His days breathing are numbered. I just need proof first."

"Proof of what?"

"Proof that he's working with Gibbons. I need to expose him to Leader Taryn. He's already gone around telling the Osjhka that I'm trying to frame him to get out of the marriage. I need concrete evidence so I can finally put all this to rest."

"What are you going to do?"

"Nothing, yet. I have to wait just a little bit longer. But you need to be careful. Markos knows you're alive again, and he knows we've ... well, you know. Or he suspects. And he isn't going to let a man who's violated his future queen live, especially not a *human* man."

"Please, Miss Summers, I can take care of myself."

"Oh, like you did the first time Markos killed you?" I shoot back, wrestling on the last of my clothes and my boots and replacing all my weapons.

"I knew Bentley would revive me. Though, getting killed definitely wasn't part of the initial plan. It is a bit of a doozy, as you witnessed."

"Gibbons isn't going to revive you this time! Don't you get it? Markos and him don't need you any more! They're fit to raise a half-breed army, and you're nothing but a human who's going to get in the way! If Markos sees you again ... he'll kill you on sight."

Dr. Havens looks me up and down, still not moving from his spot on the bed. "And what would you suggest I do, Miss Summers? If I'm truly not to trust Bentley, where does that leave me?"

"I don't know, but you can't stay here. Markos isn't going to kill you at CCU, not in front of that many people. Leader Taryn would annihilate him. But he knows where you live, so you shouldn't stay here. I think he followed me here when I brought you here to take care of you."

"I'm not leaving my house, Miss Summers. I'm a great deal safer here. I know where all the weapons are here, at least. And once Bentley enchants and returns the Drauldin to me—"

"You still seriously think you can trust him?! After all I've told you?"

"I don't see what choice I have."

I throw my hands up in the air. "You're insane. You're going to get yourself killed, and then I'm going to be ... I'll be ..."

"You'll be what, Miss Summers?" he asks with a raised brow.

"I'll be fucked! That's what!"

His brows furrow and he adjusts his glasses. "Why would you be that?"

"Because I love you! I love you and ... I don't want to lose you."

"Oh, Miss Summers," he says. He holds his hands out, leaning forward in his bed. I take his hands and let him pull me down onto the bed beside him. He's still tucked under the covers as I lay there in all my clothes and boots and weapons, snuggled up to him as he resumes petting my hair. I fight back the tears that thoughts of losing him have stirred. "You're not going to lose me."

"How do you know?" I ask.

"Because," he says, and I can hear his grin despite my face being buried in his chest, "I have a plan."

CHAPTER 29

His voice drones on from the front of the room, but all it does is pull me back to the conversation between him and Markos. Professor Gibbons yammers incessantly, but I'm hardly taking in every other word. I'm fixated on his face. His angular nose and his too-square jawline and his hairline that's started receding on one side.

He's hideous and I don't know how Dr. Haven trusts him so implicitly. What does Gibbons stand to gain from keeping him alive? At least with Markos, he stands the chance of helping raise and lead an army, of ruling over all the clans. What does he have if he stays partnered with Dr. Haven? The Drauldin and the opportunity to keep hunting?

I don't see how Dr. Haven could continue being a hunter after all this. If he's fallen in love with me, he must see that we're not all without empathy and a lust for life.

Or a lust for something else.

I remember him telling me how little drauls are able to enjoy music and sex. Clearly, the statement was half-true at best. To say I've enjoyed my encounters with Dr. Haven would be a gross understatement.

Class ends and all the other students begin to leave. Professor Gibbons prattles on about a test coming up next week, and about an assignment due in the next couple days. I don't care about any of this. I don't care about anything but confronting him and figuring out exactly where he stands and whose side he's on.

The classroom empties one by one, oblivious human students scuttling off to other classes or the library or wherever else they've mapped out in their day.

But not me.

I stay seated, watching, waiting. Looking to the front of the room as Professor Gibbons moseys about as if he isn't perfectly capable of seeing me still sat here. Several minutes pass after we're left alone before he bothers acknowledging my presence.

"Zalida," he says, and I hate the way my real name rolls wet and low off his tongue. "You have questions about the assignment? Or concerns about the test next week, perhaps?"

"Don't you dare play stupid with me, Professor," I warn. "I'm not here to fuck about and play nice with you. I'm here to apprise you of something important."

"Oh?" His brows shoot up in mock surprise. "Well! Do tell, then. Considering I saved your beloved professor and brought him back from the brink of death after your fiancé mangled him, I can only assume this is a thank-you, a way to repay me for my kindness."

"You make it sound like you saved him specifically for me. I didn't even know you had the power to do that."

He wanders over, his too-big suit jacket following him like a shadow. "There's more possibilities with the half-breed blood than you could possibly imagine," he whispers once he's in earshot. "Why do you think Markos wants to raise an army of us?"

"And yet he still insists on having me as a wife," I groan. "I'm not a human, or a half-breed. All he'll make with me are feral little monsters."

"The feral ones are better for fighting," Gibbons explains. "You need to have some ruthless ones to act as protection, warriors. And who better than family to have the utmost respect and loyalty? The feral ones will be the muscle who do the dirty work, and the half-breeds will be the smart ones, the powerful ones. Their blood will unlock endless possibilities.

"Total extinction of the human race, aptly. Eventually, there will only be select drauls left. The rest will be half-breeds. There's only one major problem with Markos's plan."

"Are you kidding me?!" I snort. "I can think of a few major problems with it."

"The half-breeds are no guarantee. Even if Markos mates with human women, the chances of any of them actually conceiving is exceptionally rare. And even my blood and my magic aren't strong enough to do anything about that."

"So, that's it then? You're just going to help him eliminate the human race, as well as Leader Taryn and the current Ancestors? That's your grand plan? And what about Dr. Haven, what happens with him?"

"Ross and I have been friends for a long, long time, Zalida. You were right in stating I didn't bring him back just for you. I didn't bring him back for you at all. Prior to Markos's little outburst, I hadn't realized you and the good doctor had grown so fond of each other. It's cute, really."

"He's my professor, and a damn good one," I say defensively. "This school deserves him. Of course I care about what happens to him."

"But it's more than that, isn't it? I think you're all too

aware that Markos has also picked up on that little fact, and he doesn't seem too happy about it."

"I'm aware!" I growl and smash my fists on the table in front of me. "None of this answers my question, Professor! Who does your loyalty lie with, Markos ... or Dr. Haven?"

"Ross is not only my friend, but a damn good hunter. One of the best in history, I'd say. If you weren't fraternizing with him, I could probably convince Markos to keep him around as long as he'd be willing to aid us in our venture. But ... I can't guarantee anything now. Your relationship with him is going to serve as a death sentence. You know how ... *protective* ... Markos is."

The thought makes me ill.

"I can't marry Markos, Professor Gibbons. And there are a plethora of reasons, most of which have nothing to do with Dr. Haven. This plan that Markos has to raise a half-breed army is never going to work, and you know it. It's a suicide mission. Markos might be able to eliminate Leader Taryn, but he'll never be able to take out the Ancestors."

"They've been around for far too long, Zalida. They're old, tired. Nearing death. He'll be doing them all a favor. Besides, their leadership is more of a figurehead than anything of tangible value. They're the ones who keep archaic laws in place, such as the one that's gotten you into this arranged marriage. It's time for them to be put to rest and new leadership to step in."

"And you truly think you and Markos are going to be able to pull this off? Just the two of you?"

"No. That's why I wanted Ross to join us. I'm not foolish enough to believe this endeavor is going to be half as easy as Markos has convinced himself it is. What that boy lacks in brains, he certainly makes up for in brawns. And enthusiasm. But then again, I don't need to tell you about how enthusiastic he is, do I?"

Professor Gibbons sneers and it takes every ounce of self control I can muster not to punch him in the teeth. "So you saved Dr. Haven ... because your loyalty lies with him, is that it? You've not really given me a straight answer, Professor, and I'm not one for childish games."

"If I wanted Ross dead then I wouldn't have saved him, would I?"

I bite my bottom lip to keep from saying anything ignorant. "No, I suppose not."

"Good. Then I'd say you have nothing to worry about. In the meantime, you best get yourself prepped and sorted for the wedding. I hear it's just around the corner, Zalida. Sorry, *Sara*."

I scowl. "Speaking of that, Professor Gibbons, I'm afraid I'm going to have to ask a favor of you before I leave."

"Oh? And what might that be?" he asks, looking positively bored.

"The Drauldin. I'm afraid I'm going to need you to give it to me. I'll be needing it to get rid of Markos once and for all."

I wince in my seat as he bursts into a fit of giggles. "Are you insane, woman? I can't just *give* you the Drauldin. Besides, it'd be useless to you. Only the blood of a half-breed can enchant that blade. Every draul knows this."

"Then enchant it first!" I roll my eyes. "I know that without the enchantment it's completely useless. But it will be my best bet in getting rid of Markos. He's too unstable to rule an army anyhow. You're better off trying to raise a half-breed army by yourself. At least you have a secure head on your shoulders."

And you best work with me on this, if you want it to stay that way.

He smirks, my compliment seeming to have had the desired effect. "Alright, Zalida Wren. And how do you suggest we bring about new order if we do kill off Markos? You must have some grand plan?"

A sharp inhale chokes my words. I hadn't thought about it, at all. I don't see the need for a new order. Leader Taryn and the Ancestors may be grandfathered in and a bit too traditional, but other than the arranged betrothal tradition, I don't have any issues with the way they run things. They know what they're doing. They've kept the farms running, kept us hidden, kept everyone alive.

And yet, they don't even know about the existence of half-breeds ... or do they?

My brain is a flurry of questions. What are the Ancestors keeping secret? They knew the Drauldin was stolen, and yet no one said a thing. Leader Taryn didn't even seem to know. Is it because the Ancestors are mostly Yedora clan members, and admitting they let the Drauldin be stolen would cause the other clans to question their strength and ability?

"What do *you* want, Professor Gibbons? What's your big stake in all of this? You want more half-breeds to be born solely so you can rise up as their leader? I don't see why Markos would be so onboard with this. He's not a half-breed."

"That doesn't mean he can't help lead them."

"Help? I don't know how well you know Markos, Professor, but he doesn't generally *help* with anything. He's not really the stand-beside-you type, he's more the do-what-I-say-or-I'll-end-you type."

"He and I have an agreement. I trust he'll stand by it," Professor Gibbons states firmly.

I fold my arms tightly across my chest. "And you and Dr. Haven? What about your agreement? Because the two seem to—"

"What about me?"

His scent hits me and I feel that familiar pull. I turn to

see Dr. Haven crossing the room toward us, his look inquisitive as he smiles.

"Ross! Impeccable timing, we were just talking about you," Professor Gibbons announces.

"Oh?" He stops once he's beside me, his hand pressing into my lower back and causing my breath to catch.

Is this his way of indicating to Gibbons I'm under his protection? Not like I need protecting.

"And what exactly were the two of you discussing?"

Professor Gibbons's gaze falls to where Dr. Haven's arm wraps behind me, but only for a split second. "Sara seems to be a bit worried about you and our alliance. She's questioning where my loyalties lie, as though we haven't been friends for several decades."

Several? Dr. Haven hasn't even been alive *for several decades. Unless he just means they've been friends since they were little?*

"Ah, I see. So you were just putting her mind at ease, then?" I examine his features, looking for any hint of distress or worry lying among them. But I see nothing, nothing but two old friends chatting as casually as if they were merely talking about the weather.

"Yes, exactly. She's convinced I would let my loyalties lie with Markos over yourself."

Dr. Haven cocks a brow at me. "Really? Even after he brought me back from the dead?"

"Thank you," Professor Gibbons chimes in. "My point exactly. If I wanted you dead, I could have left well enough alone. The job had been done for me."

"I heard you!" I hiss at Gibbons. "I was outside your house the night you told Markos to go ahead and eliminate Dr. Haven again!"

Professor Gibbons cocks his head, but then a slow smile stretches across his thin lips. "You sneaky girl," he coos. "I admit, I did say that. But telling Markos not to kill Ross would have been met with hostility. It was easier just to play along for now. You know how Markos is."

"Whatever," I snap, glaring at them both. "You'd have been just as worried in my shoes, Dr. Haven. I'm simply looking out for you."

His fingers caress my lower back and my furrowed brows soften.

I couldn't stay mad at this human if I tried.

"I appreciate you, Miss Summers. Immensely. But Bentley and I are old friends, and I trust him with my life. As he's proven I should."

"Right. Well, that's good then. That's all I needed to clarify." I stand and gather my things, Dr. Haven scooting out of the way to make room for my departure. I grab my bag, facing him when I turn to leave. "Goodbye, Dr. Haven. We should meet up later. To discuss the project."

"Project?" Professor Gibbons asks.

"A school project," Dr. Haven clarifies. His attention turns to me, and I can tell by the cloudiness in his eyes that he wishes he could kiss me goodbye just as badly as I want him to.

But he won't, I know he won't. Not at school, and certainly not in front of Gibbons.

"Yes, we'll touch base later, Miss Summers."

I nod, shooting Gibbons one last side-eyed glance before exiting the room.

I don't care what Dr. Haven thinks. I don't trust Professor Gibbons.

Not with his life ... and not with my own, either.

CHAPTER 30

I have mixed feelings about meeting at Bumpy's. On one hand, it's a very public space, which makes me feel secure in that I don't think Markos would be willing to initiate an attack. On the other hand, it's particularly crowded today, and the white noise is both overwhelming and a terrible setting for the top secret conversation that needs having.

"Are you alright?" Dr. Haven asks, concerned eyes staring at me from across the table. They're distractingly blue today, pulling me away from the question he's asked. Pulling my mind to other places. His room. His bed. His shower.

"It's just noisy in here," I say quietly, swirling the last bit of coffee in my mug.

"Want to go for a walk?"

I feel my eyes widen as I look up at him. "What? Right now?"

"Why not? The park is just across the street."

"It's too isolated. There's too many trees. If Markos wanted to attack you—"

"He'd have done so by now," Dr. Haven interjects. "And

that's not to say he doesn't want me dead. I'm certain he does, *again*. I don't believe for a second he's at all thrilled about Professor Gibbons resurrecting me from the brinks of fatality. But he's too smart to do it here. He'll wait for a more opportune time. So, come on. I'll buy you a coffee for the walk."

I give a lighthearted sigh. "Alright, Dr. Haven. But only because, if there are two things I'm weak to refuse, it's your company and some good bean water."

Dr. Haven snorts as he laughs. "*Bean water*? Where are you getting this terrible slang from? I know it's not from my class, Miss Summers." He shoots me a cheeky grin as I follow him to the counter, keeping him company as he orders one coffee and one pumpkin spice latte to go.

"I got it from Angel," I say as he hands me one of the cups a minute later. "She's got some ... interesting ... language sometimes."

"Perhaps she should be in my class," he says, to which we both chuckle.

Walking around the park together creates a deceptive inkling of some normalcy between us, as if in some parallel universe we might currently be doing the same thing, but as a regular couple. An actual couple.

A human couple.

A bit of sadness tightens in my chest as we walk. I take a sip of the bitter black liquid, trying to dull the sensation. "So what's your plan now?" I ask, trying to sound indifferent. "You and Professor Gibbons plan on ... what? Continuing to hunt us down? Even after all you and I have been through? Even after you've learned that we ... can still *feel* things, however muted."

Dr. Haven thinks about this for a minute, his fingers clenching and unclenching around his paper cup. He takes a big swig and exhales deeply. "Is there a part of you that hates me for what I've done? For killing off so many of your kind?"

I laugh half-heartedly. "*My kind* has never really been my kind, so to speak. I don't have any choice but to stay with them, not anymore. Not after Markos killed my ... my ..." My hands grow cold and clammy at the thought of him despite the warm cup I'm holding. "Drauls are forbidden from having relations with humans whatsoever. It's not allowed, the Ancestors are very strict about this. There was no repercussions to Markos for what he did to my lover. The way he and everyone else saw it, they were saving me from myself. Saving me from lingering attachment to that world."

One of his hands reaches up and squeezes my shoulder. "That doesn't answer my question."

I sigh. "I could never hate you, Sir. Regardless of what you've done, or what you'll continue to do. There will always be hunters out there trying to take us out. And there will always be us, farming and killing humans, drinking their souls. It's the same circle of life humans have with other animals. It doesn't make anyone bad, and certainly not worth hating. It's just nature."

We walk in silence for a few minutes, simply absorbing the serenity that comes with being near one another. Then Dr. Haven clears his throat. "We still have to do something about—"

"*Me*," a gravelly voice hisses down from a treetop above us. Markos jumps down, landing in front of us. His large black boots and leather pants lead up to his topless midriff, his body gleaming in the low evening sun. His frame is full of muscle, and he'd easily be intimidating to the fittest of humans, even without the knowledge of what he is. It's no wonder he was able to crush Dr. Haven, a mere human, so easily.

And now I fear he's going to do it again.

"Hello, pet," he sneers. Then he turns to Dr. Haven. "And hello to you, my pet's pet."

"He's not—" But I bite my tongue. There's no sense in arguing, especially not here, not now. Not in the middle of the park in daylight. "We can't do this here, Markos. And you best get out of here before any of the humans see you running around in this barbaric outfit. If you can even call it an outfit. It's nearly winter and you're half naked!"

"You'll eat all these words soon enough, Zalida. And I'm not here to squeeze the life out of your pet again. Not yet. I'll wait until he meets me at the new farm to do that. I'd rather an audience."

My stomach clenches. "You're not here to kill him?"

He looks at Dr. Haven, a feral twinkle to his eyes as he licks his lips. "As much as I'd get off on that ... no. I'm here as a courtesy to you, my queen. Here to offer a warning."

"What warning?" Dr. Haven asks, taking his hand off my shoulder and sticking it in his coat pocket. His blue eyes are narrowed behind his frames, and there isn't an ounce of fear anywhere in his features despite having been crushed to oblivion by the very creature standing mere feet from him.

Markos turns his attention back to me. "You, pet, are in trouble. Leader Taryn and the Ancestors have grown wise to your relationship with this human, and want word with you immediately. There's been a meeting discussing how to handle you. Your mission was to find the hunter and report them to Leader Taryn for me to eliminate, and instead ... you're *fucking* him."

My icy hands clench into fists, fury pumping through me at the audacity of his words. I completely crush my coffee cup, the hot liquid pouring over my hands and onto the ground as I throw the paper cup away. "And it would have been *you* who fed them such information, wouldn't it, Markos? You don't even have evidence of such an accusation!"

"I don't need evidence when you spent four days inside his house, Zalida! You are *my* bride! Have you forgotten that? And this plaything that you've grown attached to ..." He looks to Dr. Haven again, but this time his eyes grow dark, that smoldering deep maroon I've seen before. "Enjoy your time with him tonight. It'll be the last one he spends breathing."

"What are you talking about? You're planning to attack him tomorrow? Why would you tell us this?" I slam my hands into my jacket pockets to keep them from vibrating. "You will not touch him, Markos. I'll see to it you don't."

"You are to both come to the new farm tomorrow. After sundown. The Ancestors will be there, and Leader Taryn will take their guidance into consideration in deciding your punishment. You'll be lucky if they don't kill you, Zalida. I might just have to find a new wife."

"Should I be so lucky," I snarl, rolling my eyes. "I'm glad the Ancestors will be there. Leader Taryn might not believe me about your little alignment with Professor Gibbons and plans to overthrow them all, but maybe the Ancestors will have more sense and reason. They'll see through your facade, Markos. It's *you* who will be on the chopping block tomorrow."

"No one believes you, Zali. No one, and I mean *no one*. I made sure of that. Not a single soulless is going to believe that you are making these accusations for anything beyond getting out of the marriage. They know you would do anything to keep away from the likes of me, and they know you've failed to report the hunter's identity because you're in love with him. You're a liar and a traitor, and no one in our clan or any other is going to see you as anything but from now on.

"They'll never know about my alliance with Gibbons. No one is going to see me, the next Osjhka Leader, as someone who would sell out his own kind. I may have led Gibbons to all the farms, but it's time for our race to experience a metamorphosis. Pure-breeds are in the inferior race, Zali. Leader Taryn and the Ancestors aren't worthy of ruling anymore. And Gibbons is working on an elixir to give me the abilities of the half-breeds. It's too bad you won't be around to see it."

Dr. Haven goes to speak, but I shake my head. "We'll see, Markos," I say calmly. "We'll see. Are the Ancestors there now?"

"They will be, tonight. They'll stay at the farm with Leader Taryn until all of this is dealt with, until you're properly punished and the hunter is killed. And if the two of you think you're going to try anything stupid, like going on the run together, just know that I *will* hunt you down. I'll travel to the ends of the earth for you, Zali. You'll live in constant fear, always wondering where I am, always sleeping with one eye open. You'll never know peace again."

"I'm a monster, Markos. I don't know peace now."

His eyes dance between Dr. Haven and myself, his wicked grin flashing in the bit of sunlight left. "Tomorrow. Right after sundown. You will both be there. *Or else.*"

I nod but say no more. I watch as Markos takes off through the park's trees just before a couple humans come wandering down the path. He's a blur against the yellow grass, out of sight as quickly as he appeared.

Fuck.

I gather the crumpled coffee cup from the grass and throw it in a nearby bin, neither of us saying anything until the couple walking in the opposite direction has passed. I keep my hands in my pockets, desperately trying to ignore how cold they feel. The sun will be setting soon, and the night's have grown cold with the onset of winter.

"You can't come tomorrow," I say, finally breaking the silence. "It'll be a death sentence."

"I'm not afraid," Dr. Haven replies, glancing at me as we walk. "Besides, Markos has already killed me once. I know exactly what to expect. And we can have Bentley at the ready in case—"

"This isn't going to be like last time," I tell him firmly. "There will be no bringing you back from this. I'm not going to be able to get your body out of there before Markos or any of the others drink your soul. They'll be feasting on you before I can so much as say 'Goodbye'." The thought brings tears to my eyes, but I exhale hard and force them back.

"No one is going to be saying that," he says. I wish I was filled with the air of confidence his words carry. "I can assure you, Miss Summers, we aren't going in there empty-handed. Neither of us is."

I look over and see a curious smile on his lips, the glimmer in his blue eyes telling me he's scheming up some grand plan as we speak. "Care to elaborate? Or are you just going to continue to let me stew on all this inside my head?"

Dr. Haven pulls his hand from his pocket, the hand that had previously been resting on my shoulder. In it he grips his cellphone. His other hand comes up and presses a little red circle on the touch screen, a line on the screen that'd been moving stopping as he does. "Ta-da."

"You ... You were recording all that?"

"We'll have to listen to it and see if it came through clear enough despite my coat pocket. But Markos is quite loud, his booming voice carries quite well, I'd think. And, if all is well, there you have it, Miss Summers. Your proof."

I stand there in silence, stunned by the simplicity of it all. "This doesn't mean you can come. It *does* mean you need to send me that audio file, though. I can play it from my phone for Leader Taryn and the Ancestors tomorrow night, if it's discernable. If it is, there'll be no way for Markos to deny it. He'll be finished."

"I can't let you do this alone."

"God, could you be more cliche, Sir? There's no *letting* me do anything. If you come, they'll kill you. Maybe not Markos, Markos won't be around long once we play this. Leader Taryn or one of the Ancestors will end him. With the amount of magic they wield, they won't need the Drauldin, or any other weapon. They'll vanquish the tiny fraction of a soul he has left without needing to lay a finger on him.

"But you ... you, they'll want to take their time with. No doubt Markos has already told them that you're the one who has been hunting us. Killing you will be making an example out of you for all the clans. To show that all hunters will eventually become the hunted."

"Unless I have something they want. Something worth keeping me alive for."

"What could you possibly—"

"Information. Information that not even the Ancestors have."

I cock a brow, noting how low the sun has fallen into the horizon. I'll need to be home soon, tucked safely away where none of the humans can see me. "*You* have info, about drauls or something related to us, that not even the Ancestors know? How?"

"Hunting has taken me all sorts of places. Tracking the different clans. Tracking the farms. And thanks in part to Bentley, I have two bits of information that just might save my life tomorrow. The first is that I've been working on a formula, using Bentley's half-breed blood, to create a serum that sustains drauls without the need for souls."

I gasp. "Is that ... Is that possible?"

"I think so. I've had a single test subject, and it's worked out well so far for her."

Her?

Small pangs of jealousy course through me. "You know

another draul? There's another one you know personally who you haven't killed?"

"Well, I don't kill just for sport, you know," he says. "To be fair, I didn't know this one was a draul when I met her. She keeps very to herself."

"Interesting. So you and her are friends, then?"

Dr. Haven adjusts his glasses. "I wouldn't go as far as to say that, no. But she's been a willing test subject for some of my experiments, and for that I'm appreciative."

"I see." I want to press him for more details, but there's far more important things to be discussing than the sudden mystery woman in his life. "And the second? What's the second bit of information you have that is so grand?"

He smiles, and it's a boyish smile I can't help but reciprocate despite the seriousness of our situation. "Not even Bentley knows this," his voice is hardly above a whisper, "but I know where an entire colony of half-breeds lives."

"Now *that* is impossible," I reply. "If there was an entire colony of half-breeds out there, the Ancestors would know about it. They know about all the clans and colonies. They keep even closer tabs on any stragglers, any free-roaming drauls who don't align with any group. That's how they found me. They tracked me down and cornered me. Markos made sure I was alone and needed to join the Osjhka clan. They left me with no one. That's what they do."

His eyes find mine and they're heavy. He takes both my hands in his and squeezes. "And that's why you don't care that I hunt them."

There's a pain in my chest from reliving this story yet again, but something in his eyes settles it. "Yes."

"There *is* a colony, Miss Summers. I've seen it. I've interacted with them. They stay in hiding for good reason. They know they'd be considered a threat to the pure-breeds. Just like Bentley, he has been in hiding for a long, long time."

"Yet somehow he ended up working with Markos, a pure-breed."

"We needed information. It helps to have relations with someone on the inside. And Markos is just pompous and soul-hungry enough to fall for a scheme of that sort."

"Are you saying you guys tracked down Markos and baited him specifically?"

"Come on," he says, releasing one of my hands and using the other to pull me along the path. "It's almost dark. We need to get you out of here, lest someone see you once you switch. And yes, that is exactly what I'm saying. We baited Markos. This is why I wasn't worried about Bentley's loyalty the way you were."

I follow Dr. Haven, my chest fluttering at the way his warm hand feels wrapped around mine as we walk. "Where are you taking me?"

"Home."

"But ... 1042 Marr Street is in the other direction."

He gives me a side-eyed smile but keeps walking. "*My* home, Miss Summers."

And those words are all it takes for him to begin fanning the fires within me.

CHAPTER 31

His lips feel more than familiar as they land on mine, as though he's kissed me a thousand times before. *But it hasn't been anywhere near that many.*

I love the way he tastes and feels; Like coffee and pumpkin spice and a recklessly broken code that I never really wanted in the first place. Everything about him is stunning, and everything about him makes me wish I could be a different ... me.

"Hey, is everything okay?"

"Hmm?" He stares at me as I lay beside him on his bed.

"You seem distracted. Are you worried about tomorrow? Worried Markos isn't going to keep his word and is going to try something tonight? Still worried Bentley will betray me?"

"When you put it all that way," I laugh. "We've certainly no shortage of things to be worrying about."

He grabs my chin and pulls my face just close enough to his to peck my nose. "Here's a crazy thought: What if Markos was doing us a kindness?"

"Excuse me?" I shake my head. "Dr. Haven, Markos doesn't *do* kindness. Ever. He's ruthless, barbaric, pure insanity. If you're suggesting he gave us tonight, I assure you he didn't. If he refrained from killing you tonight, it's because Leader Taryn and the Ancestors told him to."

"Okay, fine, but regardless of the reasoning, he *did* give us tonight, right?"

"He probably ..."

I feel my sadness lurking in my features, and I can tell he does too by the way he looks at me. "He probably what?"

"He probably wanted me to spend the night with you, to make losing you tomorrow harder on me. He's confident he's going to kill you tomorrow. And I'm sure he knows that, given the option, the most likely outcome was me being here tonight. With you."

Dr. Haven's mouth finds mine with the softest of kisses and I melt. "Exactly. You *are* here with me. Right now. At this moment. And how wonderfully miraculous is that?"

I smile, borderline annoyed that he somehow always manages to say just the right thing. "You're right."

"And we checked the audio file, and it's perfect. Tomorrow is going to go smoothly. We have your evidence. We have a plan. And you're safe here, with me, in my condo. Why not just get lost in each other and enjoy the night? We can worry about everything else in the morning."

"Yeah," I say softly.

Dr. Haven props himself up on one elbow, leaning his head into his hand. "Are you sure there's nothing else bothering you, Miss Summers?"

"If I ask you something, will you be completely honest with me, even if it's not really my place to ask?"

"Of course."

"You ... The other draul you mentioned, the one who's been working as a test subject for your elixirs ... Who is she, and how do you know her?"

"Are you jealous?" he muses, but I haven't it in me to feign amusement. I close my eyes as his thumb streaks down my cheek, and then across my lips. "You remember the lady with the parrot across the street, of course."

"Yes," I say past his thumb. "Why?" I open my eyes after several seconds pass. Dr. Haven stares at me, his thumb still tracing bits of my skin, moving down along the side of my neck and onto my shoulder. "No! Her? She's a draul?"

He nods. "That's why she's only ever out on her balcony during the day."

I'm trying to process his words, but the feeling of his skin on mine as fingers join his thumb and run lines down my arms is incredibly distracting. "So she ... But you said she never talks to you."

"I did, and she doesn't. I said she never nods or waves at me. She doesn't. I said she never speaks to me. She can't. Her parrot speaks for her here and there because she's completely unable to speak. Physically incapable."

My heart pounds excitedly. "So, that's it then? She's the other woman in your life?"

Dr. Haven laughs. "There are no other women in my life. But sure. In this particular sense, yes. She's the only other female draul I interact with."

I don't waste any time plunging myself against him and kissing him fiercely. His laughing subsides as my mouth claims his, hot and full of need. Other bits of me mirror this, my entire body aching with the sort of hunger only he can satiate.

And the sort of hunger he can't.

My stomach growls loudly, Dr. Haven's mouth leaving mine as he looks at me with concern. "You wouldn't think that a creature that drinks souls and doesn't eat food would still get that sensation when hungry."

I sigh deeply. "You wouldn't think. It seems to be a part of the human system that remains along with that last little bit of soul. It's a pain in the neck, really."

"It's a pain in someone's neck ... when you bite them."

I sharply inhale in mock offense, but I can't keep from bursting out laughing at the cheeky grin on Dr. Haven's face. "That was a terrible joke, Sir. Terrible."

"Terribly funny," he shrugs. "It made you laugh, at least. I like making you do that."

"I like it too," I admit as my stomach produces more ravenous cries. "It's been a while since I've been at the farm. I should probably feast on someone tomorrow when we get there. Before everything with Markos and Leader Taryn and the Ancestors goes down."

"Or," he says, a wild look in bright blue eyes, "you could have some of my serum."

I feel my whole demeanor perk at the thought. "Are you serious?"

"It's been keeping Jezebel alive for the past few years, and she's not had any side effects that I know of."

"Jezebel? The parrot lady?"

He nods. "Would you like some?"

My heart soars at the very possibility. "Yes! Yes. Definitely. I want to see if it works on me."

"Okay, wait here."

He leaves the bed and heads to the main room. I hear what sounds like an oven door, my body vibrating with excited, nervous energy as he comes back holding a coffee mug. I cock my head. "What? No strange vial? Not even a fancy little mason jar? Just a regular old coffee cup?"

"Just drink it, would you," he says, handing me the cup as he sloughs off my teasing, "and quit being ridiculous."

I look down into the mug to find a cyan-hued liquid, vibrant and ethereal, staring back at me. There's not much in it, perhaps a few ounces, and my dull pulse races to a near-normal speed as I tip it back and let the concoction pour past my lips.

The flavor is largely bitter, with only a few sweet notes in the aftertaste, but immediately my hunger subsides and I feel the rush of a freshly-drunk soul coursing through my veins. "Oh, wow. I feel amazing!" I gush, swallowing the last of the miracle potion and setting the mug on the bedside table. "Seriously, Sir, I feel *so* good!"

Dr. Haven crawls back into bed beside me, kissing one of my temples as he lays next to me. I curl up next to him and sigh, resting my forehead on his chest. "I'm happy you seem to approve," he says as he kisses my hair. "Now you should feel refreshed and rejuvenated for tomorrow."

"Do I ever. This stuff is pure magic," I sigh.

"It literally is. Magic, and half-breed blood, and a few other things. Seriously, Miss Summers, their blood is beyond powerful. They take the best qualities from both races, and within their blood lies the key to unlocking all sorts of deeper magic. That's why the Ancestors are so wary about their existence. They're a threat."

"Oh, I'm well aware. But they've been telling all of us there haven't been any cases of half-breeds since Jalvana, the original owner of the Drauldin."

"Because they don't let any stay in existence should they find out about them. I suspect that's why they're also not keen on solo drauls hanging about. Had you been a half-breed when they found you, they'd have killed you without hesitation."

"Hmm." I stare at him, but the blueness of his eyes is disappearing behind trails of smokiness the longer he stares at me. "Enough about that," I say, running my teeth over my fangs. "I don't want to think about any of that right now. I don't want to think about any of them. All I want to think about is you, and how you're wearing way too many clothes."

"You think?" he asks nonchalantly. He undoes the buttons of his dress shirt one by one, my eyes panning down each time his fingers migrate. When the last button is released, he flips the shirt back off his arms and tosses it to the floor. "How about now?"

"Mm-mm," I shake my head, letting my hands find the button of his jeans. "Still too many."

His irises are both bright and cloudy and he stares into my eyes, the beginnings of a storm on a summer day. I miss that, miss summer, and yet by the time summer rolls around again, he probably won't be here and ...

I push the thought from my mind, trying to focus on the moment and just enjoy every second with him. My hands are down the front of his pants and underwear, but I don't immediately take them off. I let my fingertips tease him, reveling in the way they become coated with precome as I run them over his head. I feel his manhood growing against my touch, and it takes everything in me not to let my fangs sink down into his shoulder as he kisses the side of my neck.

He rolls away from me onto his back to wrestle off the rest of his clothing, and I use the opportunity to get out of my own. The way his silken sheets feel against all my bare flesh is heavenly as I close my eyes, and I relish the way he appears above me as soon as I open them again a moment later.

"Hi," he says as he stares down at me.

I giggle. "Hi." He continues looking at me, smiling, his body hovering above mine as his hands stay planted on either side of me. "What, Sir?"

"Nothing, really. Just admiring how beautiful you are."

"Even when I look like this?" I whisper.

His face comes down and kisses mine, stealing my breath and my words and everything I thought I knew about hunters. Regardless of what he's done, I know he would never hurt me.

I trust him with my life and I don't want him to go. I don't want to lose him. I don't even want to go back to face Leader Taryn and the clan and the Ancestors and deal with Markos. I want the two of us to stay here tucked safely in his condo, in this moment, forever. And I ...

I love him.

It's not as though the realization is hitting me for the first time, but it's hitting me with such intensity. Despite how hard I try to fight it, my brain races with the fact that, after today, everything is going to change. Regardless of what happens at the farm tomorrow, things between Dr. Haven and I are guaranteed to shift.

Unless ... No.

"Care to share where your brain is at?" he asks, pecking my lips softly.

"Make love to me." The words spill out before I can stop them, momentarily canceling the noise in my head.

In typical perfect style, he doesn't question anything. Doesn't hesitate, debating whether any of this is a good idea or is ultimately just making things harder. He doesn't worry about any of that, but instead lets his lips graze my neck as I close my eyes and sigh.

"Okay," he whispers against my flesh.

His hips move down between mine. My legs instinctually wrap around him, pulling him close and pinning him to me. I feel his thickness parting me as he presses inside, my walls savoring every inch of him as he takes his time, slow and patient and deliberate as I accommodate his girth.

My fingers dig into his shoulder blades as he begins rocking back and forth, his hard shaft slipping in and out of me easily with how wet I am just from wanting him. I can't help but let out a sharp gasp every time he thrusts forward. I love the way he feels, how deep he gets and how smoothly his body moves against mine. I'm completely lost in him.

My legs and fingers clench tighter and he pauses, trailing more kisses along my neck and jaw as I feel him pulsing inside me. "Are you okay?"

"Mhmm," I moan, squeezing my legs tighter and pulling him just a little deeper inside.

"Are you sure?"

"Yes." He moves again slowly and I moan. "You feel amazing."

"So do you," he grunts, his words breathy as he stills his movements. "Too good. I'm not sure how much longer I can—"

"Please fill me," I beg, letting my arms wrap around his neck as my fingers get lost in the back of his hair. "I want to feel you come in me."

His body is happy to oblige, fulfilling my request. I feel all his muscles tense as he pulls himself down on me harder, his face buried in my hair and the side of my neck as he lets himself pour into me. Every drop leaves me feeling full and satisfied, and I hold him and stroke his hair as he lays on me and waits to catch his breath.

"That ... was incredible," he sighs. He lifts his head enough to look down at me, clouds of gray parting from his irises as he smiles. "You're amazing."

"As are you," I say, and he kisses me.

He rolls off of me but curls up close, his fingers trailing down between my breasts, along my sternum, and down the length of my stomach before tenderly teasing along my opening. "You're so wet," he whispers in my ear.

"Mhmm." All I can do is agree as his thumb and forefinger wrap around my clit and gently squeeze, the rolling motion forcing my body alight with pleasurable shockwaves.

His hand slips lower and he presses two fingers inside me, bending them upwards as I squeal with delight.

His thumb continues on my button, stroking it gently as he moves his hand upwards harder and faster. My legs tremble as my hips shoot up to the ceiling to meet his hand, the pressure from his fingers intensifying as erratic moans escape my lips.

"Sir, I ... I ..."

I can't speak as a gushing orgasm claims me, soaking his hand and my thighs and the bed below. My whole body quivers with enormous sensation as I come over and over, and I am nothing but a cool, damp mess by the time I find myself nestled back down on his bed.

"That was ... uhmm ..."

"Amazing?" Dr. Haven grins, finishing my sentence.

"Yeah. That." I laugh. "That was ... It was nice."

"It was," he agrees, kissing the side of my face which is matted with damp hair. His fingers stroke along my temple, pushing my hair back behind my ear as I lay there, eyes closed, wishing I could live in this moment, beside him, forever.

"You're so beautiful," he whispers, and I know he means it.

Even when I look like this, even when I look like a monster. He doesn't see a monster. He sees something else. Sees ... me.

He goes to drape his tattooed arm over me and immediately yanks away. I open my eyes and he chuckles. "There's a very cold wet spot on the bed now."

I smile and close my eyes again. "Sorry, Sir."

"Don't be, Miss Summers. Remind me to throw all this bedding in the wash tomorrow."

I hear it in his voice, the realization that settles in alongside that final word.

Tomorrow.

Will we even be here tomorrow? Will he still be alive? Will I? What if—

"After we get back from the farm tomorrow," he clarifies. "We'll wash it then."

I turn to face him, eyes opening wide. "We?"

"Unless you don't want to come over again tomorrow night."

I smile and close my eyes. "No. I do."

"Good," he says, and the last thing I remember is the way his thumb feels stroking across my temple as he pets my hair and I drift off to sleep.

CHAPTER 32

Though I've been here before, everything feels so foreign. The abandoned town has a chill in the air that speaks to more than just the cusp of winter. There's a stillness, a coldness. An emptiness that brings about that icy feel to my hands, the one that makes my pulse drop and my fingers ache.

And it's way, way too quiet.

I keep Dr. Haven close beside me. I tried to stop him from coming today, but it was directly after assisting his coming with my mouth in the shower, and he wasn't having it. I probably should have withheld all sexual favors until he agreed not to come, but I'm not sure that would have made any genuine difference.

And in the event that one or both of us does die here today, I didn't want it to be after having denied our last opportunity to be together.

The moments from the shower flash through my mind as we walk, pulling my eyes over to him. His face is riddled with concentration. It's obvious he doesn't feel the least bit comfortable, but if he's feeling any genuine fear, he's hiding it well.

"Where is everyone? Is it always this quiet?" he asks.

"No. I don't know," I reply, keeping my voice hushed. "We need to go to the hotel on the outskirts of the town. That's where everyone is staying."

We're about to pass a small bungalow with boarded up windows when I see the front door creak open a smidge, the mellow light from inside pouring out onto the porch from behind a figure. Yellow eyes hover there, watching me. Then a hand shoots out.

"Zali, wait!"

Dr. Haven keeps close to me, his coat brushing against my leathers as we stop. "Vanthony? What are you—"

"Get in here!" he whispers, his hand frantically coaxing us inside.

"Who's that?" Dr. Haven asks, but there's no time to explain.

I take his hand and squeeze tightly. "It's okay, we can trust him."

And I hope I'm not wrong about that.

We go inside and Vanthony shuts the door. He seems frazzled, out of breath. His golden eyes glow wide, chock full of fear as he wraps his arms around me and embraces me in a tight hug.

"H—Hi?" I say, dropping Dr. Haven's hand so I can hug Vanthony back. "Are you okay?"

He breaks off the hug and grabs my shoulders. "I should have believed you!" he cries. His hands lightly tremble as he grips around my biceps and squeezes. "I'm so sorry I didn't believe you!"

"Vanthony, what are you talking about? What happened? Where is everyone?"

"Oh, Zali. Everyone is in the hotel. The Ancestors have

called everyone in for questioning. One of the Ancestors, Nalo, was murdered."

"WHAT?!" Vanthony immediately shushes me and I regain my composure before continuing. "What do you mean murdered? He's our Ancestor, from the Osjhka clan. He should be safer here with us than anywhere. I don't understand. What happened?"

"That's the thing. Markos is ... He's telling everyone that it was you, Zali. You and your," he glances at Dr. Haven, "your beloved hunter."

My chest burns, my throat stinging with the bile that my queasiness is bringing up. "Vanthony, please, you have to believe—"

"I know it wasn't you, Zali."

There's sincerity in his eyes, a look of trust and knowing that comforts me. "You do? How?"

He leans in ever closer, stopping only once our noses are nearly touching. The fear in his eyes rattles me, but I do my best not to let it show. "I saw him do it."

"Who?"

He presses his mouth to my ear, my scalp prickling with the heat of the word. "Markos."

I pull back, my eyes widening. "You saw him do it? When? How?"

"Shhh. Please, Zali. I have no proof. Markos will kill me. Nalo went into a feeding room. I was going to go in there and have a little drink before the meeting today. You know, to keep my senses sharp. And that's when I saw him. He came up behind him and sank his fangs into him. He took what little soul Nalo had, and then he used a blade to slice all around his neck, right over the puncture wounds. He's claiming that your hunter has enchanted weapons."

"That's not even true!" I hiss. "Well ... Not currently, at least."

Vanthony looks at Dr. Haven, terror still radiating from his eyes. "You're really the one who's been killing us all?"

Don't answer that.

Dr. Haven doesn't look the least bit put off by the question. "Yes. But there's more to it than that. I was hired by—"

"You were *hired*?!" Vanthony and I gasp in unison.

I slam my hands on my hips. "I thought you were just killing us because we have no souls and thus no joy left in life? I thought you were doing us a kindness? Is that not true, then?"

"I told myself that as a justification for my actions, Miss Summers. But the truth is, there isn't as much peace between your clans as your elders and leaders would have you believe."

"The Ancestors."

"Yes. I just didn't want you to become involved in any way," he says with apologetic eyes. "I've told you before, I don't hunt for sport."

"We can discuss this more later," I snap coldly, more annoyed by the fact that he's kept this from me than any ties he might have with other clans. "Vanthony, where is Markos? And Leader Taryn?"

"Everyone is in the hotel. They've set up the meeting in the lobby. I excused myself to eat, but I've been hiding here waiting for you. I needed to warn you. And I owed you an apology. I'm so sorry, Zali. I should have believed you. Even if you are sleeping with *the enemy*." He shoots Dr. Haven a fang-baring scowl.

I hug him tightly again. "Thank you, Vanthony. Come on, Dr. Haven. We need to go."

"I'm going to go eat something," Vanthony says. "I don't want Markos wise to me having tipped you off by the three of us entering together. And I need my strength in case ... Well, who knows how this is going to go down. Just know my loyalty lies with you, Zali."

"Thank you, Vanthony."

Dr. Haven and I exit the house and make our way toward the hotel, walking briskly. "That was a friend of yours, I take it?"

"He is," I nod, "and the one who kept me so well-dressed for school. He picked out all my human attire."

I look over and see Dr. Haven smiling, but he doesn't say anything. We keep quiet until we're standing in front of the hotel doors, an old, rusty set of metal doors that have somehow become the gateway to life-changing possibilities.

"Are you ready?" I ask Dr. Haven, a look of determination in his eyes.

"Yes. Let's get this over with."

I grab his hands and we immediately turn to face one another. "Dr. Haven, I ..."

He stares down at me, his gaze having grown soft. The way his eyes keep trailing slightly down tells me how desperately he wants to kiss me. "Yes, Miss Summers?"

"I ... In case anything bad happens in there, I just want to say ... I love you."

He kisses me, and it's ravenous and gentle and reckless and perfect all at once. It's everything he is and everything I've fallen in love with, and it takes all of my strength not to take him by the hand and run the hell out of there and say fuck it to all this nonsense.

"I love you too, Miss Summers. Now, let's get this over with so we can go home and wash that bedding."

I smile and nod. "Alright."

I swing the doors open and we trek through the bit of hallway before passing a large open doorway to find a few dozen drauls taking up all of the space in the lobby. Everyone from my Osjhka clan is there, including Markos, who is standing holding Leader Taryn's shoulder. Alongside Leader Taryn sat around a round table are the remaining Ancestors, four from the Yedora clan, and one from each of the other clans; Jeskla, Zoscar, Dyhrali, Edomia, and Vushma.

Nalo, the Ancestor who had represented the Osjhka clan, is gone.

"Where's Nalo?" I ask, steering potential suspicion away from Vanthony.

"Ah, Zalida. And ... is this the infamous hunter?" Leader Taryn asks. "Funny, I pictured someone a bit ... *stockier*."

Dr. Haven nods politely. "Doctor Ross Haven, your Leadership. I've come to atone for my actions. I want you to know that the members of your group that I killed were not targets of any personal vendetta. And that to make amends, and in the hopes that you'll spare my life, I've come prepared to offer you two pieces of valuable information."

Leader Taryn's head cocks so to the side that it sits at nearly ninety degrees. "Is that so, Hunter? You think that a mere human has information so pertinent to our kind that it would be worth sparing your life after all the blood you've spilled?"

Dr. Haven nods again. "I do."

"Neat," Leader Taryn hisses through a very open-mouthed smile. "We'll get to that in a moment." His attention turns back to me. "Zalida, it seems you've held up your end of things, delivering the hunter to us. And just in time, too. The full moon is mere nights away."

"Yes," I say, "but I should point out two things. One is that Dr. Haven came of his own volition tonight. And two, he did not work alone."

A few gasps can be heard throughout the group, followed by hushed whispers and sideways glances. Then a figure enters the room from an adjoined hall, and my breath hitches when I realize who it is.

Professor Gibbons!

"What is he doing here?" I demand.

Markos bursts into roaring laughter. "*You* can shut your mouth, traitor!" he bellows for all the room to hear. "You are no good, Zalida Wren. Not only are you a traitor, you've broken draul code by mating with this human. And as if that were not bad enough, he is the very human that has been killing us all off for *years*! He has been working hard to ensure our extinction, and yet you've been sleeping in his bed!"

I battle the urge to say something, anything, in my defense.

"Are you quite finished, Markos?" I seethe through clenched teeth.

"Not yet," he states. He waves an arm broadly across the spectrum of the room. "You immediately came in here and asked where Nalo was."

"Yes, because he's obviously missing. So what?"

"Why don't you answer your own question for us, Zalida? You know where he is, don't you?"

"I've no idea what you're talking about," I snap. "As far as I heard, all the Ancestors had come for the meeting."

"Nalo was killed, Zalida." Leader Taryn's voice is the honey to Markos's gravel. It's smooth and sticky and sweet, and everything about it is making my stomach turn. "Markos is suggesting you had something to do with his demise. Is this true?"

I shake my head violently. "No, Leader Taryn! Please, you have to believe me. I—" The metal doors open and through the small hallway appears Vanthony. "Vanthony! I ... You don't believe that I killed Nalo, do you?"

I'm staring at Vanthony but he doesn't once look at me. I follow his gaze and realize his eyes are locked with Markos's. "I ... Well, I ... Zalida doesn't strike me as the type." Markos's gaze narrows, his eyes two daggers that pelt Anthony relentlessly. "But ... But I'm not sure."

Great. So much for having Vanthony's unwavering loyalty. It's all on us now.

"I have reason to believe it was Markos," I say, urging conviction to reverberate through my tone. "He was the one who killed Nalo, Leader Taryn, and he has been conspiring with this ... *half-breed* ... to kill off you and the Ancestors so they can raise an army of half-breeds."

"Enough of this foolery!" Markos booms. "Everyone here is most aware that you and your little hunter have been on a rampage to destroy our kind, Zalida! Why, I wouldn't be shocked if you led him here and assisted him in taking out Nalo just so you could attempt to frame me for all of this! Sleeping with this human has driven you absolutely mad, and your feelings for him mean you will stop at no bounds to have our marriage called off!"

"You *lie!*" I hiss, my vision growing hazy and red. My eyes burn as undiluted fury courses through my veins, setting my very blood on fire. My breathing grows labored and heavy, perspiration breaking out across my forehead as I debate lunging across the room and ripping out his jugular with my teeth.

Professor Gibbons produces the Drauldin from inside his long coat. "Markos, if it would please your Leader and the Ancestors, I'd like to enchant this blade so it may aid you in ridding the world of this traitorous creature."

"You ... You ... You bastard!" I scream. I go to move, but feel a hot hand clasp tightly around my icy fingers before I'm able to move. I snap my head around, barely able to breathe through my rage, and see Dr. Haven's fingers interlocked with mine.

"It's okay," he says quietly. "Stay here with me."

It's hard to hear anything, my heavy breathing forcing the blood to rush through my ears. Everything feels hazy and distant, as though this is all a terrible dream and at any moment I'll wake up, in his bed, greeted by the smell of coffee and him kissing my forehead.

"I think it is time for the clan to release you, Zalida," Leader Taryn announces. The circle of Ancestors seated around the table all solemnly nod their heads in a long bow.

"No! I haven't done anything wrong!"

"You are not only with a human, but the very hunter who has been killing our kind!" Leader Taryn bellows.

"Fine! But I didn't plan to fall in love with him! And Markos has been working with Professor Gibbons here to orchestrate Dr. Haven's hunting! How do you think they always managed to track us so closely? No matter where we moved to, no matter how far, every new farm would be raided within a few months! You think that's a coincidence? Professor Gibbons was getting all of the information from Markos, and relaying that to Dr. Haven to send him after us."

Leader Taryn's head cocks straight back up nearly in slow motion. "Oh really?"

"It's the truth!" I cry, my voice full of pleading and hints of desperation. "Please, Leader! I have never done wrong by you. I have never been anything short of loyal."

"But it's no secret you've been opposed to this arrangement with Markos since the beginning. While I appreciate you taking on this assignment, I have to say I am concerned with how long you've withheld this human's identity. That doesn't speak much to loyalty to me."

"I wasn't certain for a long time that he was the one doing the hunting, Leader. And he wasn't, not alone. He may have been the one wielding the Drauldin, but he wasn't the one enchanting it. He needed Professor Gibbons to do that, who is only capable of that because he's a half-breed."

"I know what he is," Leader Taryn says firmly. I look to the Ancestors and see that there's no suggestion of surprise on any of their faces.

How long have they known about Professor Gibbons?

"I thought there were no known half-breeds in existence? Isn't that what you've been telling us for decades? I'm glad to see you finally believe me about what he is."

"Bentley Gibbons's half-breed status has only recently been brought to our attention. As well as other rumors, issues between the clans. Feuds and storms and potential wars that have been brewing. But that ends now. And you, Zalida Wren, must be made an example of for your disloyalty."

The rage I swallow burns my esophagus, my vision hued with the sheen of an animalistic bloodlust. "I did what was asked. I discovered who the hunter—*hunters*—are. I have no desire to harm you or the Ancestors or anyone else, and neither does Dr. Haven. On top of this, he has *proof* that Markos has been betraying you all along. Isn't that right, Dr. Haven?"

He glances from me to the Leader and nods. "Yes. And as I said, I've also come to make amends. And if Gibbons is embarking on a partnership with you, then I would love to do the same. Seeing as he's a half-blood who was enchanting the Drauldin for me to hunt with in the first place. He's not inno-cent in all this. And it is Markos who's been betraying you directly, right under your nose."

My eyes shoot to Professor Gibbons, expecting him to protest. But all he does is nod towards Leader Taryn, saying nothing.

"For the blood of our people that has already been shed," Leader Taryn demands, "you will share the information you keep that is apparently enough to forgive all their losses. But first, show me this supposed proof."

Dr. Haven nods. "Certainly." He pulls his phone from his pocket, turning the volume all the way up and holding it out toward the center of the deathly quiet room.

... They'll never know about my alliance with Gibbons. No one is going to see me, the next Osjhka Leader, as someone who would sell out his own kind. I may have led Gibbons to all the farms, but it's time for our race to experience a metamorphosis. Pure-breeds are in the inferior race, Zali. Leader Taryn and the Ancestors aren't worthy of ruling anymore. And Gibbons is working on an elixir to give me the abilities of the half-breeds. It's too bad you won't be around to see it ...

MARKOS'S CHEST is the stillest I've ever seen it as his voice carries out from Dr. Haven's phone and settles amongst the members of the room. Eyes are wide and mouths hang open as everyone turns to stare at Markos, who looks unusually, unnervingly ... *calm.*

"You've obviously staged this, Zali," he says. "You and your human." He's trying hard to sound nonchalant, but I hear it, the tiniest whisper of nervousness in the back of his voice. "It's no secret that the humans use all sorts of technology to control and manipulate each other, and that's all this is. No one is going to buy into your schemes anymore, traitor."

Everyone is silent. The room feels void of air with everyone's held breath, waiting for Leader Taryn or any of the Ancestors to speak. Markos opens his mouth again, but Leader Taryn steals the very words from him with a wave of a hand. Before he can speak, Markos's voice disappears and nothing but a small squeak comes out.

"You've said enough, Markos," Leader Taryn says. "You swear on Lisha this is all true, Zalida? This recording was in no way altered or manufactured to frame Markos and escape the marriage?"

"I swear, Leader Taryn. I would not mislead nor betray

you. If it had come to it, I would have accepted my fate and married Markos, despite my intense reservations about being his wife. I would have respected your wishes, your Leadership, had I not been able to convince you to change your mind. This recording is nothing but truth. Markos intends to kill you all, and he wants Gibbons to help."

"Markos, what do you have to say for yourself? And make it better than, '*This is clearly all staged*'. I want the truth. Who does your loyalty lie with, really?"

Leader Taryn waves his hand and Markos grasps his throat, as if he can feel the sensation of being able to speak having been restored. "I ... My loyalty is with you, Leader. It always has been."

"Good. Then you won't be upset if I ask you to prove it."

Markos takes a step back from Leader Taryn's side. "Prove it? How?"

Leader Taryn tips his chin toward Professor Gibbons. "Kill him."

Professor Gibbons eyes shoot open, terror seeping from his dilated pupils. "Kill me? But we have an agreement in place! I'm still working on the elixir that will grant you all the power of the half-breeds. You need me. You'll never be able to finish it without me!"

Leader Taryn merely shrugs, a sickening grin on his lips. "We'll manage."

Markos looks between Gibbons and our Leader a minute, bathed in indecision. "Professor Gibbons is right, Leader. He's useful to us. He—"

Leader Taryn's hand floats up with so little conviction he appears bored. He flicks a long, gnarly pointed fingernail and Markos immediately grabs his throat with both hands. He chokes and sputters, clawing at his esophagus as every vein on his neck and forehead begin to bulge. Then Leader Taryn lowers his hand, and Markos coughs and wheezes as he fights to catch his breath.

"I suggest you hurry," Leader Taryn sighs, "or I might just get bored and kill you in his place."

Markos regains his composure. His eyes, yellow in the dim lobby lighting, grow cloudy with swirling plumes of red and maroon. He bares his fangs at Gibbons, his voice hardly above a whisper. "Sorry, Bentley. Guess your usefulness has run out."

"Someone like you is not going to be able to kill someone like me, *pure-breed*. You should know by now that we are stronger and faster than you could ever be."

Markos removes a studded leather vest and a long-sleeve undershirt to reveal his frame. Rippling muscles cover every inch of his torso. Defined shoulder blades make their way into massive biceps and thick forearms. His abs are incredibly chiseled, and it doesn't take a genius to figure out that Professor Gibbons with his twiggy form, half-breed or not, is very likely doomed if Markos gets ahold of him.

"You might be a tad quicker," Markos sneers, licking his fangs, "but you *aren't* stronger."

He lunges from beside the table where Leader Taryn and the Ancestors sit, charging at Gibbons with all his might. Gibbons is quick, moving with such speed that he's little more than a blur as he dodges out of the way and into the center of the room.

Drauls sitting at tables all move back to stand against the walls, clearing the way for the battle about to ensue. Dr. Haven and I stay near the entrance, the two of us watching as Markos lets out grunts and cries as he lunges at Professor Gibbons over and over.

"You'll tire eventually, Gibbons!" he roars, his eyes sparkling with the thrill of the hunt. "You'll tire, and the second you do, this is over!"

He chases him some more, Gibbons narrowly escaping the last swing as Markos's hand grips the corner of Gibbons's trench coat and rips it. Gibbons looks genuinely pissed, staring at his damaged coat in disbelief. "This coat was a gift," he mutters, voice hardly coherent. "How ... How dare you!"

He pulls the Drauldin from inside his coat, holding it in his right hand as his left hand hovers over the length of the blade. He begins muttering an incantation, the symbol of Jalvana lighting up on one side of the steel near the hilt. Then he holds his hand out palm up, ready to drag the blade across it and consummate the enchantment.

Leader Taryn's hand shoots up, his long arm casting out to point the bony fingers of his hand in Professor Gibbons's direction. Three long fingernails shoot from the center of his hand, all three puncturing the side of Gibbons's neck. In their place, Leader Taryn has nothing but three raw nail beds, all bright red and bleeding.

The Drauldin clatters to the floor as Professor Gibbons clasps his throat, but the bleeding is already out of control. Spurts of the red liquid pour out from between his fingers as he mouths for air. His eyes, still chock full of fear, grow hazier and dimmer by the second. The Drauldin lays on the floor only a moment before Markos snatches it, Gibbons's body falling down in its place.

"YOU!" Markos howls as he swings the Drauldin up above his head with both hands. "I've been waiting to end you a second time!"

He comes flying at Dr. Haven but I throw myself between the two men, the weight of me barely enough to hold Markos back as he snakes an arm around my back and swings the Drauldin wildly. Dr. Haven jumps out of the way, tucking himself into a corner of the room as I press into Markos with all my force. He lifts the Drauldin and brings it clambering down toward my skull. I cry out as both my hands shoot up, catching his arm and holding it above my head. My arms shake violently as I try to keep the blade from touching me.

"Too bad ... you'll ... never get ... to bear my children, Zali!" Markos roars as he twists his wrist and points the blade closer to my neck.

"I ... would rather ... DIE!" I scream loudly as the blade kisses my neck, slicing a flesh wound above my collarbone that immediately begins to burn and sizzle.

"What ... How did you ..."

Markos and I both watch in awe as the blade pulses with a low blue light. It shines brighter and brighter, until the entire blade is near blinding as it hums with the energy of enchantment. A gentle ringing hums from it in a rhythmic beat, and Markos's face looks like a deer in headlights as he stands there admiring the sudden power he wields.

It's now or never!

I wrap my hands around his on the hilt and force the blade upward, catching him off guard as he stumbles back in a too-late attempt to miss the steel. The blade sings and glows red as it whizzes along his cheekbone, barely grazing him but causing irrefutable damage nonetheless.

"Arrgghhh!" He screams in agony as he drops the blade and grabs his face. Tendrils of black spider out from every edge of the cut, first across his face and then mapping out along his entire torso and arms. Within a matter of seconds his skin sizzles off in dusty flakes, and he only lets out a couple more screams before his maroon eyes turn gray and he bursts into nothing more than a handful of ash.

Leader Taryn claps unenthusiastically. "Well done, Zalida."

"I ... I don't know—"

"It seems it's not only half-breed blood that can enchant the Drauldin," Rynka says, our Ancestor from the Dyhrali clan. "It seems your girl is special."

"So it does," Leader Taryn agrees. He strums his skeletal fingers together. "We'll have to let you live now, Zalida, despite your relations with the human. We must see what else you're capable of."

"I ... Thank you, Leader Taryn. Thank you, Ancestors."

They all bow their heads silently. Leader Taryn turns his attention to Dr. Haven, who has moved from the corner and is once again standing by my side. He picks the Drauldin up off the floor and walks to their table, setting it in the center.

"This belongs with you," he says.

Before he can remove his hand from above the sword, Leader Taryn's hand shoots out and grabs his wrist. "You're so ... warm," he says through gritted teeth. "I can see why Zalida would be so fond of such a creature. You may go."

He unhands Dr. Haven, who rubs his wrist and takes a couple steps backward. "You don't want to know the knowledge I was going to share with you?"

"I've seen it all," Leader Taryn says, waving dismissively toward Dr. Haven's wrist. "Leave this place. And, if you wish to continue living, retire from your work as a hunter. Gibbons is no longer, you've no one to aid you, and you're without the Drauldin. You're lucky you're being allowed to live, given how much you know. And I will extend this courtesy only once. If our paths cross again, I will end you myself. And Gibbons won't be there to resurrect you."

"Understood," he says, offering a polite nod. "Thank you."

Vanthony gives me a thumbs up from the far corner of the room and I offer a weak smile. I don't know whether I can take Leader Taryn's word for it that Dr. Haven will never be sought after this, but I don't have much choice but to believe it for now.

And I pray to Lisha it's true.

I take Dr. Haven by the hand once he makes his way back

to me, the two of us about to head out when Leader Taryn's voice stops me dead in my tracks.

"Ah, ah. Hold on you two."

I swallow hard and turn. "Yes, Leader?"

"Markos killing Nalo means that the Ancestors are now short a representative from our Osjhka clan."

"So they are," I agree. "But how did you know Markos was the one—"

Leader Taryn points to Dr. Haven. "I saw the conversation with Vanthony."

Vanthony's eyes grow wide at the sound of his name. "I'm sorry I didn't report it to you!" he cries. "Markos had everyone so convinced, and I—"

"Hush," Leader Taryn orders, and Vanthony goes silent. "Zalida, I cannot let you leave without telling you: I have a new assignment for you."

"Already?" I gasp. "What is it, Leader?"

"As Nalo is no more, I will be stepping up to take his place with the Ancestors. But this leaves the Osjhka without a Leader."

"It does."

"*You* will be that Leader."

I struggle to find my voice as my heart pumps slow and furious in my chest. "I'm not sure—"

"I am." Leader Taryn's face remains solemn, not a glimmer of feeling in his hollow features. "You are perfect. And powerful. And it is an order, not an offer."

"Yes, Leader. Thank you."

"And as for you, Ross Haven," he says, their eyes fixated on one another's, "I would suggest finding somewhere to live as far from Lochfort as possible."

CHAPTER 33

"You're seriously not going to stay?" Meredith whines, puppy dog eyes peeking up over the edge of her coffee cup.

"I can't believe you're not going to stay, Sara! Harsh! I mean, I get it. I totally get it. It's family, you can't just not take care of your sick family. But nothing is going to be the same without you! Not school, not the house. Oh, and Dr. Haven is *coincidentally* leaving this summer as well! You wouldn't happen to know anything about that, would you?" Angel grins cheekily.

"No," I grumble, staring out through the front window of Bumpy's at all the happy, oblivious humans walking the streets and strolling the park. "It's too bad though. He's an amazing professor."

"Of course you'd say so! He gave you near-perfect marks on that big assignment and you totally aced his class. I think that's just because he had a big crush on you." I shoot Angel a stern glare and she cowers. "I'm kidding! I'm kidding. Gosh. You're testy for someone who just passed their first semester of school with flying colors!"

I force a smile. "You're right, I'm sorry. I guess I'm just stressed about having to leave and ... take care of my family."

But what I'm really stressed about is the thought of having to leave without him. *How am I supposed to go back to my clan and go on like Lochfort never happened? Like* he *never happened? How am I going to erase all these memories from my mind so I can somehow find happiness in a world where I don't get to see him at school every day?*

Where I don't get to see him ... at all.

"Yeah, I get it. That must be a lot of responsibility for you to shoulder. That sucks. Do you think this thing with your family is long term? Maybe you can come back to CCU next fall! You know, in the new year. Just take a semester and the summer off, tackle stuff with your family, and then—"

"I'm going to miss you, Angel."

She looks shocked, but a moment later her eyes begin welling up with tears. "I'm going to miss you too, Sara. And Meredith will miss you also, right, Mere?"

"Totes," she nods, a banner of latte foam settled into a mustache on her upper lip. "The house is going to be ... Well, actually, it won't be more quiet without you. You're, like, the most freakishly quiet person I know."

Angel laughs. "Yeah, that's true. You're like a ninja, Sara. Especially at night. I wouldn't even know you were home most of the time if it wasn't for your shoes by the front door. How are you always so quiet? I don't know any other girls who are that quiet."

I chuckle and sip my coffee. It warms my belly and sends a comforting feeling throughout me. It's funny, coffee has ceased to upset my stomach ever since I drank the elixir Dr. Haven gave me. It's almost as though it made me just a little bit more human again. And my once-frozen hands haven't been nearly as cold ever since Markos died and I am officially happily single once again.

Well ... Perhaps not happily.

I sigh, watching the snow outside come down in perfect little flakes. Sunlight dances off an undisturbed blanket of snow that covers the park, glittering in the bright afternoon. Christmas has come and gone, and everyone looks so happy, so peaceful.

I'm riddled with envy.

"You okay?" Meredith asks, and I nod.

"Yeah, yeah. All good. Just tired."

"It's probably because you haven't eaten anything!" Angel barks. "How can you always be full when I literally *never* see you eat anything? You realize we've been roommates for like four months now, and I've never seen you eat *anything*? Don't you think that's kinda crazy?"

"Quit bugging her about it!" Meredith pipes up. "Maybe she has deipnophobia! You never know. And even if she does, that's perfectly okay! Right, Sara?"

"I'm sorry, what are you going on about?" I reply.

"Deipnophobia!" she repeats, louder, as if the issue were one of volume and not of understanding. "You know, fear of eating in front of others! Some people are just terrified to eat food in front of other humans. So ... they don't."

The word 'humans' is exactly the problem here. You'd both be terrified if you saw what I ate.

"Is that some kinda eating disorder?" Angel asks.

"I don't know," Mere replies, "I just know it's super weird."

"Mere!" Angel gasps.

"What? It's just a weird thing to be super picky about. Who cares if someone watches you eat food? Unless you're a really gross eater who licks their fingers clean after. That's just gross."

Angel laughs. "Remind me never to invite you over to my house again."

"We live in the same house, you tard!" Mere balls up a

napkin and tosses it at Angel, who keenly dodges it as the two of them burst into a fit of laughter.

"Great, now I have to pick that up!" Angel grumbles, bending under the table to retrieve it. "You're so gross! Quit being gross, Mere!"

"You two are absolutely ridiculous humans," I tell them. "Both of you."

"Takes one to know one," Angel grins as though she's a decade younger. "We should get headed back to the house. It's supposed to snow a lot tonight, I'd rather get home before it flies. You coming, Sara?"

Angel and Meredith both stare at me with expectant eyes. I glance over at the counter and see Tobi, who offers me a friendly wave paired with an endearingly awkward smile.

"You could go say hi to him, you know," Angel coos. "Go chat him up, ask him how his day was, ask him how soul-sucking being a barista is. I bet it's the worst."

Nothing compared to the kind of soulsucking I'm used to, dear Angel.

"No, I ... I'm good. He seems nice, but he's not really my type."

"Is it the freckles?" Meredith asks.

"Rude! I have freckles. And no, it's because he's not a dreamy, older professor," Angel teases, and for once I simply roll my eyes instead of scolding her.

"See? This is what I'm talking about, Angel. You're absolutely ridiculous," I say matter-of-factly.

"Whatever, at least you aren't denying it for once."

I should be. I just don't have the energy to deny it anymore today.

"Alright, we're heading home. I guess we'll catch you later then?" Angel asks as the two of them stand from the table and start putting their coats on.

"Yeah, yeah. I'll ... I'll catch you guys at the house later."

I watch as they put their hats and gloves on and march

out into the day, still giggling like a couple of mad hyenas. I wait until they're good and out of sight before heading into the park. I pull my coat closer around myself, fix my scarf up a little tighter, shove my hands into my pockets. I let winter nip at my skin as I walk at a leisurely human pace. My brain might be sending the signals that make my legs carry me, but it's my heart telling them where to go.

It's not a big town and it doesn't take more than seventeen minutes to walk to Dr. Haven's condo building. I debate scaling the building and climbing in his window, but night hasn't fallen and Jezebel is sitting outside on her balcony.

Her parrot must be somewhere nearby.

I go in and buzz Dr. Haven's unit, waiting for the intercom to connect us.

"Miss Summers?" His voice feels distant and metallic through the little box.

"Yes, it's me."

I ride the rickety elevator up to the fourth floor and head to unit *407*, where Dr. Haven is already standing with the door held open a crack. "Come in," he says, holding the door as I enter, then closing it behind me.

Things have been calm since the night at the farm. Leader Taryn surprisingly agreed to both of us finishing the semester before I take over the Osjhka clan and Dr. Haven moves ... wherever he's planning to move to. Despite the fact we've still been intimately seeing each other, the whole topic is a giant elephant in the room. But it's not an elephant we can afford to ignore any longer.

I breathe in the familiar scent of his space. The spiciness and the woodsiness and the bitterness of freshly brewed coffee. I go and grab a mug from the cupboard, happy to make myself at home as I always do when I'm here.

I stand at the kitchen counter savoring the hot liquid when he comes up behind me. He wraps his arms protectively around my waist and nuzzles his face in my hair. "I've missed you," he says softly.

"Missed me? I just spent the night here on the weekend."

"Yeah, but that was three sleeps ago. Three sleeps is too many to go without seeing you."

I chuckle as I sip my coffee. "Alright, fair. You already know I agree with you."

"Have you met with the leaders again?" he asks, obviously needing a topic change. "Has Leader Taryn explained how and when you're going to take over Osjhka?"

I take a big gulp and shake my head. "No, but it'll be soon. Very soon. Now that the semester is officially over, there isn't anything left to wait for. I have to head back to the farm tonight."

"Tonight?" His voice spikes with panic as he squeezes me tighter. "Why tonight? Why not tomorrow? You should ask if tomorrow would be okay."

I crane my neck back. "Why? What's tomorrow?"

"Tomorrow I ... I have a train ticket. In a week's time, I'll be on the other side of the country. A fresh start after all that's happened, you know?"

I try to mask the heartache in my voice when I tell him how great that is, how happy I am for him, but I can tell by his expression he isn't buying it. "What are you going to do for work?" I ask, trying to lighten the mood. "Work at another university?"

He kisses my hair and I turn back to drinking my coffee. "Yeah, I was already offered a position at a fairly prestigious school. It pays quite a bit better than what I was making here. Which is good because the housing prices out there are ridiculous." He forces a laugh, but I can't muster the strength to join him.

"Are you selling the condo then?"

Dr. Haven sighs, resting his chin on my shoulder. "I

suppose I will. Your Leader made it pretty clear that I'm not welcome anywhere near this town. I don't think it'd be in my best interest to push my luck and stay. I feel lucky enough that they let me live. After all, I did kill a lot of drauls, especially from your clan."

My clan—Soon to be even more my clan once I become Leader. A buttload of headache and responsibility that I want exactly zero part of. I never even wanted to be part of a clan, never mind in charge of one. I just want—

"You could come with me, you know," he says, and while part of me is elated to finally hear him say this out loud, another part of me really, really wishes he hadn't. My chest burns with overwhelming sorrow. To think tomorrow is the last day I'll see him feels like the weight of a million moons on my chest. I bite my bottom lip to keep from sobbing, my voice wavering as I try to form words.

"I ... can't. You know I can't." I hardly recognize myself with how fragile I sound, how raw. Everything about him drains the killer instincts from me and leaves me vulnerable and exposed and, though I wish I hated it, I've grown to so love this about him.

"Why not? What's the reason? You think the Ancestors would forever hunt you?"

"No, I *know* they would forever hunt me. You heard Leader Taryn. The position wasn't an offer, it was an order. He wants to know the clan is in good hands. They need level-headed drauls running the sectors, or else chaos breaks out. There's already whispers of a war brewing between us and the Yedora clan in the mountains. Savage, feral beasts they are."

"What if we asked the Ancestors to give you time to train someone else as Leader? Do you think they'd be open to letting you go if you could offer a suitable replacement?"

Hope pings in my chest, but it quickly fades away as I assess the feasibility of such a thing. "Where would I find someone like that, Sir? I know everyone in our clan. The only draul who's half-decently stable is Vanthony, and he's scared of his own shadow. They're not going to see him as a worthy Leader."

"What about Jezebel?"

My heart freezes. "Jezebel?"

"Yeah. She's older, but you'd be amazed by how tough she is. And, being older, she could likely garner a lot of respect in a position like that. Sure, she's been clanless for a long time, but wouldn't the Ancestors also appreciate having one less free-roaming draul out there? Plus, she's wise as hell, and she doesn't need access to a farm because she has my elixir to sustain her."

"I can't believe you agreed to keep producing it for the Ancestors indefinitely. How are you even going to get it to them from across the country?"

"They'll send someone," he says. "Leader Taryn will make the arrangements personally. I just wish they'd let me make enough for everyone to have it, not just the top drauls. Then none of the clans would need farms anymore. Mind you, growing enough herbs is difficult. Gibbons never understood that either."

"They'd never let you anyway. The farms are how they control us. It's how they keep us chained to a source, unable to break out on our own. Once you become accustomed to the convenience of it, going back to hunting feels so daunt-ing. Except for the really feral ones, like Markos. But we're not supposed to hunt anyway. It's forbidden, too likely to expose us to the humans."

"Mhmm," he agrees. "You didn't answer my question."

"About?"

"Whether or not you could suggest Jezebel as a suitable replacement."

I spin around in his arms, letting myself get lost in the

blues of his eyes. "Would she even want that? I can't just ... *donate her* ... for my own selfish reasons. She seems content across the way in her apartment, doesn't she?"

Dr. Haven pulls me against him a little tighter, his delicious scent and warmth enveloping me as he smiles. "Only one way to find out. I guess you'll have to ask her."

I furrow my brows at him. "It was your idea, why don't you ask her? You've far more of a relationship with her than what I have."

"Yes," he says, pecking my forehead between words, "but you ... are the clan leader ... and ... she ... likes ... you. Plus, let's be real, you're the much prettier one out of the two of us, and people are more keen to listen to pretty people."

I laugh and roll my eyes. "Except that Jezebel isn't a *people*, is she?"

"Sort of," he grins. "Just ask her. See what she says. Or rather, what her parrot says."

"Right." I wrap my arms around his waist and press my head into his chest. The soft fabric of his cardigan hugs my ear as we stand there and I close my eyes and listen, taking in every beat of his heart. "I don't want you to go," I say quietly.

I never want to let him go, and the way his arms keep me pinned to him tells me he feels it too, an inevitability that neither of us wants to come to terms with. That a world where forces are set on keeping us apart isn't going to be an easy world to live in.

That it'll be hell.

"You can keep my condo."

My head snaps up in surprise. "What?"

Obviously I must have misheard him.

"You can keep it. I don't really want to sell it anyway. Why don't you stay in Lochfort? Go to school. Finish your degree. I know you weren't planning on actually being a full-time student, but why not? You've passed off as one this long. I'd say you're the real deal by now."

"I don't ... but the clan—"

"Oh, come on. You can run the clan and still go to school. You're a draul, I know you have memory and recollection well beyond any human. School is easy for you, almost trivial."

"Then why would I do it?"

"For something to do?" His face comes down as he kisses my lips, but it's too brisk and leaves me needing more. "Either way, the condo is yours to live in. If you want it. I'd rather know someone is here taking care of the place while I'm away."

"I don't know what to say. Thank you, Sir."

"My pleasure, Miss Summers."

I hook my arms around his neck, using them to hoist myself up enough to kiss him again. Our lips peck several times, but I can't stand to let him get away with just that. I slip my tongue into his mouth, savoring the coffee on his palate as his tongue swirls around mine.

He urges me backward with his hips, his hands grasping my waist tightly as he hoists me onto the kitchen counter. Impatient fingers fumble with the button of my jeans, my regular human jeans that I've grown to love wearing as much as my leathers, and he anxiously pulls my pants off my legs and folds them neatly before setting them next to me.

His forearms push my knees apart as he leans forward, his hot breath tickling my inner thighs. Kisses trail up each one, forcing gentle quivers as the front of my panties grow damp with anticipation. He slides a finger along my pelvic bone, hooking it onto the side of my panties. He pulls the lacey orange fabric to the side, exposing me as his mouth hungrily claims me.

I place my hands back behind me, the smooth granite cool on my fingertips as I brace myself. My hips jut forward with every flick of his tongue, and I cry out sharply when I feel one, and then quickly two, fingers pressing deep inside me.

It doesn't take him long to make me come, his hands and mouth having grown expertly in tune with all my sweet spots and triggers. I'm panting when he stands fully up from between my legs, his face finding mine after he adjusts his glasses. I kiss him back despite my breathlessness, loving the way he always lets me taste myself on his lips immediately after.

"Come on, let's go to bed," he says, taking my hands in his.

"Now? But it's only," I glance at the stove, "ten o'clock in the morning."

"Does that mean you don't want to get in bed with me?" he grins.

"Wait, are we *going to* bed, or are we *getting into* bed?"

"Does it change your answer?"

I laugh. "No. Not at all."

"Good," he says, pecking my nose. He stares into my eyes, those swirling grays filling his blue irises as we sit in this moment, just taking one another in. "I love you."

"I know," I say softly. "I love you too, Sir. Hey, can I ask you something?"

He pecks my lips. "Always."

"You never told me what you were going to ask me that one day at Bumpy's."

He cocks his head. "What day?"

"It was a long time ago. That day that Angel showed up and interrupted our meeting. That day she saw Markos sitting at the bus stop across the street. You said you wanted to ask me something right before she showed up. And I only recently remembered that, and that you never ended up asking me."

"Ah, that. Yes, I remember." He smiles.

"Okay, so what was it?"

"I wanted to ask if I could take you on a proper date after the semester was over, but the question ended up being pretty unnecessary with how things unfolded."

"Oh." I smile. "I see."

"So? Are you going to tell me what you would have said?"

"You already know it would have been an emphatic 'yes', Sir."

"Good." He kisses me gently. "Come on," he pulls my hands and urges me off the counter. "Come to bed."

"Yes, Sir," I say, not wanting to think about tomorrow.

At this moment, all I want to think about is him.

CHAPTER 34

He leans in just as I smile and ends up kissing one of my fangs. "Sorry!" he blurts, and it's awkward and perfect and I want to laugh and cry simultaneously. I resist the overwhelming urge to throw him over my shoulder, carry him back to his condo and handcuff him to the bed so he can never leave.

I lean in and kiss him deeply. "I'll miss you."

"And I you," he says, pressing his warm lips to my forehead and holding them there a second too long before looking down at me again. "It's not like it's forever. I'll stay in touch."

"I know. It won't be the same, though."

"It won't," he agrees. He checks his phone. "I have to go, I'm going to miss my train."

"I know." I give him one last giant squeeze, happy when he returns it just as hard. "I love you, Sir."

"And I love you, Miss Summers. I'll message you when I arrive safely."

He gives me one last kiss before exiting the alley, leather

briefcase and his suitcase in tow. I watch as he disappears around the corner, then scale the building and peer down from the roof, watching as he gets on the train. The doors shut, but I watch through the windows until he takes his seat. Then I watch as he sits there and reads, enjoying the view of him until the train finally departs.

He instantly feels so far away even while the train is still well in sight. The wind is cold and blustery. I pull my jacket around myself tighter as I leap from rooftop to rooftop, eventually heading back down to the ground in the direction of the condo.

I whizz through the night, careful not to let anyone see me. I don't stop until I'm in front of Jezebel's building. I leap from the ground and make my way up to her balcony, surprised when I find the sliding glass door open a crack.

"Hello?" I say as I open it wider, peering inside. I step in and shut the door behind me. I find Jezebel sitting at a small kitchen table just off the living room, her wrinkled hand hovering above a half-finished puzzle. Her fingers grip a piece that she easily places in one of the upper corners.

"Hi, Jezebel," I say to her. I can't help but smile at the sight of her, thinking about how Dr. Haven and I weaved her into our story for the *Human Nature* assignment. Though, we left out the part about her parrot speaking for her.

"Hi!" her parrot squawks, but Jezebel doesn't look up from her puzzle.

"I'm sorry to burst in on you like this."

"*SQUAWK!* Was expecting you!"

"Oh ... Kay. I don't know if you know anything about the clans—"

"Yup! *SQUAWK!*"

"Okay. Well, the Leader of the Osjhka clan is joining the roster of Ancestors, and he wants me to take his place. I've never had any interest in the clans or their politics. I only joined one to ensure my survival, really. But I'm over that now. Dr. Ross Haven's moved away, and I want to—"

"Go! *SQUAWK*! Want to go!"

"Yes, exactly. I want to go be with him. But the Osjhka clan will need a suitable Leader. Someone smart and calm and calculated, someone the other drauls can respect. And ... Dr. Haven suggested I might ask you, so. Here I am, asking if you'd be interested in leading a clan."

"Can do! *SQUAWK*! Yup! Can do!"

The parrot's head bobs up and down as it watches me. Jezebel's still completely engrossed in her puzzle. If you didn't know any better, you'd think she had no clue I was even in the room.

"Really? Oh, that's amazing! Thank you, Jezebel. I'm headed to the farm now. I can talk to Leader Taryn about it when I get there. I'll come back and visit you tomorrow."

"*SQUAWK*! Tomorrow! Yup!"

"Thank you, Jezebel." I turn to leave, but I've only made it a step past the kitchen doorway when her parrot screeches behind me.

"Wait!"

I turn and look, my eyes meeting Jezebel's. She smiles, and it's the warmest, most genuine smile I've ever seen on a draul. "Yes?"

"Congrats! *SQUAWK*! Congrats!"

"Congrats? For what? The leadership?"

Jezebel rubs her stomach, a different puzzle piece clenched in one hand. I stand there, confused, but she just keeps rubbing her stomach.

"Food? Are you hungry, Jezebel? Do you need more elixir?"

"*SQUAWK*! Congrats, baby! Yup!"

Jezebel sets the puzzle piece down and makes a large half-circle motion in front of her belly.

"What are you ... Are you saying I'm—"

"Congrats, baby! Yup!"

And just like that, everything changes in an instant.

Oh, shit.

EPILOGUE
PART TWO

My mother's voice has always been so soothing. It's strange, but it seems to pop into my head more often ever since I started using Dr. Haven's elixir regularly.

Or perhaps it's because I too will be a mother soon.

I rub the slightly convex curve of my stomach. The ladybug is well out of sight, but I don't bother shutting the bedroom window. The sunlight is warm, and the air is filled with the freshness of spring flowers beginning to bloom.

I grab my laptop and go curl up in bed, propping myself up on a pillow as I open the essay I'm working on for school. I scratch the back of my neck, immediately wincing at the feel of the brand. It's the only reminder of how close I was to marrying that beast, Markos. I can't imagine how things would have unfolded with him in hindsight. Would we have raised the baby as our own?

I push the thought from my mind. It doesn't matter now. Markos is gone, and the half-breed inside me is going to be raised with nothing but love and tenderness. I settle against the pillows and inhale deeply. The smell of coffee wanders from the fresh mug I've got sitting on the bedside table, and the only thing that could possibly make this Sunday more perfect is ...

Him.

ABOUT SCARLETT MORO

THE PROFESSIONAL VERSION

Scarlett Moro is what you get when you pair a love of the paranormal with a little too much coffee. She spends her caffeinated energy playing with her kids, putting off laundry, and creating fantastical romance about shifters, spirits, and other spookums.

Hailing from Alberta, Canada, Scarlett lives in a love-filled house with her nesting partner, their three humans, and three fur-babies.

THE GRITTY VERSION

Hello, Fellow Human. I hope you enjoyed reading this title! I can't express how infinitely I appreciate your support. Whether you paid or read for free through Kindle Unlimited, I adore you. You're a cool cat. Thank you. Being a creative human isn't easy. My brain is always a million places at once, full of far more ideas than time to write. Thanks for your patience when I'm overwhelmed or slacking.

ONLY AFTER DARK
SCARLETT MORO

Feel free to creep Scarlett @ www.scarlettmoro.com to browse her other titles and sign up to her newsletter. Seriously, she loves creepers.

THANKS FOR SUPPORTING
AN INDIE AUTHOR!

FOR THE READER

9 781069 110824